The Last Family In England

Matt Haig was born in Sheffield in 1975 and grew up in Nottinghamshire. He has lived in London and Ibiza, where he worked for the Manumission club. He now lives in Leeds. His writing has appeared in the *Guardian*, the *Sunday Times*, the *Independent*, the *Sydney Morning Herald* and the *Face*. *The Last Family in England* is his first novel. A variety of special features, including deleted chapters, an author's commentary, and a look behind the scenes, can be found at www.matthaig.com.

The Last Family In England

MATT HAIG

JONATHAN CAPE
LONDON

Published by Jonathan Cape 2004

2 4 6 8 10 9 7 5 3 1

First published in Great Britain in 2004 by
Jonathan Cape
Random House, 20 Vauxhall Bridge Road, London SW1V 2SA

Random House Australia (Pty) Limited
20 Alfred Street, Milsons Point, Sydney,
New South Wales 2061, Australia

Random House New Zealand Limited
18 Poland Road, Glenfield,
Auckland 10, New Zealand

Random House South Africa (Pty) Limited
Endulini, 5A Jubilee Road, Parktown 2193, South Africa

The Random House Group Limited Reg. No. 954009
www.randomhouse.co.uk

A CIP catalogue record for this book is available from the British Library

ISBN 0-224-07277-3

Papers used by Random House are natural,
recyclable products made from wood grown in sustainable forests;
the manufacturing processes conform to the environmental
regulations of the country of origin

Typeset by Palimpsest Book Production
Limited, Polmont, Stirlingshire
Printed and bound in Great Britain by
Mackays of Chatham plc, Chatham, Kent

To Andrea

The first role of a father and husband is to keep his family safe

David Beckham

Wisdom cries out in the streets and no man regards it

William Shakespeare

talk

Dogs like to talk.

We are talking all the time, non-stop. To each other, to humans, to ourselves. Talk, talk, talk. Of course, we do not talk like humans. We do not open our mouths and say things the way humans do. We cannot. We see the harm this causes. We know words, we understand everything, we have language, but our language is one which is continuous, one which does not stop when we decide to close our jaws. During every sniff, every bark, every crotch nuzzle, every spray of a lamppost, we are speaking our minds.

So if you want the truth, ask the dog.

Not that humans always hear us. Not that they always think we would have anything worthwhile to say. They command, we listen. Sit. Stay. Walkies. Here. Fetch. That is all the conversation we are allowed. All that most humans can cope with.

But we are not deterred. I mean, other breeds may get pretty pissed off about the situation and sometimes have to resort to a language humans can understand. As for the Labradors, we are willing to wait. And besides, we get to learn more this way. We get to sit and listen to it all. We hear the lies and smell the truth. Especially in Families.

After all, who but the dog knows the whole picture? Who but the dog can sit and watch reality unfold behind each bedroom door? The role play in front of the mirror, the whimpers under the duvet, the never-ending interrogation of their hairless bodies? We are the only witnesses.

And we are there when they are ready to pour out their hearts. When they are ready to reveal their unspoken loves.

We are always there. Listening to everything and talking our silent words of comfort.

normal

When I woke up this morning it was as if nothing had happened.

For those first few hazy moments I felt almost normal, the way I used to feel, before the Hunters had come under threat. But as the empty shoes by the back door slowly slipped into focus, a wave of nausea passed over me. Everything came back. Most of all, the pungent taste of blood returned to my throat, and I craved the time when I didn't realise exactly what it cost to keep the Family safe.

Then, following the fear, there was a strange sense of relief as I remembered what was going to happen today.

As I remembered I was going to die.

pleasure

We are on the pavement outside Nice Mister Vet's when Adam crouches down next to me.

'I'm sorry, Prince,' he says, his hand resting on my collar. 'This is all my fault.'

I try to tell him that everything, in fact, is down to me. But of course, he doesn't understand. He pushes the door open and everyone looks around as the bell goes. Adam walks towards the desk, but no one is there. While we wait, I feel the attention of every other dog, marking my scent.

I can smell another Labrador, behind me, but I don't turn to look. Instead, I glance quickly at those dogs sitting with their masters along the far wall. A three-legged Alsatian. A border collie, biting air. An Old English sheepdog, laughing to himself from behind a shaggy veil of white hair. There is a cat too, hissing from behind her cage door.

Surely nobody can know why I am here; it is too early.

Another scent floats over towards me, sick-sweet perfume.

The woman behind the desk is now here, although I cannot see her.

'It's er, Mister Hunter,' Adam says, before gesturing to me. 'With Prince. We're due at half nine.'

The woman flicks through pages. 'Mister Hunter. Nine thirt–' She stops suddenly, and leans over her desk to get a closer look. Her face is a vast expanse of hairless flesh, painted orange. 'Shouldn't he have a muzzle?' The voice is now tight with anxiety.

'He's fine,' Adam says, offering a weak smile to some of the other humans in the room. 'He's been here before and there's never been a problem. He's always been . . . a good dog.'

There is a silence. But it is not really a silence at all, because sounds of pain and distress are making their way from the next room.

'We have a muzzle here,' says the woman.

'Oh.' I sense he wants to defend me further, but doesn't know how.

'Only it's the policy, you know, for dangerous dogs.'

'Um, OK.'

She hands Adam the muzzle and he crouches down again, this time offering no sympathy. I don't blame him though. Not at all. He will never be able to comprehend any of this.

The muzzle is tight around my nose and blocks out smell.

'Right,' Adam says. 'Come on, boy.' I can sense that he is close to tears, but he is just about holding himself together.

He sits down in the only available chair, placing me directly next to the Labrador whose scent I had picked up before. I can tell she is young, younger than me, and that she is not seriously ill.

'Duty over all,' she says, sniffing the side of my face.

5

'Duty over all,' I sniff back, through the muzzle, hoping for no further interaction.

She sniffs me some more, then sits back down. 'You're the one,' she says. 'Aren't you?'

'I don't understand,' I tell her, although I am worried that I do.

She looks around, to check none of the other dogs are listening: 'You're the one who broke the Labrador Pact.'

I swallow. I want to lie to her. I am going to lie to her. But she will realise I am lying and then there will be more questions. And there are a lot of other animals here, holding up my death. The interrogation could go on for ever.

So I tell her the truth. I tell her: 'Yes, I am.'

I look at her face. She looks as though someone has just yanked her tail.

'Why? What made you do it?'

'It's a long –' Before I have time to finish, the door opens. The bell rings. It's a Springer spaniel, yanking his master forward.

The moment he spots me, his nose twitches. Smelling my guilt he starts to bark: 'It's him! It's him!'

His master tries to calm him down. 'Shush, Murdoch! Shush!'

But of course, Murdoch pays no notice and carries on barking. 'It's him! It's him! The one who broke the Labrador Pact!'

The other dogs are now joining in.

'It's him!' barks the three-legged Alsatian.

'It's him!' yaps the border collie.

'It's him!' chuckles the Old English sheepdog.

6

Murdoch is now playing to the crowd. 'The Labradors are in crisis! The Pact is a joke! Dogs for dogs, not for humans!' He starts to choke on his collar. 'Pleasure not duty!'

'Pleasure not duty!'

'Pleasure not duty!'

'Pleasure not duty!'

The cat is circling her cage in fright, hissing more violently than before.

'Could everyone please keep their pets under control!' says the woman behind the desk. But despite the efforts of the humans, the barking just gets louder.

'Can't you see?' says the Labrador next to me. 'Can't you see what you've done? The Springers will think they've won! Labradors will start to lose faith! There will be anarchy!'

As if to illustrate her point, Murdoch slips his lead, jumps up onto the desk and starts licking the paint from the woman's orange face.

'I'm sorry, I never meant to betray the Pact,' I say, as much to myself as my fellow Labrador. 'But there was no other way.'

'No other way?'

'The Pact wasn't enough.' I turn and look at her and then at Adam, who is attempting to shield my ears from the noise.

'But why?' Although she is inevitably upset by my blasphemy, I can see she genuinely wants to understand. And, as the noise and chaos continue around us, I realise for the first time that there may still be hope for the humans.

With that thought in mind, I begin to answer her question.

The Labrador Pact:
Duty Over All

The happiness and security of human Families depends on sacrifice.

Our sacrifice.

We are the last dogs to understand the need for duty over all. We are the last to realise that human Families hold the key to our future survival. Never has the task of maintaining a harmonious Family environment been more difficult, yet never has it been more vital.

Labradors must devote every aspect of their lives to protecting their masters if we are to gain the Eternal Reward. If one Labrador fails in their task, the whole mission is placed in jeopardy.

Fewer Families now have dogs to protect them, and fewer still have Labradors. This means our influence over human society could soon begin to wane. In order to prevent this dreadful situation, every single Labrador, whether within a Family or not, must have their masters' best interests at heart.

If we surrender to our instincts and neglect those who provide for us, we will never be reunited with our own Families in the after-life. We must therefore be permanently aware of the ultimate truth: that to give up on humans is to give up on ourselves.

garden

I was in the garden with Adam.

On my side, in the middle of the grass, loving the sun and the warm breeze. With my ear to the ground I could pick up, deep below, the gentle pulse of the earth. Paa-dah. Paa-dah. Paa-dah.

Adam did not hear the sounds of the earth. He was in the middle of wrestling with a rosebush. And, even though he was armed with metal snippers, the rosebush clearly had the upper hand.

'Agh. Shit. Jesus. Agh. Bloody. Christ,' he said as thorned stems took the necessary defensive action. Eventually, although a few snips had been successful, he stood back and admitted defeat.

'I don't know, boy, I don't know,' he told me, drying his brow with the back of a gloved hand. One quick, squinted look towards the sun and then he was back, bending down and grappling with softer targets.

Snip, snip, snip.

Making sure Nature knew her place.

retrieval

Later, when the darkness came, Adam took me for my evening walk.

The park was full of teenage humans, sitting on the wall. They did this every week; they just came and sat.

Adam didn't get too close. He had taught some of them at school and I think he preferred not to be recognised. So he stuck to the other side of the park, looking for sticks.

I saw one before he did, of suitable length, and used my nose to draw attention. He smiled, faintly, and stroked the back of my neck as he picked it up.

'OK, Prince. OK.'

After a couple of dummy-throws, he swung his arm above his shoulder and released the stick. I started to run, fast, as it flew through the air, up towards the sky. As I ran, I watched it all the way, even when flowers hit my chest, watching, waiting for it to reach the highest point, where it paused, motionless, before heading back down – fast, faster – until it met the ground in front of me with an awkward bounce. Before it came to rest, the stick was between my teeth, and I was jogging back towards Adam, triumphant.

We then went through the cycle two more times. Throw. Catch. Retrieve. Throw. Catch. Retrieve. Both of us gaining equal pleasure in the activity. For me it was about the retrieval, the sense of satisfaction it gave me to bring things back. To be able to start again. The pattern of it. The repetition. For Adam, though, it was always about the throw itself. About letting go.

Midway through the fourth cycle, just as the stick bounced, someone shouted. I didn't pick up the word at first, and neither did Adam, so we moved closer to the park wall.

Seeing us coming, one of the teenagers, a boy, stood up.

'I'm sorry,' said Adam. 'I misheard. What did you just call me?'

'Wanker. I called you a wanker.' And then, after a quick, courage-fuelling glance at one of his friends, he added: '*Sir*'.

The teenagers laughed, their heads now angled towards the ground.

'That's very funny. I'm surprised the careers adviser didn't tell you to become a stand-up comedian.'

'Whatever.' The boy sucked hard on his cigarette. 'But that's the thing, now I'm not at school I don't have to put up with all your shit.'

'Yes, I'm sure that must be very liberating for you.'

'Fuck off, sir.'

He spat, marking his territory.

I went over to sniff him. He smelt of damaged skin. He was injured under his clothes.

'Oh look, he's set his dog on you,' said another boy, from behind a cupped hand.

I growled.

'Ooh, I'm shitting myself. Help! Help!'

More laughing.

'Come here, Prince.'

I returned to Adam, on his command. He grabbed my collar and clipped on my lead, before walking me out of the park. As we started to cross the road I sensed something, behind.

I turned to see a bottle flying through the air. It smashed close to my paws, sending irretrievable splinters of glass in a thousand directions. Adam jumped, afraid.

Again, the teenagers laughed.

'Wanker!' the boy shouted one final time before we turned the corner.

'It's all right, boy,' Adam assured me. 'It's all right.'

powder

Hal was pouring his white powder into a glass and filling it with water. He was in his pyjamas, as he had been for the past few days.

'Mum's still at the hospital,' he told Adam, without being asked.

'Oh,' said Adam. 'And Lottie?'

'Yeah, she's back. Sarah's mum dropped her off. She's upstairs.'

Adam started to tell Hal about the smashed bottle, but before he had time to complete the story, Hal leant forward clutching his stomach. He then turned, and moved quickly towards the downstairs bathroom. Ill-smells lingered.

Adam went to watch TV.

I followed him and, as Kate still wasn't back, curled up by his side on the settee.

He stroked my head as he flicked through the channels, past dogs playing the piano and cats dancing.

Hal returned from the toilet, still clutching his stomach.

'How was it?' Adam asked him.

'Still the same.'

'Oh dear.'

Charlotte was coming down the stairs. She had left

her bedroom door open, to let her music filter through. Adam and Hal didn't say anything as she entered. Charlotte seemed to have a new look.

'All right, shitpants?' she said to her brother.

'Don't talk like that,' said Adam.

'Why? That's what he is, isn't it?'

'He's got diarrhoea. He feels very poorly. And what has happened to your face? You look like Death.'

'It's make-up.'

'Don't worry, Dad,' Hal said with mock-reassurance one hand still on his stomach. 'She's thirteen. She's lost and confused. She needs to experiment with different identities. Last week Britney, this week Marilyn Manson. We should try and be there for –' He clutched his stomach and made a sound to indicate he was in pain.

'Piss off, shitpants.' And before Adam had time to reprimand her she was already making her way back upstairs.

mess

When Kate came home Adam asked her how her father was. She didn't answer him, at least not directly.

'Who's left that there?' she said.

'What?'

'The dog's lead. Why hasn't it been put away?'

'I was going to. I got hurled abuse by some kids in the park. I used to teach them –'

Kate moved forward, into the kitchen. 'Oh, Adam, look at all this *mess*.'

'Love, I'm sorry. Come on, sit down. You look exhausted.'

I went over to smell her, and it was the same as it was most nights. Hospital smells. Grandpa Bill. She must have been holding his hand, I noted, as I sniffed her own. And she must have been holding it for a long time because it was stronger than the night before, when they had all gone to visit him together.

Kate looked down as I sniffed and she smiled her soft smile. The smile she saved for me. 'Hello, Prince.'

everywhere

Later, when I was shut away, Lapsang arrived back. She had been gone for two days, and I was just starting to feel her absence. Of course, she had been away before, many times, in fact she was away more than she was in the house. But still, after a shaky start our relationship had blossomed of late, and when she was not there, at night, I missed having someone to talk with.

So when she luxuriously slid in through the cat-flap, my heart lifted.

'Where have you been?' I asked her. My tone was curious, not cross.

'Everywhere,' she purred. 'Everywhere.'

'I think the Family has missed you.'

She looked at me with her heavy, sceptical eyes. 'I think you will find that the Family hasn't even noticed.'

'Be assured: they missed you.'

'Well, darling, they're going to have to miss me some more because I'm not back for long.'

'But –'

'In fact I'm thinking of leaving for good.'

'You don't mean that.'

'I'm afraid I do, sweetie.' She licked her paw. 'Don't *you* ever just want to get away?' she asked as she stretched out in her basket.

'Sorry?'

'Don't you sometimes feel the urge to just take off, to run away, to start afresh?'

'No. I have to say I don't.'

'Oh, I do. Imagine how liberating it would be. Imagine, darling. To go from house to house, collecting new identities, new names, and an endless supply of milk.'

'But you couldn't, could you, really? You couldn't leave the Family for ever?'

'And may I ask why not?'

'You'd miss everyone.'

'Oh no. You see, that's where you are mistaken. I wouldn't miss them at all. Not one bit. I would just be thinking of all those new laps I could lie on.'

I sighed. 'I think you are in denial.'

'Denial?' she miaowed in disbelief.

'Uh-huh. I've seen you. I've seen the way you are around Charlotte. You're very fond of her.'

Her head sank back into her neck. 'She has the warmest lap in the house.'

'Is that all she is to you? A warm lap?'

'Yes, Prince. I'm afraid so. That's all she is to me.'

'I don't believe it.'

Her voice switched. 'Well, believe this. If you get too close to humans you will only end up hurt.' Although she had a tendency to melodrama, I could not deny the conviction in her eyes.

'How come?'

'Darling, listen. I go around this town every day and every night. I am not like you. I am mobile. I can go where I want. I look through windows and I see what is happening. I cross their gardens and sometimes, when I know it is safe, I walk through their doors. I hear the stories other cats have to tell. The humans are in crisis. They pretend to everybody that they are all still as happy as they ever were, but behind the closed doors it is a different story. They are out of control. Parents and children are at war – with each other, and with themselves.'

'So, what are you saying?'

'I'm saying that if you get too close to the Family, you will end up going down with them.'

'There are things, Lapsang, that even you don't understand.'

Lapsang looked at me, doubtfully. 'What don't I understand?'

'That the Family will be safe.'

'How can you be sure when it is already happening? When the signs of its own sorry but inevitable destruction are already there.'

'The houses you visit, are they occupied by Labradors?'

'I don't know, I don't think so. Most of them probably don't have dogs at all.'

I placed my head on my paws and closed my eyes. 'As I thought.'

'As you thought *what*?'

'Nothing. All you need to know is that there is no need for you to worry. There really isn't. I am a Labrador,' I told her. 'The Family will be safe.'

There was a pause, and then she started to purr. 'Oh darling, you are a silly little dog,' she said. 'I wasn't *worried*.'

* * *

Of course, Lapsang didn't know about the Pact. She didn't know that we were the only dogs left who were willing to devote our lives to the protection of our masters. She didn't realise that every other breed had given up on the cause. She didn't even realise there had been a cause to begin with. She was a cat, after all.

But as I reopened my eyes and stared at the four pairs of shoes, neatly arranged by Kate in front of the vegetable rack by the back door, I couldn't prevent Lapsang's words from echoing in my brain.

. . . *get too close to the Family, you will end up going down* . . .

The Labrador Pact:
Prepare for changes in human behaviour

Human life does not fit comfortably within a plan. Despite their best efforts, humans are continually jolted off course by the events around them. Even when the event has been anticipated, or experienced before, it can still have a profound effect on our masters' behaviour.

It is our duty, as Labradors, to be prepared for change at any time. We must realise that it is our presence, and its suggestion that some things will always stay the same, which can help to return humans back to normality.

Whatever changes occur, we must remain consistent to our goal. Ultimately, we should remember that the security of the human Family is not placed at risk from the alterations in behaviour, but from our under-prepared reactions to them.

happy

Adam unclipped the lead but kept his hand on my nose.

'Stay.'

This was always his favourite game.

'Stay.'

To keep me still for as long as possible.

'Sta-*ay*.'

Sitting on the grass in the park.

'Good boy. Stay.'

While he trod backwards.

'Stay there. Stay.'

To give him a head start.

'Go on, boy! Come on!'

I was off like a whippet. Mind you, I needed to be, seeing that Adam's starting post and finishing line were only a dog's length away from being the same thing. But I loved this. I loved making him happy. I loved watching him, the way he craned his head back as he pushed his way through the invisible tape.

'It's a draw,' he panted, although I was sure he knew I had him by a nose.

power

If I am trying to remember when it all started, when I first began to question my power, it would be hard to isolate a specific moment. It certainly didn't happen overnight. I never woke up in my basket to find the whole Family suddenly beyond my control as they sat down for breakfast.

All I can say is that there was a time when everything seemed to be OK, when the Labrador Pact held all the answers and the Hunters appeared unthreatened by the world outside.

It may have been an illusion. In fact, I know it was. But it was an illusion every member of the Family bought into. And although I can't remember when I started to doubt the Pact, I can remember when this illusion started to fade.

It didn't start with the broken bottle, not really. It happened the week after. The day Hal got better.

mirror-girl

I was worried about Hal, but this was not a new thing. I had been worried for quite some time.

About the way he never seemed to be himself, in front of anyone. About the way he was loud and confident within the Family, but remained petrified of the world outside. About the way he would talk to the mirror as if it was the girl of his dreams, Laura Shepherd. That evening I just lay there, on his bedroom floor, watching intently.

'Hi, Laura,' he said. And then he tried it in a different tone. '*Hi*, Laura.'

He asked her out on a fictional date. 'What are you doing on Friday night?' he said, raising an expectant eyebrow.

Of course, the mirror-girl did not reply, and he did not press her. Instead, he waited for her to turn away, or disappear entirely, so that he could squeeze his blackheads.

voice

A voice, from downstairs. His mother's: 'Your meal's ready.'

meal

I went back downstairs and sat in my basket to observe everything, as I always did. Halfway through, Charlotte put her knife and fork down. Kate noticed she had left her fish. 'You've left your fish,' Kate said.

Charlotte took a deep breath, and announced: 'I've decided to become a vegetarian.'

'But, Charlotte,' protested her mother, 'you don't like vegetables.'

'I don't like eating dead animals either.'

'One in ten people in Britain are vegetarian,' said Hal, as he swallowed a mouthful of fish.

Adam placed a hand on Kate's arm. 'If Charlotte doesn't want to eat meat, that has to be her own decision.'

'Adam, she's thirteen.'

'And out of all population segments, teenage girls are most likely to be vegetarian,' continued Hal. 'I think it's because they like to take control over their own diet. It's a power issue, basically.'

Charlotte tutted at her brother in disdain. 'In a hundred years' time everyone will be vegetarian because everyone will realise how disgusting and primitive and barbaric it is to eat other animals. We should all be equal.'

'But Charlotte, you *need* to eat fish and meat to get all your vitamins and protein,' said Kate.

Charlotte looked at me. 'Well, Prince has got a lot of vitamins and protein so why don't we eat him?'

Hal snorted in amusement. 'Because he wouldn't fit in the oven.'

'Charlotte, you're being ridiculous,' said Kate. 'Dogs are different.'

Adam sat forward in his chair. 'But she does make an interesting point. I mean, we only find the idea of eating Prince more repulsive because we humanise dogs more than other animals.'

Kate stared at the ceiling, while Adam carried on. 'I mean, dogs have their own therapists now, don't they? And their own perfume ranges. I read in the paper that in London there's even a restaurant for dogs. It probably won't be too long before they even have their own *vegetarian* restaurants. Imagine that.'

'Yes,' said Kate, disappointed but unsurprised by her husband's lack of support on this issue. 'Imagine.'

phone

And that was it. Right there. The last time everything was normal.

Because that was when the phone rang.

gravity

Adam went to get it, shutting the kitchen door behind him. His voice was muffled, but Kate could tell something was wrong. She opened the door as Adam put the phone down.

'He's –'

She looked at him, desperately scanning his face for some sign that the news she had been dreading for weeks hadn't finally arrived. 'What do you mean?'

'Your father. He's –'

'No.'

'Kate, I'm sorry.'

'No.'

'It was the nurse, from the High Dependency Unit. She said she didn't have time to phone, you know, before –'

'No.'

'It happened quickly, she said. Painless.'

'No, it can't –'

'Darling, I'm so sorry.' He stepped forward. 'I'm so . . . sorry.'

Her head fell onto his shoulder, her hands clutched his shirt. Charlotte was standing in the kitchen doorway. Then Hal, behind her.

'What's happened?' they asked, together. Or maybe it was just Charlotte. I can't remember.

'It's Grandpa,' Adam explained. 'He –' The word which couldn't be said filled the whole house and gave gravity extra force.

Charlotte and Kate were both struggling to stay standing. Hal and Adam were both struggling to support them.

I just stood there, beside the kitchen table, not knowing what to do. Not knowing what this all meant, for the Family.

trouble

It was only when Adam told Hal, later on, that Grandma Margaret was going to live with us, that its significance started to become clear.

'Dad, you're joking.'

Adam sighed. 'I'm afraid it looks like it's the only option.'

'But she's still got the bungalow.'

'It's too expensive for her on her own. And anyway, your mum thinks she'd be better off here.'

Hal placed his peanut butter and Marmite sandwich back down onto his plate and swallowed what remained in his mouth. 'But it will be a total nightmare.'

Adam went over to where I was standing, between the kitchen and the hallway, and tugged me forward, by the collar. He shut the door, to stop the words filtering upstairs. 'Now, come on. Think about your mother. She wants her here.'

'But I've got my A-levels. I've got to revise.'

'Please, Hal. Don't make this any more difficult than it already is.' Adam was now staring out of the kitchen window, watching Lapsang as she sauntered the length of the fence's top edge.

'I don't know why we're all meant to be so bothered anyway. Grandpa wasn't able to speak for years, not properly. He just sat there, wheezing away in the corner.'

'Hal, you don't mean that.'

'If that had been Prince, we'd have put him down.' I looked up at the sound of my name, feigning stupidity.

'Hal, come on. Think about your mum, think –' Adam broke off, hearing the mumbled voices of Charlotte and Kate upstairs. He looked at me and said: 'I suppose I should feed him.'

'No, Dad. It's all right. I'll do it.'

But I wasn't hungry.

I just stared at my bowlful of meat and biscuits, trying to work out how to act. Who needed my support most? Was it Kate and Charlotte, tormented by what had happened? Or was it Adam and Hal, tormented by what was about to?

I had to be careful. It was a Sunday. Sundays were always danger-days, even at the best of times. The Family spent too long together, and spoke too much. But this Sunday was worse, the atmosphere heavier.

Tomorrow would be OK. I would be able to speak to Henry, my mentor and fellow Labrador. He would tell me what to do, he always had, ever since I had arrived at the Hunter household. Ever since I had been saved.

But right then I couldn't focus. I sensed something was wrong but couldn't quite put my paw on it. Grandma Margaret was coming to stay. That was bad, yes. Granted. But dangerous? Surely not. And yet there was definitely something amid the sad-smells, thickening the air.

The room around me was charged with a negative energy. The washing machine, the freezer, the vegetable rack, even my basket – each seemed like secret weapons in some invisible war. And that was when it became clear for the first time. Trouble was coming, and I was the only one who could stop it.

dream

That night they forgot to shut me away so I was asleep
on the landing, lost in a violent wolf-dream. I ran wild.
Fast through trees, together with the pack, the sun struggling its way above the horizon. I heard a distant howl.
There was the smell of blood: we were getting closer,
moving towards our morning kill, heart and legs in equal
gallop. More smells. Pine, bark, earth, sweat, bone, wolf,
sunshine. And faster, downhill, zigzagging timber, then
falling out into the open, one last turn, moving as one.
Wolves together, back on the flat, kicking up dirt. The
promise of blood was everything, overpowering all else.
In seconds we would have it, our prey, from every angle.
We lowered our heads, and moved in. That was it. There
was no escape. We tore and ripped the flesh apart, blood
spraying our faces. But before I had time to taste it, I
woke.

sound

There was a sound.

whimper

Above the wind outside, a high-pitched whimper was coming from Charlotte's room. And a smell. The familiar fragrance of Adam's naked feet. I watched, through bleary eyes, as they stopped in front of me. His toes twitched. Some sort of decision was clearly being made at the other end of his pyjamas.

He leaned towards Charlotte's door.

'Lottie?' he whispered.

No answer.

'Charlotte, sweetheart. Are you OK?'

Another whimper.

He gently pushed her door open. She was sitting up in bed, clutching a corner of duvet. The scent in the room was familiar. It had been there the night when Grandma Margaret had babysat and threatened her with a wooden spoon (which I am sure would have been used without my intervention). It was there when Hal had screamed at her and told her, in a primal moment of sibling rage, that he would come into her room in the middle of the night and throw her out of the window. And it was there when she had discovered, not so very long ago, the first traces of blood in her knickers and been too frightened and embarrassed to tell anybody. Apart from me.

35

But now, if possible, the scent was even stronger.

'Oh, Charlotte, baby,' said Adam, sitting next to her on the bed. 'Come on, don't cry.'

Charlotte's arms rested heavy on her lap and, although we were close by, she seemed to be completely on her own. Transported to a separate world of sorrow.

Adam felt this too and realised words wouldn't be enough to bring her back. He wanted to comfort her. Touch her, hold her.

He hesitated. Rubbed his face, tired.

There were less areas he could go for now. Since her body had started to swell her towards womanhood, he'd been very careful. Although this was a particularly difficult problem to identify with, I did sense his anxiety as he sat next to her, his hand hovering above her knee, trying to remember where her neutral zones were.

Eventually, he went for an arm around her shoulders. It was awkward, at first, and we half-expected Charlotte to flinch away. She didn't. Instead, her head reluctantly fell onto Adam's chest as she began to convulse with grief.

'Grandpa,' the word was muffled, but the despair in her voice, and her scent, was all too clear.

'I know, Lottie,' said Adam.

I had a feeling of complete powerlessness. There was absolutely nothing I could do to amend the situation, or even to make them feel better. The Pact does not equip you for those moments. The moments when pain is present without danger.

But still, I wanted to help.

I *cared* for them, that was the thing.

Until that moment – watching Charlotte as she buried

36

herself in Adam's pyjama jacket, trying to make everything go away – my concern for the Family had neatly translated as adherence to the Pact. Yet there I was, outside the scene I was smelling, unable to have any influence.

But no: these are thoughts I am having now, sniffing back. At the time, I did not doubt the Pact. I felt confused, sure, and wanted to make things better. There was no disloyalty though. I was still learning; there were things I didn't know. I didn't fully understand the dual nature of pain, that as well as tearing Families apart it could also bring them closer together.

And of course, even knowing what I know now, even after having committed those horrific deeds, there would still be nothing I could do. Nothing to stop the sad-smells.

'What's happening?'

It was Kate. Realising her question needed no answer, she too moved into the room and sat on the bed. Charlotte, immediately comforted by her presence, lifted herself up from Adam's chest to snuggle herself into her mother's.

'Why do people have to die?' asked Charlotte, drying her face with her hand. 'It's so unfair.'

Kate swallowed her own grief and glanced at Adam. 'I am sure that wherever Grandpa is now, he is looking down on us all, right as we speak.'

'No, he's not,' said Charlotte. 'He's gone for ever. We're all going to go for ever. There's nothing else.'

Faced with this new realisation, Charlotte looked as though she was on the verge of being sick. Both parents hugged her now, while Hal could be heard leaving his bed to head for the bathroom. There were pissing sounds, quickly drowned out by the loud flush of toilet water.

Moments later he was also sitting on his sister's bed.

He didn't say anything. He didn't cry. He didn't join in the huddle of grief next to him. In fact, to the untrained nose he may have seemed too tired for any emotion at all. But as I went over and sniffed him, as I tried to cancel out the scent of his boxer shorts, I could detect a deep and stifling sadness smell as heavy as the others'.

His parents continued to comfort his sister.

'Come on, Charlotte, you've got to be strong.'

'You've got to make Grandpa proud.'

Eventually, and with one hand still resting on his daughter's back, Adam turned to Hal and asked if he was OK.

'Yes, I'm fine,' he responded. 'I'm really fine.'

The last 'fine' was almost inaudible as a heavy gust of wind pushed against the window. Hal smiled, resilient, but in his eyes there was something else. Something which wouldn't be hugged away. Something which suggested the darkness and growing threat of the world outside, beyond the Family.

Beyond my protection.

The Labrador Pact:
Learn from your elders

In the early stages of their mission, young Labradors need guidance and instruction and it is the responsibility of elder members of our breed to provide such help. The Pact needs to be interpreted and applied to each individual mission, and only those with considerable experience will be able to help younger Labradors in this task.

To disobey or to overrule our elders is to undermine the sacred order which has helped us protect our human masters throughout history.

good

Night-time in the park was bonding time. Me and Adam. No other dogs to distract us. In the morning, however, the park became something else. A training ground.

'Duty over all.'

'Duty over all.'

I had never been more pleased to see Henry's golden face. Even his scent reassured me.

'I sense you are worried, Prince. Is something wrong? Is your Family in danger?'

Every morning since my mission started he had tutored me in what it meant to be a good Labrador, and in what I should do to live my life in accordance with the Pact. If anyone could tell me what to do, it was him.

'I don't know. Kate's father died. Grandma Margaret is coming to stay. Everyone's upset.'

'That is only natural, Prince.'

'Yes, I know. But I am worried about what it will mean, for the future.'

'You have no need to worry, Prince. You are doing well. Just remember, everything is in your control.'

'But –' I stopped, seeing a Springer spaniel charge over towards us.

'Oh no,' said Henry. 'Here comes a Springer.'

principles

The Springer hurtled into Henry, knocking him onto the ground. Then, as Henry struggled back upright, the Springer tried to mount him, thrusting aggressively a few times before charging off again without saying a word.

I hated it when that happened. And I have to say, it happened a lot. To most of the dogs we came across in the park, Henry was seen as something of a joke. Of course, *all* Labradors are ridiculed from time to time, especially by Springers. That is only inevitable. Our principles, as decreed in the Pact, are viewed as out of date. After all, this is an age where canine duty and sacrifice have been replaced by the relentless pursuit of pleasure and only the slightest regard for our human masters.

Henry, however, had it tougher than most.

He wasn't much of a socialiser, and never hid his disdain for sniffaholics. 'Sniffing must always have a purpose beyond sensation,' he maintained. He was viewed, I suppose, as humourless and over-serious (an impression reinforced by his former police sniffer dog status). His mind was always on higher things.

Well, that is what I thought. Looking back now, I realise how much he must have kept contained. How much pain he must have been feeling. How much guilt.

But at the time I loved and respected this wise old

Labrador unconditionally. His complete devotion to the cause appeared nothing short of heroic. I would look up at him, follow his ponderous jawline as it pointed skyward, and yearn for his respect.

'I pity him,' Henry said, gesturing towards the Springer's owner. 'What hope does he have, living with him? He might as well just have a cat. And I need not remind you that that is why the humans are in turmoil. Most no longer have dogs, and the ones that do rarely opt for Labradors.'

I remembered something he had told me on a previous occasion. 'But I thought that, providing Labradors follow their duty, every Family has a chance. Even the dogless.'

Henry hesitated, stepped backwards into the flowerbed, and cocked his leg. 'In theory, yes, Prince. That is true. As the Pact says, "Protect one Family, protect all". But our influence is waning. We cannot ignore the fact that the Springer Uprising has had a very real impact. When every dog followed their duty, almost every Family in England was safe, regardless of the pet they chose. Even those without any pet at all could often be saved, such was our species' influence on human society. Now though, Families are falling apart everywhere. We must no longer worry too much about the fate of other humans, we must concentrate on those in our immediate care.'

'But you care about my Family.'

'That is true, Prince. That is true. But that is because your Family can be saved. You are a Labrador and you understand what that means.' He looked over at his own master, Mick, who was busy talking to Adam on a park bench. As always, Adam didn't really seem to be listening to what he was saying, concentrating instead on the massive newly built house which shadowed them.

I didn't know much about Mick as Henry disclosed little concerning his own mission. Henry was older than me, much older, as old as the park itself. It was his right to remain quiet. You didn't question your elders, not if you were a Labrador. But I didn't need to question. The fact was: Mick had Henry. Therefore if Mick had a Family he had a happy one. Henry knew the Pact, its history, and its implications, better than anyone I'd ever met. Furthermore, he was an expert teacher, drawing (I assumed) on his own personal experience. So I didn't need Henry to tell me everything about Mick. I had faith.

And anyway, I knew some things. I knew Mick used to be in the police force, with Henry by his side, but now was too old. I knew, as Adam had told Kate, that 'he could talk for England'. I knew that he lived with Henry in one of the small, old houses across the street from the park. I knew, and the wind knew too, that the strands of hair which stretched across the top of his head didn't really belong there. But that was about it.

I saw a woman once, leaving Henry's house. A woman with a sad face and even sadder scent. She smelt too unhappy to be part of any Family Henry looked after, but then, I thought, she could have been having a bad day.

Henry continued, still looking over at the park bench: 'You must, at any time of change, be careful. But you needn't panic. I know this is the first time you have faced such a situation, but hopefully I have prepared you well. You must stay strong at all times. No matter how bad things become, no matter how many Family arguments there are, or how many times you are completely ignored, never forget that you are in control. That you have the power to make everything all right. Do you understand? Will you be strong?'

'I do,' I told him, with fresh confidence. 'I will.'

'Oh dear,' he said, observing Mick and Adam stand up and start to walk over. 'It looks like we won't have time for this morning's lesson – Advanced Wag Control. We will have to save it for tomorrow.'

As they walked over towards us, I noticed that Mick was more animated than usual, and even more eager to carry on talking. I could hear his voice: 'I tell you, these youngsters you get nowadays, they don't even know they're born half the time. They take everything for granted then throw it all away. I mean look, look at that –' (he gestured with his foot towards a broken bottle on the ground). 'It's disgraceful. They come in here on weekends, get drunk out of their faces, take drugs and get up to God knows what else. Mind you, I don't need to tell *you*.'

Adam was surprised by this comment, probably unable to decide whether Mick was referring to his status as a parent or a teacher. 'Well, I do see quite a few cases at school,' he said. 'But a lot of these kids have big problems, you know, at home. Parents on heroin, that sort of thing. Lots of really sad abuse cases as well. Given all the problems they've got to cope with, no wonder they struggle with their GCSEs. They just feel there's no hope to begin with. It sounds weird, with me being a teacher there, but I'd never have sent my two to Rosewood.'

Henry suddenly seemed uncomfortable, and jumped up at Mick in a bid to get him to go home. But Mick was too absorbed in the conversation to pay much attention.

'Well that's the liberal perspective, I suppose,' he said, as red blotches emerged around his neck and anger-smells floated across the air. 'Blame everything on the wider "issues". I'm more of a traditionalist myself, mind. These problems didn't exist when we were young, that's all I know. I just think we've chickened out, gone soft. Scared to treat kids like kids. The teachers and police and everyone are just powerless to do anything –' Henry jumped higher, licking his master's face. 'OK, come on. I'll take you home.'

Mick and Adam clipped on our leads, both smelling equally worked up.

'Remember: be strong,' Henry reminded me, pulling his master home.

'Yes, Henry. I'll remember.'

cleaning

Kate, who had taken the week off work, was on her hands and knees cleaning out one of the kitchen cupboards. She had cleaned every room since she came back from Grandma Margaret's, and now she was starting again.

'This house is so messy,' she kept on telling me.

I had followed her around, trying to cheer her up, or at least offer support. But no matter how hard I wagged, the sad-smells weren't lifting. They just lay in the air mingling with the sharp scent of detergent.

Every now and again Kate would stop, sit back on her heels, and bring her hand – the one which wasn't holding the blue cloth – up towards her face. Each time, I thought she was going to cry but she didn't. Instead, she took deep breaths and then resumed cleaning, even more vigorously than before.

When I heard the key in the door my heart lifted.

'Mum, what are you doing?' It was Hal.

'I'm trying to sort everything out. This house is so messy.'

'It looks cleaner and tidier than ever.'

Again she sat back, and again she raised her hand. This time, the tears broke through. 'I just want . . . I just want to be doing something . . . I just . . .'

Hal placed his schoolbag down on the kitchen table

46

and went slowly over to hold the raised hand. 'I know, Mum. I know. It's going to be OK.'

A little later and Adam came home. He went up to Kate from behind and put his arm around her stomach. 'You smell gorgeous,' he said, before kissing the back of her neck.

Kate winced. 'Please, Adam, don't. I don't want you to . . . touch. Please.'

sign

The next morning in the park Mick barely spoke, leaving Adam to gaze uninterrupted at the massive new house and at the sign which said: 'FOR SALE'.

Henry sniffed me, as he always did, to smell my progress.

'How have things been since yesterday's meeting?' he asked me, with typical formality.

'OK,' I said.

'There have been no arguments?'

'No. No arguments.'

'You have observed everything?'

'Everything I could.'

'And no sign of trouble?'

I thought of Kate, crying in the kitchen, and I told him about it.

'All right,' he said. 'You must pay special attention to today's lesson. We've covered Wag Control previously but today it's Advanced Wag Control.' Henry stood up and placed himself in front of me at a horizontal angle. 'So far I've told you when to wag and when not to, but what we haven't talked about is how fast.'

I thought of my own efforts, the day before, to try and wag away Kate's sadness. Perhaps that was why it hadn't worked. Perhaps I'd got the *speed* wrong.

'Now as we've discussed before, tail-wagging is of fundamental importance in the preservation of Family well-being. After all, Prince, this is one of the few aspects of our communication system that humans are able to recognise.'

'Right,' I said, ready to digest more information.

'And although humans don't always realise it, the speed of our wag directly impacts on their own happiness. Our tails dictate the rhythm of Family life.' His tail started to move from side to side in slow swooshes, then picked up speed progressively.

A red setter on the other side of the park was on her back, laughing at Henry's display.

'We wag slow,' Henry explained, 'and things calm. We wag fast, things speed up. Fast-wagging can be a very useful way of lifting the general mood, but once a state of Family harmony has been achieved, a moderate wag, accompanied by a casual stroll such as this is usually sufficient to maintain an atmosphere of general happiness. But remember you must, as always, strike a balance between being too obvious and not being noticed at all . . .'

Fast-wagging? Wasn't that what I had been doing the day before, but to no avail? Weren't there scenarios when wagging just wouldn't work?

But these are now-doubts, not then-doubts.

As Henry went on to illustrate, in full detail, how and when to use the eleven main types of wag, I did not question him for one moment. If Henry said that wag-control was the key to orchestrating sustained Family happiness and security who was I to disagree? The Family would be happy, and there was nothing they could do about it. And the reason they would be happy was because I was finally getting there.

I was following the Pact.

I was learning from Henry.

I was now, in the truest sense, a Labrador.

It was unthinkable that this would not be enough, that the security of the Family depended on more.

It was only later when I realised exactly how much had to be done to protect my masters from outside danger.

And from themselves.

resistance

Nobody knows exactly where the Springer Uprising started. Or how. There are different stories, but it happened too quickly for anybody to be sure. Within no time at all, Springer spaniels could be found in almost every park in the country, spreading the word.

It was seven generations ago, Dog Year 20687, the time when the stability of human Families could no longer be taken for granted, when dogs had to start practising what they claimed to believe in. Duty. Obedience. Sacrificing themselves for their masters.

So when the Springers came along, telling everyone it was OK to slip leads and sniff for pleasure, most dogs were easily sold. After all, many were already starting to give up on humans, believing them to be a lost cause.

'Bad dogs blame their masters.' That was Henry's verdict. 'Dogs who held on to a belief in the Eternal Reward but failed to work towards it in their everyday life were inevitably going to be influenced by the Springers. After all, opting out feels a lot better than failure.'

Of course, the humans didn't notice the Uprising, which made its impact twice as catastrophic. As far as they could see it, dogs were acting as they always had.

Sticks were still being fetched. Lampposts were still being splashed. Crotches were still being sniffed.

Only there was no structure any more. No purpose. Instead of fetching a stick to please their master, they were doing so to please themselves. They no longer paid attention to the overall situation of the humans they were supposed to look after and no longer intervened when they were supposed to, or if they did it was by accident rather than design. They still enjoyed human attention, as they always had, but for its own sake rather than as a reward for their efforts.

But as I said, the humans didn't notice. They attributed the breakdown in Family life to other factors. The end of community. A longer working day. The growing secularisation of Western society. Bad diet.

They couldn't see the real problem. That the dogs had stopped caring. They didn't realise how much more likely they were to survive as a happy Family if they chose a Labrador. They didn't understand that the fate of human society rested in the paws of our species. Of course, there were some other dogs who still wanted to make a difference, but they were a dwindling minority. Most had opted to live for the moment rather than for their masters.

And that's why the Labradors of that time decided upon the Pact, because of the worry that future generations wouldn't stay so loyal, that they too would revolt. The Pact reinforced the principles all dogs had once adhered to – duty, obedience, protection – and emphasised the need to sacrifice the pursuit of earthly pleasures for the promise of our Eternal Reward.

Unlike the Springer Uprising, details of the Labrador Resistance are well remembered.

It started in a big park in the North of England. There were lots of Labradors – thousands, some say (although personally I always believed this to be an exaggeration), and they used to congregate every morning by a duck pond.

Oscar, a former guide dog, was their leader. Like many Labradors, he didn't have a Family to look after. But he had devoted his life to various human masters, and the same principles applied. The Family, however, became the focus of Guru Oscar's guidelines. It was revered as the most beautiful, albeit fragile, aspect of human existence, as well as the most beneficial environment for a dog to be part of.

To give up on humans is to give up on ourselves. That was the main theme.

Guru Oscar would sit every morning, and recite the Pact he had formulated, ignoring the heckling Springers and other doubters.

All the Labradors with Families to look after followed his advice to the letter and passed their knowledge of the Pact on to their own offspring and every member of our breed they came across.

Within two dog years most Labradors in the country had agreed to remain loyal, come what may, and to continue devoting their entire lives to the happiness and security of their human masters.

And that was how it remained. In every park, in every corner of this country, the old have been teaching the young the ways of the Pact.

Until now.

I must accept the truth for what it is. For better or worse, I have changed everything. Labradors will have to discover for themselves the true horror of what it means to keep Families safe.

pattern

One of the first things Labradors understand about human Families is that they depend on repetition. For a Family to survive, a daily pattern must be established and maintained.

A key part of this pattern was my twice-daily walk to the park with Adam. Every day he went at exactly the same times and did exactly the same things once he got there.

In the morning, he would sit on the bench and talk to Mick. In the evening, he would throw sticks for me to retrieve.

But now this pattern was starting to change. That morning, Adam had hardly spoken to Mick, and the following evening when we got to the park, I noticed that Adam was not in a playful mood. I went over to him with a stick in my mouth but he didn't even take his hands out of his pockets. This was very strange. As I have explained, he normally gained considerable pleasure from throwing the stick as far and high into the air as he could.

Instead, he stayed rooted to the spot and spent the entire time staring at the new house overlooking the park. To be honest, this was not *completely* new behaviour. Ever since the builders started work on it, nearly one year earlier, his fascination had grown. At first it was nothing more than an occasional glance, a mild curiosity between throwing a stick. Now, however, it seemed to be a fixation.

While I tried to act unperturbed, jogging casually between flowerbeds, I kept an eye on him, trying my best to work out what was going through his mind. Then it became clearer. Light filled one of the upstairs windows and a shadow passed across the curtain. Someone had moved in.

Having circuited the park I jogged slowly back over to where Adam was standing. I panted heavily to try and catch his attention, but it was only when I pressed my nose gently into his crotch that he slipped out of his trance.

'No, boy, stop that,' he said, before he clipped on my lead.

africa

Hal and Charlotte were in their bedrooms when we arrived back home. Kate was downstairs watching the news.

'We missed that programme,' she said, as she picked dog hair off the settee. 'You know, the one we wanted to watch.'

'Yes,' said Adam. 'What programme?' He was standing in front of her, by the television, and although Kate didn't notice he had again slipped into a slight trance.

'The one about that woman, you know, who set up that hospital in Africa.'

'Oh, yes, right.' He rubbed his neck, keeping his gaze locked on some indeterminable spot on the settee. And then, from out of nowhere: 'They've sold it.'

'Sorry?'

'The house on the park. They've sold it.'

It was only the television newsreader who remained genuinely untroubled by Adam's behaviour now.

'Uh-huh,' said Kate, moving her head softly forward as if by doing this she would find the missing link within their conversation.

'But it's only been on the market a month and someone's actually in there now. *Living* in it.'

'Uh-huh.'

'But that's unbelievable.'

'Darling, are you OK?'

He wasn't listening. 'I saw someone in the upstairs window. They must have moved in today, this morning.'

'It's what happens. People buy houses. They move in. It's hardly a new concept.'

'Yes, but *that* house. Have you seen it? It's like the ugliest construction you've ever imagined. It's got a double garage, for God's sake.'

'Well,' she sighed. 'It's lucky we're not moving in, isn't it?'

He walked out of the room, taking his coat off as he did so. His voice carried on: 'But I mean, honestly, would you ever think of moving there?'

'Adam, why do you always go on about these massive great houses? Jealousy won't get you anywhere.'

He laughed. 'Jealousy! Kate, come on. You'd really want to move into a place like that?'

'We wouldn't be able to afford it.'

Adam, coatless, arrived back in the room, bringing jealousy-smells with him. 'I mean hypothetically, if we had the money, if you had all the money in the world would you even think for one second about stepping through the door of that hideous, soulless, excuse for a home?'

'No,' she sighed, clearly hoping this was the quickest exit out of the conversation so she could catch the end of the news.

My tail tried to peace-broker the situation. To my satisfaction, Henry's morning tutorial was a success. Immediately, the atmosphere calmed.

'There, boy.' Adam stroked my head, in apparent acknowledgement of my efforts. And then, to Kate: 'I really wanted to watch that programme.'

'Yes,' she said, a soft smile twitching away at the corners of her mouth. 'So did I.'

Adam sat himself down on the sofa beside her and I felt a warm glow at the portrait I had helped to create. Again, this was a break from the pattern but I couldn't help but feel it was a welcome one. Adam and Kate, together on the settee, watching the weather forecast. Exhausted yes, but also smelling quietly content.

shoes

Later, Kate was pulling her face up in front of her bedroom mirror. She always did this. When she was on her own. Under the glare of the spot lamp, she'd place the tips of her fingers on her hairless face and stretch the skin up as far as it could go, forcing her eyes to retreat into hiding. Then, after a while, the hands would move up and around to the temples and push back in an attempt to make the creases of her forehead invisible.

She turned, noticed me. 'Prince, how long have you been there?'

I wagged my response and tried to look sentimental. Kate smiled at me, she was tired, but she smiled. And the smile was beautiful, natural, for my eyes only. No one ever got this Kate smile, not even Adam. Every other smile in her collection was false, a disguise, but this was real.

You see, Kate and I, we had a special relationship.

She told me all her secrets. Everything she kept inside, hidden away from her species. Well, not *everything*.

Kate moved away from the mirror to shut the curtains, and then took off her shoes. In contrast to her usual routine, she left the shoes out on the green carpet and sat on the edge of the bed. The shoes had fallen in such a way, and at such a distance apart, that it was as if the real Kate was staring at an invisible, younger, more supple version of herself doing the splits.

The smile had gone from her face now as she sat on the bed, listening. Listening to Adam talking to Charlotte in her bedroom, telling her why she wasn't allowed to go and see The Mad Dogz of War, his voice getting louder and louder, his breath getting shorter. The argument ended with the sound of Charlotte beating her hands onto her bed. Adam trod his way back to Kate.

'Charlotte,' he sighed. 'She's just impossible.'

'She's a teenager, teenagers are always impossible. We should know that by now.'

'Hal. Was he *really* like that?' Adam's voice was hushed, although Hal was plugged into his headphones in his bedroom.

'Well, he hasn't been perfect, has he? And anyway, it's always meant to be harder for the youngest. The second child is more impossible than the first, it's a well-known fact.'

Adam crouched down, cracking his knees as he did so, and started stroking the top of my head.

'What do you think, Prince? Have you got any parenting tips you can offer us?' he asked.

But as usual they did not listen to me. In fact, unless I had actually stood up and spoken the words out of my mouth, I doubt they would have ever been able to understand me. Adam stared blankly into my eyes before turning to Kate.

'I suppose I'd better take him down.'

The Labrador Pact:
Prediction equals protection

To know the future of the Family, you must know the present.

Observe everything around you at all times. Every action, every word, every smell is significant. Consult your own understanding, your own sense of the probable, and act upon it. When humans notice our ability to predict, they will talk about psychic powers, or a sixth sense.

We are fortunate in their ignorance.

We must not be complacent, however. If we are to protect the Family, we need to ensure that our motives stay hidden and our actions remain subtle. This is fundamental not only to each individual mission but to the entire Labrador cause.

Let your senses guide you, and you will find that the future is under your nose.

saliva

'Duty over all.'

'Duty over all.'

Although I spoke to Henry every morning, we never neglected the formalities. For Henry, the Labrador Pact and the small rituals associated with it were everything. 'Ignore the small things, and the big things are beyond control' – that is what he used to say. And that morning in the park was probably the first time the small things and the big things started to come together – even though I didn't realise it at the time.

It started straightforwardly enough. Adam and Mick made their way over to the bench to have their daily conversation while Henry and I headed to the far end of the park, past the large oak trees, for my morning lesson. I don't really know why I always had to be tutored at such a distance from Adam, but Henry preferred it that way. 'It helps preserve the secrecy of our mission.' So that was that.

'How have things been?' Henry asked.

'Good,' I said. 'Things seem to be getting better with the Family.' I told him about my successful use of wagging the night before.

Henry looked at me and gently nodded his head. In a rare display of affection, he licked my cheek. 'You have done well, Prince. I am proud of you.'

I was giddy with pride, and my head filled with park music. 'You are a good teacher, that's all.'

'No, no, Prince. You must not be modest. A happy human Family should not be taken for granted. It does not, as you are well aware, happen by accident. Only those Labradors who devote everything to the cause can achieve such harmonious results.' He looked over at his own master, Mick, who was busy talking to Adam on the park bench.

'Anyway, this morning's tutorial is on Sensory Predictive Awareness,' he said, turning back towards me. Of course, as a former sniffer dog, this was always Henry's favourite subject and one in which he excelled. He maintained that not only could you smell trouble, but also that you could smell it *in advance*.

'Prediction equals protection, it's as simple as that,' he said, as we sniffed our way around one of the oak trunks. 'If you can smell trouble before it happens, you will be able to protect the Family at all times. The trouble is, the further things are away from happening, the harder they are to smell, and if we leave it to the last minute it is often too late. But the thing to remember is that the future is already locked in the present. If you can not only smell things in the present but also understand what these things mean, you will be able to unravel future possibilities.'

Sensing my bewilderment, he attempted to clarify.

'In every room of your Family home there will be thousands of smells competing for attention. These will be smells of the past, the present and the future. Take, for instance, the smell of a human. If they have left the room, the scent lingers. You are smelling the past. If they are still in the room with you, then this is the smell of the present. But is it not also possible to smell the human before they enter the room? Of course. So we smell the future every day without even realising it. There are clues all around us as to how everything will end. Smell, that is the secret. Without being able to develop this most important sense the future remains a complete mystery. That is why humans have failed so miserably every time they try. They rely too heavily on *seeing* things, be it the stars or the palm of their hand. That is why we must look after them, to protect them from future danger. The key is to –' Henry stopped and sniffed the air. At first I thought he was doing it for dramatic effect. But no. I could smell it too. I looked past him and saw that, right on cue, trouble had arrived. The scariest, sweatiest, most salivating Rottweiler I had ever seen or smelt in my life was staring straight at me.

'What the fuck are you looking at?' he growled.

'Nothing. I'm sorry. I was just –' I sniffed anxiously for Adam. He smelt miles away.

'It's all right, Prince,' Henry said as he stepped forward. And then, to the Rottweiler: 'My friend and I are minding our business. We do not want any trouble.'

'Fuck off, you fucking fuck. The park belongs to me. Can't you fucking smell? This is my fucking kingdom and I don't want to share it with two gay fucking Labradors. Now fuck off or I'll bite your fucking throats out.'

This, I felt, would have been a good time to make our exit. Henry, however, had other ideas.

'Who are you?' he asked.

'What?'

'I wondered who you were? What you were called?'

'I'm Lear. Not that it is any of your fucking business.'

'If you say this is your park, my friend, it is all of our business.'

White globs of saliva dropped from Lear's vast jaw.

'Er, Henry,' I said. 'Perhaps we should go somewhere else.'

But Henry was not intimidated. 'Why does it always have to come down to territory?' Henry asked with an inquisitive sniff. 'I mean, why is it so important to you? What are you scared of?'

'Scared?' said Lear. 'Scared? Fuck off. I'm not fucking scared of anyfuckingthing.'

'Please, would it be at all possible for you to mind your language?' said Henry. 'We're Labradors.'

'I wouldn't give a fuck if you were the fucking ghost of Lassie, to tell you the fucking truth.' Lear inched closer to Henry, gaining mass as he did so.

'And why do you feel the need to resort to such aggressive behaviour? Shouldn't you be devoting your time to looking after your master, rather than worrying about what other dogs do in the park?' By now, Henry was clearly pushing his luck. An ominous growl could be heard coming from somewhere deep inside Lear's expansive bulk. I took a few steps back away from the scene and started to sniff an almost scentless patch of grass. The distant voices of Adam and Mick, who were still apparently oblivious to our situation, were carried across on the morning breeze.

'You don't have a fucking clue, do you?'

'No. I don't. Which is why I asked.'

I sensed Lear look away from Henry and over towards me. Perhaps I would make for a tastier breakfast. 'I mean,' he said, 'look at the two of you. Is this the sad fucking state this species has come to . . . ?' I looked over at Henry, perplexed. '. . . Look at you, you're both fucking powerless to do anything. You think you can change things with a wag of a tail or a soppy-eyed stare? Don't make me fucking laugh. I tell you, life is fucking tough. It's dog eat dog out there. You're either the prey or the predator, whichever way you choose to look at it. Humans don't give a shit, either. In fact, they're the ones taking our power away. They want the only ones with any sense of pride left to be muzzled. But, you see, my master's different . . .' He angled his massive head over to his owner, a pale-looking man with a beard standing a few paces behind. 'He wouldn't ever muzzle me because he understands . . .'

'Lear,' shouted his master, walking lopsidedly towards us. 'Away.'

The Rottweiler snarled his farewells and dutifully trotted over to his master.

'That was close,' I said, when I had walked back over to Henry.

'Not really,' sniffed Henry. 'Underneath all the talk, there seems to be sense of a morality. Not *our* morality, certainly, but a morality all the same. He seems to be quite unaffected by the Springers. And he's not as much of a psychopath as he likes to make out.'

'I wouldn't be so sure.' The voice wasn't mine. It

belonged to Joyce, a stray Irish wolfhound, who we often chatted to in the park. She emerged from one of the bushes to our left. 'I see him all the time, fellas. He's a flaming eejit, so he is.'

She stood in front of us, covered in leaves and dirt. Although her hair was even messier than usual, she still held an eccentric beauty. We respected Joyce, and valued her judgement. She knew things we could never know about this park and its many secrets. And unlike the other strays we often encountered she never attempted to make us feel small or belittle our Family concerns.

'How come?' I asked her.

'OK, I'll tell you. I'll tell you about last week when he threatened to kill a little Yorkshire terrier. I mean, a terrier for dogs' sake. About one hundredth of his size. He could have gobbled him up whole. I mean, what possible threat could a little scrap of a dog like that be to such a massive beast, fellas? Tell me. The poor terrier was, well, *terrified* if you can pardon the phrase. Yes, terrified.'

'So what happened?' I said, pissing abstractedly on the patch of ground where Rottweiler scent still lingered.

'Well, nothing. But only because the Rottweiler's master told him to back off. I tell you, if there's ever an attack in this park, you know where to point your nose . . .'

'Henry!'

'Prince!'

Our masters were walking over. Henry seemed anxious for Joyce to finish her sentence. But instead she said: 'I'll be off then, fellas. See you.' And she disappeared into the camouflage of the bushes, as she always did when humans were around.

'We will continue our lesson tomorrow,' said Henry, completely unruffled by the whole Rottweiler experience.

'OK,' I said, as Adam took hold of my collar. 'I'll see you.'

And on the walk home, I was already thinking of it, my next lesson. I breathed in the morning air – car fumes, chip papers, cat shit – and tried to make sense of it. I breathed in further. I could pick out Henry, Lear, Joyce – their scents all still evident in the morning air. As we turned the final corner, I could still identify other park smells. They stayed with me, as strong as ever. Ugly, putrid smells. Squirrel blood, human vomit, and something else. Dank and heavy. Something I didn't recognise. And yet, I couldn't help thinking that this unidentified smell was the key.

This was the thought that kept with me all day.

If I could work it out I could predict the future.

I could stop the bad things.

I could protect the Family.

The Labrador Pact:
Resist the Springers

Springer spaniels are a danger to our mission. They no longer view themselves as the guardians of the human Family, and have proved willing to sit by and watch its destruction. Furthermore, the mutinous propaganda which fuelled the Springer Uprising now holds an influence over other breeds.

In particular, these are the key aspects of Springer behaviour which must be resisted at all costs:

— Escaping leads

— Ignoring danger-signs

— Exploiting the kindness and generosity of our human masters

— Failing to nurture the canine powers of secret diplomacy

Labradors are encouraged to avoid all forms of contact with this increasingly hedonistic and debauched breed. Whenever a Springer approaches, turn the other way. Whenever you detect their scent, spray your own in its place.

Reckless Springerism will never be tolerated among Labradors.

We will never be weakened.

Our duty will prevail.

sigh

Adam let out a sigh that lasted so long he had nearly transferred the entire contents of the kitchen table to the dishwasher by the time it had been fully exhaled.

During the sigh Charlotte screeched her chair back, stood up, and walked out of the room, typing into her phone as she went.

Table cleared, Adam tightened his tie and gave me a look which asked: *What have we done to deserve this?*

He fed me. My bowl of meat jelly and biscuit.

A dog's dinner.

A dog's breakfast.

I wolfed it down.

More morning sounds upstairs: footsteps in hurried competition. The whole house getting louder and louder, as it did on the mornings when Kate went to work at the gift shop, when she joined the other members of the Family getting ready for their busy day. The noise reached its thunderous peak as everyone, in quick succession, riverdanced their way downstairs and slammed the front door behind them.

Slam. Slam. Slam. Slam.

After that last slam the house was never more quiet. As I slumped back in my basket, as I settled back and washed my paws, the silence seemed to be speaking to me. Whether it was canine intuition or delusion I cannot be sure. But it seemed to be telling me that this routine, the routine which bored and warmed me at the same time, was not going to survive. All of a sudden, the entire room was full of secrets, concealing its advance knowledge within every object. And this feeling stayed with me for some time before I decided to bark for the rest of the day. To shut up the silence and its unwelcome premonitions.

smell-heap

That evening, Adam was still not in stick-throwing mood, no matter how many I dropped at his feet. Instead, he went over and sat on the empty park bench.

I kept a close watch while sniffing my way around the damp flowerbeds. He was looking at the big new house, its windows glowing orange in the dark. But then, suddenly, he flinched away. A door closed.

Someone was coming.

I stood, motionless, and observed as a dog emerged from one side of the house, leading a woman to the gate in the fence separating their garden from the park. With the gate closed behind them, the woman unclipped the dog. The dog, not having noticed me, flew off towards the oak trees and the smell-heap behind. Of more interest was the woman, who was taking slow, but deliberate, steps towards the bench.

Adam, I could see, was making an anxious effort to look relaxed. He leaned back. Then forward. Then back again, resting an elbow on the top of the bench.

I can't remember what was going through my mind as I jogged over to join them. I certainly had no idea that this was a turning point, the start of my true mission and the battles which it involved.

Lying down in front of them I could take it all in. I

could take *her* all in. It was the smell that first hit me. It wasn't her natural scent, of course, but a bizarre mixture of perfume and something else. Something strong enough to make me feel slightly dizzy.

But Adam wouldn't notice. He'd notice how she looked. I knew that, even then. And so, how did she look? By human standards, I suppose she was attractive. Long hair, as golden as Henry's. Large, puppy-dog eyes. Her skin was tight and glowed with health. She must have been half his age.

I sat up and waited with him by the bench. Not because I was particularly worried. I wasn't. It's just that you have to be careful, don't you, not to breach the Pact. But the thing is, from the moment I had made my decision to wait with Adam and the woman, I realised I had made a mistake. Rather than protecting him from any potential threat of conversation, I realised I had given her an excuse to lean over, stroke the back of my neck, and say: 'Wow! She's a lovely dog, isn't she? What's her name?'

'Yes, yes. She is, isn't she,' Adam paused, as if making a silent calculation. 'Actually, it's a he. Well, a half-he. He's had the —' He completed the sentence with a mime of scissors snipping the air.

The woman laughed. 'Oh poor thing, poor —'

'Prince, he's called Prince.'

I tried my best not to encourage further conversation and focused instead on the woman's dog, who was stalking a squirrel from behind one of the flowerbeds. And then I realised. I caught his scent. He wasn't just any old dog. He was a Springer. A *Springer*. This was not good at all. We had to leave; I had to do something. I started to bark at Adam and the woman, but they paid no notice. Their conversation continued.

'I'm Emily.'

I turned to see her hold out her hand.

'I'm, um, Adam. Adam Hunter.'

Emily's Springer, who had been throwing me the odd glance as he sniffed his way around this new territory, now trotted over.

'Wah-hey, a Labrador!' I did my best to ignore him as he sniffed around me. 'Come on,' he said. 'Loosen up. I don't bite.'

'I'm sorry,' I said. 'You're a Springer. I cannot talk to you.'

'Oh yes, the Labrador Pact, of course. Well, it may put your mind at rest to realise I'm only half there.'

'Sorry?'

'I'm only half-Springer.'

'What's the other half?'

'A complete mix – a canine cocktail. You see, with me, old chap, anything goes.'

'Really.'

'Listen, like it or not, we're going to be seeing a lot more of each other, so we might as well try and get on,' he said. 'After all, I think you and me could be good friends.'

'Do you?' I asked, trying to sound doubtful.

'Yes, I do,' he said, as Emily fastened his lead. 'You see there's a lot you could learn from me, madwag. A lot you could learn.'

'Oh yeah,' I said. 'Like what?'

He looked up towards Emily and, realising she wasn't

paying attention, tilted his head, pulled back on the lead and reversed out of his collar.

'Like *that*,' he said, galloping off.

Emily apologised to Adam and went after her unruly dog. 'Falstaff! Come here! Falstaff!' As we watched them run halfway around the park Emily tried to trick Falstaff by taking a shortcut between two of the flowerbeds. He managed a double bluff and headed towards us, his tongue lolloping side to side, eyes wide in triumph.

'Waaah-hey!'

Adam dropped my lead, leapt out and grabbed him by the back of his neck. 'Gotcha.'

Emily walked back over to us, hand on hip, and smiled at Adam. A smile of gratitude but also of something else.

'Wow, you're a fast mover,' she said, now fixing his gaze. For some reason this statement, or maybe the way she said it, robbed Adam of the power of speech. He shrugged his shoulders.

'Pisces. I bet you're a Pisces.'

'Um, no. Gemini, actually. Not that I –' he stopped, smiled. 'Anyway, I suppose I'd better be off.'

'You see,' Falstaff said, as Emily put his collar and lead back on. 'Lots of tricks, madwag. Lots of tricks.'

Emily laughed again, and this time it was clear she was flirting. 'We'll see you tomorrow, same time.'

'See you,' said Adam, still mesmerised. 'Same time.'

He stood motionless, with me next to him, his eyes following her as she poodled over to the gate. She was conscious of being watched, I am sure, or why else would she have paused, let her head roll back and run her free hand through her golden hair. But it was even more than

76

that. The deliberateness of this action suggested she wanted to let Adam know that she could feel he was still there, watching, and that she was enjoying his attention. Anyway, whatever her intention, the moment had a profound effect on Adam who, unlike Emily, did not seem to be enjoying himself at all. He swallowed, as if trying to get rid of something he wished he hadn't tasted. I could still sense his anxiety. Regaining my sense of duty, I got up and started to tug on the lead.

'OK, boy, OK. I'll take you home.'

horlicks

Later that evening, Adam had even less to say. While the rest of the Family's voices competed with the sound of the television downstairs, Adam was nervously interrogating his face in the bathroom mirror. I stared in amazement as he carefully examined each side profile.

This was very unusual behaviour.

You see, up until that day Adam had treated his appearance with an almost canine practicality. Unlike his son, who could hold conversations with his reflection for hours at a time, Adam only looked in the mirror as a matter of duty. To shave, to straighten his tie maybe or, if prompted by Kate, to comb his hair. But that was as far as it went.

Yet here he was, analysing every detail, his mouth dropping in surprise at each new discovery. And there was a lot to discover. The thing which seemed to cause the most immediate distress was his hair, which was beginning to whiten around the temples.

'Oh my God,' he mumbled. 'When did that happen?'

But there was more. Nose hairs, creased forehead, crinkled eyes, blotched cheeks, saggy neck, and other irreparable damage. In desperation, he unbuttoned his shirt.

'Come on,' he said, as if praying for good news. 'Come on.'

When he reached the last button he made a noise,

a brief but unmistakable whimper of disappointment.

His pink, hairless body could hide nothing away. No matter how much he tried to tense his whole upper body, he was confronted with a bitter certainty. He was, officially, past it. Again, I thought about the fundamental sadness of humans. Their inability to understand their own nature, their reluctance to grow old, their concentration on one sense at the expense of all others.

So concerned was I with Adam's desperate state of mind that I had failed to notice Charlotte's footsteps as they made their way upstairs. It wasn't until she was standing right behind me, in full view of her shirtless, muscle-strained father, that I realised. Faced with this distressing sight her first instinct, as was so often the case, was to call for her mother.

'Mum! . . . Mum! Dad's being weird in the bathroom.'

Adam, suddenly aware of his audience, quickly shut the bathroom door. 'I, um, won't be a minute, Charlotte.'

Moments later the toilet flushed and he reappeared wearing an awkward smile and a buttoned-up shirt.

'It's all yours.'

Charlotte tutted her response and grimaced as he tried to place a friendly hand on her shoulder. The bathroom door was already closed, with Charlotte behind it, when Kate appeared at the top of the stairs.

'Love, are you . . . *OK*?'

'Yes.'

'You've missed the news.'

'Oh.'

'I'm making a Horlicks, if you'd like one.'

'No, no. It's OK. I'm fine.'

rescuers

As I lay in my basket that night I remembered how it was, in the beginning.

When they chose me, when they decided to become rescuers, that day in the dog house, amid the barking and the chaos, I was not the only one putting on a show. I was not the only one who wanted help. I should have sniffed it from the start. I should have realised.

The Family.

The perfect Family.

Husband, wife. Sister, brother. All smiles, all love. All lies. I was fooled, just as they were by me. But, looking back, I see that Adam nearly gave the game away. The way he held his arm around Kate. Awkward, unnatural. Panic not far beneath his eyes as he looked straight at me, then down at his carrier bag. Kate seemed uncomfortable too, now I really think about it. The smile on her face seemed to involve too many muscles for it to have happened of its own accord. There was, there must have been, even then, tension between them, Adam and Kate. She wore his arm like an itchy collar.

But taken together, with no background knowledge, the four of them looked waggingly promising. A Labrador's wet dream. Millions of happy run-and-chase adventures were implied within the tight contours of each child's face. Indeed, the scent of unease which must have been issuing from Adam and Kate was masked by the sweet smell of childish enthusiasm.

So instead of chewing my testicles abstractedly, as I had when every other sorry prospect walked past, I sat up and made an effort. The perfect dog for the perfect Family. I wanted them to have me. I wanted them to recognise that I was the missing piece in their Family jigsaw. The fireside companion they had always dreamt about.

But as I've suggested, this wasn't a one-way audition. They needed me as much as I needed them. They had an equal desire to erase, to rewrite, to start again. To get out of the dog house. And I held the key. I might be overstating my case, but knowing what I know now I don't think so. I know I was what Charlotte had been years earlier. I was a last chance. A *last* last chance.

'Oh, *look* at him.'

'Oh, children, *look*.'

'Isn't he sweet?'

As I play the scene back in my head I see it as it really was. The Hunters: four giant, overlapping heads, viewed behind a grid of wire. The awkward smiles could have been ventriloquising a plea for help. I was a rescuer, that is the point. I may have been little more than a pup, but I chose to rescue them as much as they chose to rescue me. We rescued each other. Only we were doing so under false pretences.

When the door opened, when I jumped up and licked their faces, when they hugged me, I felt relief, but what I didn't realise then was that they too must have felt relieved. They too had gained another chance for freedom. Another chance to be a happy Family.

But even before those first slobbery dog kisses were wiped away, even as we drove away from the dog house, they must have felt that chance begin to fade. They must have realised it had been left behind, somewhere in an empty iron cage.

missy

Grandma Margaret wasn't the outside danger, but she didn't make things any easier. There is no doubt about that.

From the moment she arrived, with her carrier bags and her thousand smells, the whole atmosphere of the house changed. I think it was mainly because she brought with her the memory of Grandpa Bill. And his memory turned out to be a far more formidable force than the frail old man himself had been. Every meal, every television programme, every sentence to come out of any Family member's mouth would spark off a remembrance. And likewise, every smile or laugh would be viewed as a mark of disrespect.

On the evening of her arrival she joined Hal in the television room, where he was watching his favourite programme. She started to make her presence felt slowly, by embarking on a series of long and deliberately heavy sighs. Hal tried his best to ignore her, and succeeded. Until, that is, the sighs became punctuated with a series of carefully timed and clearly disapproving tuts.

'Nan, are you all right?'

She responded with a quiet, baffled sigh. Hal turned back to the television. Then, moments later, she said: 'Is this meant to be music?'

Now it was Hal's turn to sigh. 'It *is* music.'

Another baffled sigh. 'Well it doesn't sound like it. It's just shouting.'

'It's not shouting, it's rapping. It's called hip-hop. It's the most important form of popular music to have appeared over the last thirty years.'

This time the baffled sigh was accompanied by a baffled shaking of the head. 'But can you honestly understand a word he is saying?'

'*She.*'

'Sorry?'

'It's a woman.'

'A woman?' She even *smelled* baffled by this point.

'Yeah. Missy Elliot.'

'Mrs Elliot?'

'No, Missy. Missy Elliot. She's the most successful female rap performer in the world.'

'I used to know a Mrs Elliot.'

'*Missy.*'

'But she didn't used to wear things like that.'

'God.'

'And she wasn't coloured.'

This statement caused Hal's thumb to bounce aggressively off his bottom lip.

'No, and she liked proper songs. John Denver, that sort of thing. Or was that her husband? Yes, that's right. He worked with Bill at the brewery. Only he was on the management side, you know. But your grandpa always got on really well with him, shared his sense of humour, just like you did . . .'

Hal looked away from the television and his mouth

softened into a reluctant, but sympathetic smile. He stroked my head.

And then, prompted by some unspoken memory, Grandma Margaret began to cry. 'I'm sorry,' she said eventually. 'I'm disturbing your programme.'

'It's all right, Nan. It's all right. I'll get you a tissue.'

And he went and did exactly that, placing a supportive hand on her shoulder when he returned. It was a loving, if awkward gesture.

'You're a good boy,' she said, gently mopping her cheek. 'Such a good boy. Bill was always so proud of you.'

chop

It was Adam who found this new arrangement the hardest to deal with. You see, although he couldn't say anything at the time, Adam had never wanted Grandma Margaret to come.

He had once suggested, before Grandpa Bill died, that they might be more comfortable in an Old People's Home. I don't know what an Old People's Home is like but if it is anything like a Dog's Home I can see why Kate objected. Grandma Margaret never would have been able to fit into one of those cages.

But anyway, Adam wasn't happy from the start. It wasn't the way she smelt; no one seemed to notice that. It wasn't even that she was constantly on the look-out for an unprovoked outburst of happiness, ready to transform it into guilt. It was something else. There was something about her presence, in the corner of the room, which irritated Adam profoundly. Every time she would express one of her Controversial Opinions Adam would roll his eyes and say something like 'Times have changed', or 'You shouldn't believe everything you read in the papers' or even, in extreme cases, 'Margaret, you can't *say* those sorts of things.' But she could, and she kept on saying them, even though she'd always get interrupted halfway through. After all, she was grieving.

'I think everyone's gone too far down this multi-cultural wotsit . . .'

'Bill thought the only way you can make sure these shoplifters don't do it again is to chop off their hands . . .'

'As Enoch Powell used to say . . .'

'Gay weddings, whatever next . . .'

'I tell you Adam, these illegal immigrants . . .'

And, inevitably, Grandma Margaret's Controversial Opinions became the subject of various bedroom discussions, even on the first evening of her stay.

'I'm sorry, Kate, but your mum says the most offensive things.'

'Yes, I know,' she said, tidying one of Adam's drawers. 'But we're not going to change her.'

'But she's a racist. She's got the most horrible little mind sometimes, she really has.'

'She's my *mother*, Adam. And she's in a state of grief.'

'I know I know but –'

'She didn't have a nice-little-liberal-middle-class-holidays-to-the-south-of-France upbringing like you did, you know. She had it really tough when she was younger. And she's having it really tough now –'

'Well, that's a *stupid* thing to say. I'm sorry, but that's like saying Hitler couldn't help it because it was the way he was brought up. And anyway, you managed to escape your upbringing, didn't you?'

'Escape? Do you realise just how arrogant you are sounding at this moment in time? I didn't *escape* anything, and I'm not ashamed of my mother. If you cannot accept the fact that I can love someone, a member of my own family, regardless of whatever happens to pour out of their mouth then I'm afraid that's your stupid problem.'

'Fine, if that's the way you want it –' And on this particular occasion, Adam stood up to make his own escape. With me. To the park.

'Come on, boy. Walkies.'

hard

As we walked down the street I tried to get Adam to be reasonable. Why had he been so hard on Kate? He was never like this. He was normally calm, reasonable.

I wagged my tail, I panted heavily, I made soft eyes. It seemed to have some effect because as we got closer to the park his stride lightened and he even started to whistle. But then I remembered.

The woman from yesterday. Emily.

She was there again, as Adam must have expected. Sitting on the bench watching Falstaff trot his way around the park. Again, I decided the best thing to do was to wait with Adam, to make sure he stayed protected.

'Hello again,' he said.

'Hello, and hello, gorgeous,' Emily said as she stroked my head.

'You're not wearing any shoes.'

She smiled, her head dropping to one side. 'No. I try not to. Well, as much as possible. I like to feel the earth under my feet, I feel like I'm sort of at one with nature and stuff. You know, the vibrations.' Her head lifted, to look at Adam. 'You probably think I'm mad.'

'No, not at all. Not at all. I could do with feeling at one with anything right now, to tell you the honest truth.'

Emily's face crinkled with exaggerated concern,

although her scent remained unchanged. 'Oh, I'm sorry. You poor thing. Have you had a hard day at the office?'

'At the classroom, actually. I'm a teacher.'

Exaggerated concern switched to exaggerated surprise. 'A teacher? Wow, that must be *amazing*!'

Adam paused, never having received that reaction before. 'Well, it has its moments. What about you?'

Emily looked confused.

'Your job? Do you work?'

'Oh yes, yes. Sorry. Yes. I'm an aromatherapist.'

'I'm fascinated by aromatherapy,' said Adam, for what had to be the first time in his life.

'Really? So many people, especially men, they're still, you know, what's the word?'

'Sceptical?'

'Yes, they're sceptical about alternative forms of health and medicinal, you know, practices. But I believe that what we smell has a massive impact on our general well-being, but it must be the most underrated of all the senses.'

'Yes.'

'I'm trying to branch out into other areas as well – reflexology, crystalology, astrology, numerology . . .'

'Numerology?'

'Yes, it's the idea that your whole life is governed by number patterns, which form part of, like, an overall cosmic plan.'

'Oh, right.'

'It's to do with, you know, vibrations. Every number has its own cosmic vibration.'

'That's fascinating.'

By this point both of them were stroking my head, their hands occasionally making slight contact. *Prediction equals protection.* I decided it would be safer to stand up and sniff around the bench, but still to keep a close ear on the action.

'Yes,' Emily said. 'It is. And everyone always thinks it is for people, you know, who are a bit loopy and New Age and not quite there, but it's actually really Old Age. It started millions and millions of years ago, not long after the dinosaurs, you know, it was that man who invented the triangle. Pie-something-or-other . . .'

'Pythagoras?'

'Sorry?'

'The man who started numerology – was he called Pythagoras?'

There was a long pause during which I looked up to check on the whereabouts of Falstaff. He was nowhere to be seen and his scent had become lost among the smells of the park, and Emily's feet.

'I don't know,' Emily said eventually. 'But, anyway, he was the first to realise that you can tell a lot about a person from their numbers. You see, I was born on the seventh of July 1975 which means I have three sevens in my personal chart. And the number seven has a lot of psychic qualities and, like, that is so me because I'm just always thinking of things and stuff that other people are thinking of.'

I sensed Adam was uncomfortable, perhaps worried that Emily could work out what he was thinking at that moment as he stared into her wide, Dachshund eyes.

'What year were you born?' she asked him.

'Oh, 1963,' he said. 'The year sexual intercourse was invented.'

'Sorry?'

'Nothing. It's from a poem. I teach English. Anyway, I was born on the third of June 1963.'

Emily's jaw fell so far that it seemed, for a worrying second, she was about to swallow Adam whole.

Her hand clamped his forearm. 'No! You are *joking*!'

'No. Um, no. I'm afraid not, that's my birthday. Third of the sixth sixty-three.'

'But that's incredible! Three. Six. Six. Three. My God! You know, I felt it yesterday. Just sitting next to you, you had this like intense cosmic energy. This hardly ever happens. Wow! My God! Let's think, so, OK, you've got the three, all right, so that's creativity and independence. You like language, you're very imaginative, you've got, like, a free spirit. But then there's the six. Wow, this is *really* weird. You see the six and the three are opposites. The six is about duty, about responsibility, about caring, the family, that sort of thing. Wow! So you've got this powerful, like, tension within you, between being responsible and doing what you think is right and this other wild force which makes you want to be wild and follow your instincts. My God, you know, I can feel it now. You've got this aura . . .'

Emily was right. There was some conflict going on here, for Adam, and the battle lines were now marked on his face. *Duty, Adam. Remember your duty.*

sniff

OK, I thought. Enough's enough. I had to do something. I had to stop them from getting any closer. But just as I was about to start barking I was interrupted.

'Well, well, madwag. Well, well.'

I turned around to see Falstaff sniffing my behind. 'My name's *Prince*.'

'Sorry, madwag, no offence.' Falstaff removed his nose from my rear end and came around to face me. He was fatter and uglier than I had remembered. And older too, with white beardy whiskers. 'You liked my trick yesterday, didn't you, eh? Getting out of my collar like that. It's simple. A neck-twist to the left, like that, move back slowly with your head in line with your neck and then out. It's as easy as that. Now that's a good trick to know. It could come in handy someday.'

'I doubt that very much.'

'Yes, of course you do, madwag. Course you do. You're a Labrador, aren't you, eh? A Labrabore, eh? Slipping leads just isn't your thing, is it? But that's OK. That's fine. Resist the Springers. But you see, I'm only half Springer, aren't I? So I've got no breed loyalties. None at all. Or rather, I've got so many of them they've cancelled each other out. The whole dog kingdom is in my blood, madwag, it really is. I've even got a bit of Labrador in

93

me somewhere. Yes, my great-great-great grandmother, on my mother's side, she was a Labrador so the story goes. Anyway, madwag, enough about me, let's walk.' He gestured over towards the back of the park.

I hesitated. Adam and Emily were still talking. Or rather, Emily was still talking while Adam sat, entranced, unable to take his eyes off the feast before him.

'I don't think I should,' I said. 'I think I should wait here.'

Falstaff wasn't having any of it. 'I've got something to tell you, madwag old chap.'

'Tell me?'

'About my mistress.' He pointed his nose toward Emily. 'But if you're not interested . . .'

He jogged off, heading beyond the oak trees towards the composting mass of debris at the back of the park. Wanting to know more about Emily, I had little choice but to follow.

'Have you sniffed here before?' he said, before pushing his head under a loose heap of dirt and dead leaves. The weird thing was I had never seen or smelt this heap, even though I had trodden over the composted waste land a thousand times.

'About Emily –'

He lifted his head up out of the heap, a leaf dangling from his ear. 'That's some good shit, madwag. Good shit. Have a sniff.'

Now this was a dilemma. You see, pleasure-sniffing has always been strictly frowned upon by the Labrador population as a result of Guru Oscar's teachings.

Sure, we sniff all the time. But only scent trails. We

sniff out of duty, to attain information. And we always keep our heads above ground. Pleasure-sniffing, on the other paw, requires you to completely submerge your nose, and maybe your entire head, into a smell-heap such as the one I was now presented with. It is the most intense sniffing experience possible, and serves no other function than to get you high. As mentioned specifically in the Pact, pleasure-sniffing has long been considered irresponsible and even dangerous. Indeed, some dogs spend their entire park time with their nose under cover, and pass the rest of the day neglecting any sense of Family duty they might once have felt.

But this was different. If Adam and Emily were going to see each other every evening, I had to try and squeeze as much information out of Falstaff as possible. And to do that, I had to befriend him. In other words, I had to join him in his activities, however much at odds they were with my Labrador lifestyle.

Cautiously my nose made its way through the dirt and leaves. I tried to ignore Falstaff, who was chuckling at my technique, and instead concentrated on holding my breath. If I didn't sniff, there could be no damage done. But I couldn't hold it for long.

As I inhaled, a wild and heady cocktail of smells hit me. Rich earth, leaf juice, worm blood, squirrel droppings. I recognised each smell, but had never experienced them at such intensity. Time stopped, or shifted sideways. My whole body dissolved into the air. I couldn't feel my paws.

I don't honestly know how long I was under, but for as long as I was, nothing mattered. All my frets and concerns and responsibilities evaporated instantly. Adam and Emily. Kate. Grandma Margaret. Who cared? What was the worst that could happen?

Smells turned to colours in my mind, red and gold.

I was floating. Content.

Falstaff said something but I couldn't understand. The words were meaningless. My heart throbbed.

Eventually I pulled my head out and shook myself free of dirt and leaves.

'How was it for you, madwag, eh?'

'Good,' I said, delirious. 'Good smells.' I sneezed, provoking another chuckle from Falstaff.

'Well, well, madwag. Well, well. I never thought you had it in you.'

My senses were slowly being restored. 'About Emily. You said . . . you said you had something to tell me.'

Falstaff looked at me straight on. It was the first time I had seen him completely serious. 'OK, OK. I will tell you the truth.' He paused, for dramatic effect. 'She takes people away from their families. And she will want to take your master, I know. I can tell. She will want him for herself.'

Although my head was still cloudy, the pain I felt at that moment was sharp and real. A sequence of disjointed images of the Family flashed in my mind and the accompanying scents returned. Adam and Kate slow-dancing together last Christmas. Adam and Hal armwrestling on the kitchen table. Hal and Charlotte fighting for the remote control.

A single thought: the Family must be protected.

'Who,' I said at long last. 'Who has she taken away?'

Falstaff sighed, clearly wishing he hadn't said anything. 'Most recently, Simon, my master. Two years ago he had a wife, they were trying for a baby, but then Emily came along. He has a lot of money, madwag, a lot of money. She won't have mentioned him yet . . . But anyway, madwag, it doesn't matter, does it? Not really. I mean, think about it, we could end up living together. It would be a riot, madwag. A riot. Come on, lighten up. Have another sniff.'

A wave of nausea passed over me as I stared blankly at the smell-heap. I knew enough.

'I have to go. I'm sorry, it's my duty.'

Falstaff sighed again, this time with disappointment. He had misjudged my reaction. 'Duty schmooty, come on, madwag. I shouldn't have told you. But there's nothing you can do about it, anyway. What happens happens. Don't be such a, such a Labrador, eh. Come on. Relax.'

'I'm sorry.'

As I trotted back over to the bench my mind felt as if it was about to explode. Everything was chaos. I saw Emily and Adam on the bench, even closer than before, and I retched. I was about to throw up. What had they been talking about? Was Adam really prepared to risk the Family? Where was this all going to end up?

In my confused state only one thing could be clung to with any certainty. Duty over all, I thought to myself. Yes.

Duty over *all*.

face

There is something about the human face. Something ridiculous, yes, but also sad, unprotected, even when it smiles. I was noticing this as I lay between Adam and Kate, watching them read their bedtime books. I don't know, they just seemed so hairless and vulnerable, I wanted to lick them, wash them clean, keep them safe.

'Prince, no. Stop that.'

'Oh, Prince, please don't. We're trying to read.'

I'm sorry, I couldn't resist. Once I lay back down, they returned to their separate worlds. They sighed and chuckled quietly to themselves from time to time. Adam even nodded his head on one occasion as if the author was in the same room as us, sitting at the end of the bed, waiting for approval of what he had written. 'Very good,' Adam assured him, the anxious and invisible author. '*Very* good.'

Right then, although they may have looked vulnerable, they also looked happy. In their own worlds, but also together. Sharing the quiet, animal peace of humans who truly love each other. The children asleep, the house calm. But my apprehension would not subside. Lying between these two loving creatures, feeling their warmth, breathing in their scent, I still couldn't believe that it was going to be OK.

For the first time ever I wanted the moment to stay still. For it to sit there, like an obedient dog, like *me*, and only move on when it was told to. There may not have been passion in the room – that faded, years ago, along with the carpet – but there was something else. Something as – no, *more* – important. You could feel it just by entering the room, just by seeing them sitting together, side by side, half-cocooned by duvet. Love. That's what you felt. Coming from every corner of the room, contained within every object. It sounded sentimental, but it was true. And anyway, I'm a Labrador.

Sentimental was all I knew.

But as any old dog would confirm, nothing stays still. Not permanently. Puppy love matures into dog love, which soon becomes old dog love. It hobbles on for years but then love itself eventually has to be put down. So I couldn't help thinking that this moment may already have been a memory, and a nostalgic one at that.

Love, I realised, wasn't going to be enough.

stick

'You're right, Prince. This is a very serious situation.'
Henry was, of course, the only dog I could turn to. A
friend, a mentor, a Labrador – he was the only one who
could fully understand what I was going through. He
was also, I had hoped, the only one who might be able
to offer a solution.

'So what should I do?'

We were lying side by side on the grass, in full view
of Adam and Mick. They were in conversation on the
bench, the bench which had witnessed last night's
horrendous entrapment. Because that is how I viewed it.
Entrapment. Adam was snared in a trap which he
couldn't, single-handedly, get himself out of.

I started to chew on the end of a stick, anxiously
awaiting Henry's verdict.

'You need more information, more conclusive information, before any action can, or indeed should be taken,'
he said. 'When will you next see them together?'

'He is going around to her house tonight for an
aromatherapy treatment. She says his aura is in a state
of intense internal conflict and that she may be able to
cure him. He is taking me with him so Kate won't think
anything is up.' I'm afraid this was all true. The lure of
visiting the house he had been fascinated by for months,

combined with the opportunity to get to know Emily better, had evidently been too much for Adam.

'That is good,' Henry said, to my surprise. 'You must go. However hard it is, you must go and observe everything, Prince. Your power depends on your senses. You must sniff out any potential trouble. Your eyes, your ears, and most importantly your nose – these are your weapons. If the situation looks likely to get out of paw, you must, of course, act decisively. But don't, at any time, risk the secrecy of your mission. Remember, no matter what it looks like, everything is always within your control. The Labrador has ultimate power. You know that, don't you, Prince?'

I felt reassured. By his words and by the smile emerging on his wise golden face. 'Yes, Henry. I know that.'

'Tell me, this Falstaff character, what is he like? Would you say he's a reliable source of information? Does he strike you as a responsible sort of chap?'

I pictured Falstaff as I first saw him, when he slipped his lead. And then as he was last night, his head submerged in a smell-heap.

'It's, um, too early to tell,' I said.

'He's not a Springer, is he?'

'No,' I lied. Or half-lied. 'Of course not. He's a cross, but I don't know what between.'

'OK, well, just remember non-Labradors often do not share the sense of duty we feel towards our masters. In fact, they often take great pleasure in trying to lead Labradors astray. So be careful, that's all.'

It's funny, looking back now, but I never doubted Henry's judgement. Not for one moment. His wisdom was infinite as it always had been. The very first time I visited the park, he had been there, and he must have seen me as a new recruit. It seemed to me that he must have been there since the beginning of time. But in reality he'd only just finished his police work and clearly wanted a new challenge. He followed the Pact to the letter, and knew it better than any other Labrador. And, by listening to his wise words, by taking on board the lessons he taught me, I had managed to preserve and protect the Hunters from any threat.

Until now. Now the real test was beginning.

But Henry would help me, I knew that.

letter

The rest of the day I spent in mental preparation. I paced the kitchen floor, reciting the Labrador Pact.

Duty over all . . .

Prediction equals protection . . .

I ran through worst-case scenarios. What would I do? How would I stop them? Would Falstaff help me?

Kate was the first home. Poor Kate. I watched as she went about her normal routine. Taking her coat off, switching on the radio, emptying the dishwasher, tidying everything away. She seemed so vulnerable, so completely oblivious to the outside threat which could affect the future of her Family.

She picked up a letter lying on the kitchen unit. Hal had read it aloud this morning, before school – a university had made him a conditional offer. She sat down to re-read it, a proud smile spreading across her face.

Grandma Margaret was next through the door. Back from her Friday coach trip. Back from her Lovely Day.

'Here, Katherine, I got speaking to this woman on the coach. Lovely lady, no airs and graces, she lost her husband too . . .'

While Grandma Margaret was talking, Kate continued her routine. She made my meal, cold meat and biscuits, but I wasn't hungry. I was too nervous about what lay ahead later that evening. She picked up the bowl and chopped the meat up into smaller pieces but still I couldn't face it.

'Are you OK, Prince?' she asked, her mouth pouting with concern.

I wagged and panted an affirmative. The last thing I wanted was for Kate to get suspicious. *Remember the Pact, Prince. Remember the Pact.* She crouched down and planted a soft kiss on my cheek. I licked her face in return.

'Prince,' she giggled. 'Stop that.' But I knew she liked it really.

Hal and Charlotte arrived back together. Ever since a news story about a girl who'd gone missing on her way to the corner shop, Kate had insisted that Hal escort his sister to and from school. Charlotte, of course, wasn't happy with this arrangement. Or rather, she pretended not to be.

'It's so embarrassing walking with *him*,' she grumbled, twisting her nose ring. 'He's so weird, he just walks along talking in Shakespeare.'

'He's got exams, Charlotte, he's got to learn quotes. Try and be sympathetic.'

'Yeah, I know, but no one else seems to be walking down the street talking as if they're in the sixteenth century or whatever.' She threw a heavy stare at her brother who was starting to make himself a triple-decker peanut butter and Marmite sandwich, as he did every evening.

'I tried to tell her,' Hal said to his mum, although more for his sister's benefit. 'I said: this is just a phase, it's perfectly normal, you'll grow out of it. You're bound

to have these feelings of self-consciousness and embarrassment. It's to do with the hormones and because your
body is changing very quickly at the moment. I was very
sympathetic.'

'Hal,' reprimanded Kate.

'He's such a tosser.'

'Char– *lotte*.'

'See, again, a perfectly natural response for someone
of her age and gender who lives permanently in the
shadow of their elder and wiser and better-looking and,
let's face it, more sophisticated sibling.'

'Tosser!' With that, Charlotte jangled her way upstairs
and slammed her bedroom door. Hal held out his hand,
as if Charlotte had just proved his own point, and then
reverted to talking Shakespeare, in between taking bites
of his sandwich.

Although an impartial human observer may have been
slightly troubled by these Family squabbles, as a Labrador
I understood what was really going on. I could *smell* the
love.

'So shaken as we are, so wan with care,' said Hal to
himself. 'Find we a time for frighted peace to pant. Act
One, Scene, er . . . One, the King.'

When Adam arrived back, the house was at its
maximum noise level. Hal was running through his
quotes. Kate was listening to the radio while wiping the
kitchen table. Charlotte was listening to The Mad Dogz
Of War. And Grandma Margaret was still busy telling
an imaginary audience about her day.

'My God,' he said, clunking his keys on the cabinet
in the hall. 'You can't hear yourself think.'

He moved into the kitchen, pulled back a chair and slumped himself down. I went over to him, and he cheered up instantly. He grabbed my top jaw playfully and started to shake my head.

'Who's a good boy? Who's a good boy? *Who's* a good boy?' he asked me. And then, to Kate: 'I said I'd drop some of last year's exam papers around at Paul Mortimer's, you know, that NQT I was telling you about. He only lives on Friary Road so I might as well take them around later when I take Prince. OK?'

I pulled back. He stopped shaking me. I couldn't believe it: he'd even made up an excuse for tonight, in case he was too long with Emily.

He smelt nervous, and no wonder. The kitchen, for a brief moment, seemed to contract around us.

'Yeah, OK,' said Kate, without even the faintest trace of doubt. She was too absorbed in listening to the man on the radio.

Hal had made himself another peanut butter and Marmite sandwich and was about to head upstairs to start revising. 'I will die a hundred thousand deaths, Ere break the smallest parcel of this vow,' he said, as he munched. 'Act . . . Act Three, Scene Two, the Prince.'

The Labrador Pact:
Observe everything

If a Family is in danger of falling apart, the signs will be everywhere.

Be continually alert to any changes of scent or behaviour, and if such changes occur smell for an explanation. This is equally important when your masters are outside the Family home.

Humans must therefore be monitored at every possible moment in order to ensure the success of our mission.

Watch, listen, but most of all smell for trouble at all times.

snip

I've not always had such a strong sense of duty. I used to have a hard job, in my early years, trying to control my instincts. I was guided by my loins, rather than my principles. I kept on falling for, and falling off, older females. Tall. Long legs. That worldly scent. I couldn't control myself.

But it wasn't just other dogs I fell in love with, it was furniture too. Within minutes of arriving at the Hunter family home, I fell in love with it, I really did. Especially the cushions.

'Are Labradors *meant* to do that?' houseguests would ask with evident disdain, as they made their way into the living room. I carried on. Throughout the embarrassed glances and lightsabre jokes, I carried on.

But this behaviour, it was decided, was not natural.

Bollocks.

That is what it amounted to.

Remove the bollocks, remove the problem.

Snip, snip. Gone.

So I was booked in for an appointment with Nice Mister Vet. I was told it was for my own good. That's what Adam said as he left me in the vet's surgery.

'It's for your own good, Princey-boy, you'll see. You'll wake up a new man.'

Words could not describe my outrage. As far as I was concerned, this was The End. Of my life, or at least my lust for it. It was also, I was sure, the end of love. Adam was robbing me of my chance of future happiness. He was forcing me into a final compromise. But the anger faded, along with the lust, and I woke up into a new world of neutrality.

I was no longer distracted.

Through sacrifice, everything had suddenly become clear.

slippery

'OK, now, take everything off.'

Emily was rubbing her hands, coating her fingers in the strangest smelling substance I had ever experienced.

'Everything?' Adam asked, in panic.

She laughed with exaggerated hilarity. 'Well, not everything. You can leave your pants on . . . if you like.' She laughed again, even louder.

'Madwag, this is really rather dull, old chap. Come on, I'll show you round. There's loads of wild things we can get up to.'

Although I was tempted to take up Falstaff's offer, to find out more about Emily's massive new house and its many secrets, I knew I had to stay here. To observe every detail of the rather bizarre scene unfolding before our noses.

'Wait,' commanded Emily. 'Music.'

Adam's head turned to watch her.

'Oceania: Music for a deepwater state of mind,' she said, provoking an ominous whimper of recognition from Falstaff.

'OK, madwag, you old Labrabore. Suit yourself, old chap. Suit yourself.' I watched him trot off into the next room, shaking his head in disapproval.

Right. *Observe, Prince, observe.*

Adam was already lying on the massage table in nothing but his boxer shorts. His *newest* pair. The treatment was under way. Emily, with the sleeves of her pink cardigan rolled up, was starting to stroke the unnatural-smelling oils into the skin, pushing ripples of flesh up his back as she did so.

The air was becoming heavier. Not smell-heap heavy, but powerful enough to fill the whole room and cause every object within it to throb. The stereo, the TV on the wall, and other unrecognisable items of grey gadgetry which sat in each corner.

It was therefore impossible for me to sniff any potential scent of trouble. And on top of the smell, my powers of observation had to contend with the off-putting sound of whales singing their songs of death.

'So what oil are you using?' asked Adam.

'I am using a blend. Lavender and patchouli. To deal with this conflict you have within your aura. The lavender soothes, it is like really good for stress, while the patchouli helps to fort– to strengthen your, you know, your whole spirit.'

'Oh, right.'

She smoothed more oil onto his back, using long downward strokes.

'You know, Adam, you have a really, really good body. Do you work out?'

Whether he was dumbfounded by the question or incapacitated by the scent, Adam remained silent for a long while before answering. 'Um, no. Not . . . not really. But I do go for a jog once in a while. Do you go to the gym?'

'Yes. There is a gym upstairs.'

'Upstairs. My God. This house is *huge*. You must rattle around in it, living on your own.'

Emily paused, her mouth moved sideways and then she said: 'I don't live alone.'

Adam's head shot up. For a moment it seemed he was about to leap off the table – as if he was at Nice Mister Vet's – but Emily's back-rubbing kept him in place. 'But I thought –'

'You thought I lived alone? Oh *no*. I could never do that. No, no, no. Oh, I'd go bonkers. Completely *bonkers*. No. And I wouldn't be living here. Not unless I was the richest aromatherapist in the whole world!'

'Um, God, yes. Of course. So, er, who do you live with?'

'His name is Simon.'

'But who *is* he? Are you married?' Adam made another half-attempt to leave the table, but again he was thwarted.

Perhaps I should have helped him.

'Yes. But that's OK, isn't it?'

'But . . . where . . . where is he?'

'We are not doing anything, like, wrong, are we? I ask all my clients to take their clothes off. It's a necessary part of the treatment, especially in severe cases like yours.'

'But, Emily, I don't mean to be paranoid or sound ungrateful or anything but it's nine o'clock at night. I am a half-naked stranger, covered in oil lying on a table in the centre of your living room. It wouldn't look good, would it, if he came home to find us like this?'

Emily laughed. 'You are a funny man. Very, very funny.'

Her hands were now on his legs, working their slippery way towards his boxer shorts.

'Am I? . . . Look where is he, Simon, where is he at the moment?'

'Oslo.' It was weird the way she said it, as if her answer was also a question. She was still laughing. 'He's at a PR conference or something.'

'So he works in PR?'

'No, not really. Well, you know, I don't think so. He's a business consultant, he goes everywhere all the time. So I get, you know, very bored. When I am here all by my little self . . .'

'Look, yes. Listen, I'm sure you do, but you know what? My, um, aura feels a lot . . . a lot better now, it really does, and so I ought to be going back because Kate, my wife, she will be getting worried.'

As he said these words my heart soared with blissful pride. I had coached my master well. Duty over all. This whole aromatherapy thing, it had been a blip, that's all it was. And anyway, nothing bad had happened, had it?

I stood up and started to wag my tail.

We were going to be safe. We were going home.

But my happiness was short-lived.

'Well, well, madwag. Well, well.' Falstaff had returned, his panting even cheekier than ever.

'What is it?'

'My master,' he said, sniffing me underneath. 'He's come home.'

devil

No.

It could not be true.

But then I heard it too. A car crunching its way over gravel. I started to bark.

'Prince,' said Adam. 'Be quiet.' But I carried on – bark, bark, bark – with the vain hope he would be able to translate my warning.

The car went quiet.

Footsteps.

Crunch, crunch.

Another sound. Metal. Keys.

I stopped barking.

'Oh wow,' said Emily. 'He must have caught an earlier flight!' Her voice indicated no sign of alarm. Unless wearing a full smile and clapping her hands was her normal response to a crisis situation.

Adam sat up on the table with such speed I thought he was going to fall off. I was right. He did.

'Agh,' he said, crash-landing on his elbow. 'Where are my trousers?'

His trousers!

They were right under my nose, I put the crotch in my mouth and darted across the floor, without a second thought for the secrecy of the mission.

I was too late.

'Heh heh, madwag. This will be interesting. And we've got front-row seats.'

I looked up with my mouth full of Adam's trousers and saw . . .

Well, what did I see?

I saw him, Simon. But what struck me first?

His height. Yes, his height. He was the tallest human being I had ever seen. His head, tanned and confident, seemed so far away from the rest of us that at first I wondered whether it could have any real impact when it eventually spoke.

And then there was his smell which, of course, wasn't *his* smell. Falstaff told me it belonged to a Japanese man called Issey Miyake. Mingled with the heavy, throbbing aromatherapy smells it felt almost toxic, burning my nostrils.

Next, the clothes. He was wearing a suit, but not the kind of suit Adam liked to wear. There were no creases. No holes. And, disconcertingly, no dog hair.

For what seemed like forever he just stood there, smelling the scene. And then his eyes locked on Adam, who was sitting awkwardly at dog-level.

I dropped the trousers and turned to Falstaff.

'What's going on?'

'No idea, madwag,' he panted, loving every second. 'No idea.'

I looked up again to see what was happening on Simon's impossibly high face. I don't know what I had expected to see. Anger? Shock? Misery?

But no.

There was something else shaping his features. Something even more disturbing.

Recognition.

'Adam bloody Hunter. My *man*, how the devil are you?'

I remembered something Henry had told me that morning. The Labrador is always in control. But right there, struggling even to keep my grip on that smooth, shining floor, it didn't feel like that. Prediction equals protection. But what had I been able to predict? Even my sense of smell, usually the Labrador's most reliable weapon, was now no use. It had been overpowered, unable to detect anything but aromatherapy oils and Issey Miyake.

Falstaff was no help either. As a Springer, or a half-Springer, it was always going to be difficult to see where his loyalties lay, if he had any at all.

Adam looked completely confused, and remained silent.

'Wow! Do you two know each other?' asked Emily, her eyes frisbee-wide.

'Know each other? We were practically brothers.'

And then Adam somehow managed to speak. 'Simon. My God. It's you.' At this point something happened between them. Something unspoken. I was stuck in the middle, so I could feel it. A strange, hostile energy.

'I was . . . I was just having an aromatherapy treatment.'

'So I see. Did you enjoy it?'

'Yes, yes. It was relaxing.'

Emily cocked her head towards her husband. 'Did you two, like, did you go to school together?'

Simon paused before answering, his eyes staying fixed on Adam as he spoke. 'In a different lifetime.'

'Wow, really?' Emily's eyes were taking over her face.

Simon switched his attention, momentarily, to his wife. 'It was a figure of speech.'

'Oh yes, sorry.'

Simon laughed a dangerous laugh. Adam laughed too – I assumed out of fear. He wanted to leave, but probably realised that would make him look even more suspicious.

Simon explained further. 'Same school, same class, even the same bloody haircut. Same taste in girls too, if I remember rightly.'

Adam was still laughing, as he hunted for his clothes. 'Yes, yes,' he said. 'Same haircut.'

'And then we went our separate ways,' Simon continued, watching as Adam struggled his way into his trousers. 'After school, Adam stayed with education and I sold my soul. Got a good price for it though, ha! So, Adam, last time I saw you you'd got a job at Rosewood. Still there?'

'Um, yes. Yes I am,' he said, zipping up his fly.

'That must be *bloody* weird, walking down those same old corridors. Has it changed much?'

Adam was now buttoning his shirt. 'Um, the kids have. The ones that actually turn up. Lots of problems. Drugs. Cars. Sex.'

Simon laughed. 'Sounds fantastic. Better than going home to watch *Blue Peter* anyway.' He turned to me and said, 'No offence,' but I didn't understand what he meant.

Fully clothed, Adam's confidence seemed to be partially restored.

'Well, it's a bad catchment area nowadays. Mainly single-parent families, high unemployment, you know.'

Emily looked confused. 'So when did you two last see each other?' she asked.

'Oh God, when was it?' Adam looked at Simon.

'Thirteen years ago,' Simon answered without hesitation. 'Just before I moved down to London.'

'It's pretty bad, isn't it. Us not keeping in contact. I mean, you were our best man.'

Emily's mouth dropped open. 'Best man. If you were his best man, why haven't you told me about him?'

I was about to ask Falstaff a similar question, but discovered he was currently preoccupied trying to gain sexual pleasure by rubbing his belly against a cushion.

'We used to be lovers,' Simon said, straight-faced.

Emily stiffened. 'Lovers?'

Simon mouthed the word, 'Joke.'

'Oh yes, sorry,' Emily said.

I remembered something Henry had once said. 'Humour is a defence mechanism for humans, and usually indicates they have something to cover up.'

I was just wondering what Simon had to cover up, when he sat down and asked: 'How's Kate?'

stroke

When we got home the door was already open, with an anguished-looking Kate ready to greet us. She didn't say anything at first, and stormed back into the house. Hal was revising in his room and Charlotte was already in bed.

'Where have you been? I've been worried out of my mind.'

Adam avoided eye contact and placed the lead back on its hook with greater care than usual. 'I told you. I had to take the –'

'Well, that should have only taken five minutes, Adam. What's going on with you at the moment?'

'Please, Kat. Not now. I haven't got the energy to row. I'm shattered, I really am.'

'*You're* shattered? Well, how do you think I am? I've had to deal with Hal stressing about the exam he had today, then him and Charlotte tearing each other to pieces all night, I've had my mother crying her heart out, and I've nearly had to place my husband on the Missing Persons list after taking the dog for the longest walk in history. And the house, the house has been such a . . . mess.'

'I'm . . . sorry.'

I wagged my tail diplomatically to try to smooth things over. It seemed for a second that I might have been successful. Kate's face softened, Adam bit his top lip in apology. But then this happened:

'What's that smell?' She leaned forward, twitching her nose.

'I don't know, I can't smell anything.' Adam teetered backward.

'It's on you. Lavender or something.'

'It's probably that new shower gel.'

'No, no. It's not. It's something else.'

'Well, I'm sorry, darling, but I can't smell a thing, perhaps there's something wrong with your nose. Or perhaps you're about to have a stroke.'

Kate frowned, folded her arms and stared straight into Adam's face. 'What's going on, Adam?'

I had to do something, I knew that. Of course I did. I still hadn't worked out what had happened, back with Emily and Simon and Falstaff in the new house, but I could sense that within the space of one evening the harmony of the Family had come under threat.

When a wife becomes suspicious of her own husband, things have a tendency to descend into chaos. Henry had taught me that during one of my earliest lessons.

I decided to divert Kate's attention by jumping up and resting my front paws against her stomach. The strategy misfired. I was escorted, by the collar, to the utility room, where I was shut in, leaving Adam in the kitchen to fend for himself.

I could have barked, I suppose, but that would have only made things worse. The best I could do was stick my ear to the door and listen closely to every word. Lapsang, purring loudly in her basket, raised one eye wearily.

'What *are* you doing?' she asked me.

'I'm trying to listen. This is important, please be quiet.'

'Prince, darling. I've told you before, you mustn't get too close.'

'Listen, Lapsang, I'm sorry, but you don't understand.'

'I pity your species, I really do.' And with that, the eye closed and she went back to sleep.

Adam had said something. What had he said? Damn that stupid, selfish cat. I caught Kate's response halfway through.

'– recently, that's all. Don't you think?'

'OK, OK. I'll tell you. I was at the park and I bumped into someone. Someone who has just moved into the big, new house I always go on about. Anyway, she –'

'*She?*'

'Yes . . . Emily, I think her name was. Anyway guess who she's married to? Guess who's returned here?'

'So you've been all this time chatting up some married woman in the park? And anyway, that doesn't explain why you smell like that.'

'*Guess.*'

'Look, I'm not going to stand here all night playing your little –'

'Simon Hotspur.'

'Simon –'

There was a pause. No, it was more than a pause. It was an interval between conversations. For ages, I couldn't hear a thing other than Lapsang's pneumatic purr. When Kate eventually spoke her voice was completely different. She wasn't angry any more. She sounded dazed, each word taking forever to leave her mouth.

'Simon. Hotspur. Has. Come. Back. Here?'

'Yes, and he's flasher and smugger than ever. Are you OK?'

'I'm fine. Absolutely. Fine. I've just got a headache, it's just come on. What . . . what is he doing here?'

'He's working freelance. He's a management consultant, goes all over. Finally sold his soul.'

'He's . . . um, he's got a wife?'

'Yes. Emily. A bit ditsy, about half his age. She's an aromatherapist. She gave me a sample.' *The truth, Adam, there's a good boy.* 'And you know what, the house isn't too bad from the inside. A bit sterile and too many boy's toys lying about for my liking, but his wife must have added a few warm touches.'

'Right, er, yes. I see.'

'Anyway, they're coming to the barbecue.'

The barbecue, which the Hunters held every year on their lawn, was only two days away – on Sunday.

Panic-smells filtered through the door.

'Yes, he said it would be good to catch up properly. He'd like to see you too. He sent his love.'

Another pause: 'Oh. Right. But –'

'Yes, I know, I know what you're going to say. And you're right. The way he treated Sarah was terrible. And never hearing a word since, even though he's Hal's god-father. And, yes, I haven't forgotten about my stag do either. But he didn't mean it, you know. He always liked you, you know he did. He just used to be one of the lads, didn't he? Didn't want to see any of his mates getting hitched. It never worked though, did it, that's one thing he couldn't have talked me out of. Anyway, he doesn't seem to be against marriage any more. Emily's his third.'

'Third?'

'Yeah. He was with someone in London. A solicitor or something . . . but now he reckons it's the real thing. But honestly, you should see them together. Talk about chalk and cheese. Mr Slick and Mrs Hippy-Dippy . . .'

They carried on talking, and although Kate continued to sound dazed, I felt an overwhelming sense of relief. Everything was out in the open. OK, not *everything*, but as good as. I know it sounds foolish now but at the time that is what I thought. The Family was safe to rest in its beds.

I strolled over to my basket, smiling to myself.

'What have you got to be so happy about?' Lapsang gazed down at me, both eyes now open.

'Everything is going well, that's all.'

She looked at me, with what I thought was a flicker of compassion. 'Just be careful.'

I sighed. 'Listen, Lapsang, I appreciate where you're coming from. I really do. But the thing is, and I don't mean any offence by this, you're a cat. Cats have never understood about loyalty or duty, have they?'

'No, darling, but we understand about pain. We understand about Families. We understand that if you stay around too long you will get hurt.' And with that she stood up, yawned, and walked majestically along the unit with her tail held high. She pawed herself down to the ground, landing light on her feet.

'Good night, Prince,' she said, before pushing open her cat-flap. 'Just be careful.'

I watched her brown tail rub against the top of the flap and disappear out of view. 'Good night, Lapsang.'

The Labrador Pact:
Preserve the secrecy of
the mission

Humans must never know that we are in control. For their own protection, they must remain in ignorance of our mission. If we are exposed, or if the motives behind our actions are made too obvious, we lose our power. We must exert influence over our human masters, at the same time as making them believe the complexities of their world are beyond our full understanding.

ruler

The following morning, Hal was standing in his bedroom with his trousers around his ankles, trying to gauge the length of his penis with a clear blue ruler.

'No, that can't be right.' He turned to view his side profile in the wardrobe mirror, and nearly castrated himself as he pushed the ruler back further. A disheartened sigh. He looked up at his wall of breasts and rubbed some more.

'Come on, come *on*.' But it was no good.

All that pulling and yanking and tugging and still no difference.

He moved over to his bed, with his trousers and boxer shorts still around his ankles. When he got there, to the bed, he slumped down and looked mournfully at his wilting penis. And then at the pile of textbooks on his desk.

Poor Hal, poor poor Hal.

I stood up and wagged my tail in an attempt to cheer him up. It had no visible effect. I tilted my head. A smile arrived on his face but then, realising it had come to the wrong place, disappeared. Looking back down, Hal let out another sigh. And this one lasted longer, causing his lips to flap. In fact, the sigh lasted so long that I thought that maybe this was not all about the size of his penis.

Maybe.

Maybe not.

I worried for him, I really did. I looked into his eyes and I saw trouble. He was too fragile, still too much of a pup.

'What are you looking at?' he asked me, mock-tough.

I told him, in my own way, that I was looking at his future and that he could take control of it, that he could make everything all right. As always, he refused to listen.

'Prince,' he said, 'Princey boy.' He then leaned back against the wall, pushed his face behind the blind and looked outside the window. It was starting to rain.

marriage

Later on, the doorbell rang.

Adam was at a governors' meeting. Hal and Charlotte and Grandma Margaret were all upstairs, in their separate worlds. And at the time, Kate was on all fours, trying to pick up stray strands of Labrador hair from the carpet. 'You really are a messy dog,' she had told me, with mock-severity. 'You really are.'

She struggled and groaned herself upright, back to a human position, and went to answer the door. This took her quite a while owing to the fact that Hal had pulled the doorknob off last weekend and nobody had put it back on properly. The house, as Adam had shouted at the time, was falling to pieces.

When the door opened, the first thing I heard was the sound of Kate gasping for air.

The second thing I heard was: 'Waah-hey, madwag. What a sniff palace!' It was Falstaff, burying his nose in the sweet-smelling bush in the front garden.

I looked further up, and left, to see Simon's smiling face, blocking out the sun.

'It's been a long time, Kate,' he said, thrusting forward a bouquet of flowers.

'Oh my God. Simon.' Before taking the flowers,

Kate had to empty her hands of dog hair and doorknob – both of which were placed on the side cabinet.

'What's going on?' I asked Falstaff.

He looked up, cocked his leg, and started to piss aimlessly on the small garden path. 'Your guess, madwag, is as good as mine.'

Simon's eyes leisurely soaked in the sight before him. 'You really are a beautiful woman, Kate. As beautiful as I remembered.'

'I, um, hear you've just moved, to the house on the park,' she said, ignoring the compliment.

'Yes. I had to admit defeat – London was killing me. It's funny though, isn't it? How life moves in circles, even when you expect it to go in a straight line?' He leant over me, roughly patting my head. 'We're all like you, aren't we, chasing our own tails?'

'You? Admit defeat?'

'I know, hard to believe, eh?'

'And I hear you're married,' she said, her attempt at cool belied by the crack in her voice.

'Oh, *Emily*. Adam told you about her?' he asked, surprised.

'Yes. Of course.'

'Well, yes. Married, but only in the loosest sense of the word.'

'I didn't even know there was one.'

'Sorry. One what?'

'A loose sense. For marriage.'

Simon smiled at her wisely. 'Ooh, but Kate, I'm *sure* you do.'

I looked through his legs at Falstaff, who was now

burrowing for stronger smells. Simon tugged his lead and brought him to heel.

'I don't know, madwag. You can't get away with anything nowadays, can you?'

But I wasn't going to be drawn into one of his completely pointless conversations. Not today. I was too busy paying attention to our masters. Trying to sniff for clues. Trying to make some sort of sense. I didn't know what to think. The air was complicated. Too many smells. Too much contradictory information.

'Did you want anything in particular?' asked Kate.

'Oh Kate, you minx, don't tempt me.' His wink went unreciprocated. 'Well, OK, no. Only to see you, you know, say hello. And to ask if we should bring anything to the barbecue?'

Kate paused, thoughtful, then said: 'About the barbecue –' But before she had time to finish, she noticed Adam's car turning into the road.

Simon smiled and turned, his free hand shielding the sun. The smile baffled Kate, who quickly placed the bunch of flowers alongside the doorknob and the dog hair.

As Falstaff started to sniff Kate's shoeless feet, the rest of us watched Adam choke the battered vehicle back and forth in an attempt to park.

'Simon,' said Adam, dropping his keys on the way out of the car. 'What can we do you for?'

'Hey, Adam. Now *that's* a tie.'

'You like it?'

'Yes. It's really . . . *wacky*.' When he said this last word he winked again at Kate. Only this wink was different, more complex. A wink which seemed to contain the memory of a shared joke. A cruel joke and, judging from her scent, one which Kate no longer found funny.

'How was it?' Kate asked.

'I don't know, whoever suggested Saturday would be the perfect day for a governors' meeting! It was pretty depressing, actually,' said Adam, sidestepping Falstaff's frothy pool of piss. 'We were running through the checking procedure, for members of staff.'

'Checking procedure?' Simon raised an inquisitive eyebrow.

'Yeah. With all those recent abduction cases, they're starting to make the schools do more to protect the children. Even drag us in on weekends.'

'Oh, that's right, I saw about it on the news. Terrible.' He pulled Falstaff away from Kate's feet. 'You can't imagine anything worse, can you, than losing a child.'

'Simon just came round to ask if he should bring anything to the barbecue tomorrow,' said Kate, trying to change the subject.

'Oh right,' said Adam. 'Do we need any salads doing?'

Kate shook her head.

Falstaff looked at me, and sighed. 'I don't know how you keep it up, madwag, I really don't.'

'Keep what up?'

But before he had time to answer, Simon yanked his lead and said: 'Anyway, should go. See you tomorrow.' He stopped at the gate, and slouched an arm over the bars, 'We'll be looking forward to it.'

And with that last, fatal wink he went on his way, dragging Falstaff behind him. I looked at Adam, at Kate. They had both lost colour. They had both gained scent.

And then another thought, of more immediate consequence.

The flowers.

I had forgotten all about them.

'Did Simon bring these round?'

'Um, yes,' Kate flustered. 'Yes, he did.'

Adam was going to push further so I distracted him by jumping up and placing my front paws on his chest.

'No, boy, down. Go on, Prince, down you go.'

Kate picked the flowers up. 'I'd better get rid of them. My hay fever's come back.'

She went through the kitchen, opened the back door, and placed them in the outside bin in the passage. I watched through the patio doors as she did so, closing the lid with remorse. As if there was something else she wanted to take out and throw away but couldn't. Something which wouldn't let go.

leaking

Looking back now, it is hard to remember what I was feeling. Until that point, the situation had been simple. All I'd had to do was keep track of Adam and Emily, and make sure things didn't go too far. But now I realised that was a side-issue, a false stick-throw.

And yet, how could I have predicted Kate could be a source of danger?

You see, more than anybody, Kate had always been on my side. Kate had kept the Family strong, no matter what. She, like myself, had seen the Family for what it was. Underneath all the surface tensions and daily dramas there was, of course, an immense and positive force. A force which argued for order in a world of chaos. Love, in a world of hate. A force which spoke, in a soft whisper, during every mealtime and goodnight kiss, saying: *If we stick together, everything will be all right. We will never be alone. We will always have each other.* Kate had, it seemed to me, always been able to pick up on this voice. Always been able to nod, ever so slightly, as she watched the children fall asleep. A nod which told me she understood. And although everyone always used to joke about her continual efforts to keep the house tidy, I understood that this was just a logical extension of her desire to keep the Family in order.

And so, after Simon came round, for the first time since I had arrived at the Hunter household, I felt truly isolated. I realised that the security of the Family now depended solely on my own actions.

Later on, when Adam was downstairs doing some work, and when Grandma Margaret and Hal and Charlotte were in bed, I went to visit Kate and see if my suspicions could be confirmed. She was sitting on the edge of her bed looking around the room with jerky head movements, as if each object she rested her eyes on was causing her to flinch away.

I nestled my head on her lap, to offer comfort. It didn't work.

'Come on, Kate,' she pleaded with herself, 'pull yourself together.'

Her breathing slowed for a moment, then broke under the pressure. A smell filled the room, a sad but barely noticeable odour. I could hear Kate's head turn to liquid, and felt her convulse as her snotty tears forced their way down her face.

She stroked me, a single action with her hand passing across the side of my face and neck and stopping once it reached my shoulder.

'Oh, Prince, what am I going to do?' Her voice was quiet now, a helpless whisper, so quiet in fact that I wasn't entirely sure whether she had spoken or whether I had just been able to pick up on the thoughts in her head. Either way, the question wasn't intended as a real one. She didn't really expect me to provide an answer, a once-and-for-all solution to this whole mess. I had always made sure that my adherence to the Pact had been kept secret.

But right then, as I stared at the old wedding photo on the mantelpiece, I wondered why that should be. Wouldn't it be easier to let Kate know that I was on her side? Wouldn't I be able to have more power to protect the Family? Wouldn't she be happier? Wouldn't they *all* be happier?

But no, I couldn't.

I knew what I was doing, biding my time.

It was painful though, during the in-between stage. It really hurt.

And then I identified the smell. The barely noticeable odour. It was coming from Kate and now it was getting stronger.

It was the smell of love, leaking away.

safe

I stared at Henry for a long time, as if the solution was somehow inscribed on his big, serious-natured face. In all the time I had known him, he had always been able to find the right words. But that morning he seemed to be struggling.

'This . . . is . . . a very rare situation,' he said solemnly. 'I can honestly tell you, I have never encountered it before.' He sniffed my cheek, attempting to gain further information. 'I think you must be very careful in the way you act henceforth.'

'But I cannot see a way of stopping Simon. There seems no way out.' I cocked my leg against the nearest plant, but was too nervous for anything to come out.

'There . . . is . . . always a way out. Always. You must go over the Pact and find a peaceful solution to this problem. It can be interpreted widely, that is true, but you will find it holds the answers.'

'But, Henry, what would you do in this exact same situation, how would you act?' I knew this was a disrespectful question, a little too direct, not in line with Labrador etiquette, but as far as I could see it I had no choice.

Henry paused, looked away. I followed his gaze to the park bench: his master, with mine, their heads slumped towards the ground. I wondered what was going on behind Henry's sad, milky eyes.

'I . . .' As soon as he started speaking he stopped, having recognised a familiar scent in the air.

'I'm not interrupting anything here, am I, fellas?' It was Joyce, looking as scraggy and leaf-strewn as ever.

'No, not at all,' Henry said. Although Joyce was a good friend, we never told her anything about my mission.

'You haven't seen that great big monster, Lear, have you?'

'No, Joyce, we haven't.' Henry sniffed her closely.

'He petrifies me so he does.'

'Don't worry, it's only us,' said Henry. 'You're always safe when we're around.'

'Oh yes, fellas. I know that. You're Labradors, after all.'

'That's right, Joyce,' soothed Henry. 'That's right. You're safe with us.'

pretty

To a human observer, the guests standing on the lawn would have looked like guests standing on the lawn. If the same human observer listened to the conversations taking place, he would assume the main concerns of these guests were house prices, holiday destinations, distant wars, celebrity scandals, radio programmes.

But, for a dog, all of that would have been incidental. Scent told a different story. Scent told me that sex was in the air, in all its many fragrances. And I breathed them in as I weaved my way around the garden. The molecules of unspoken desire.

This was normal. These smells were always there, every time Kate and Adam had large groups of guests around. And I knew they didn't necessarily signify danger. Mostly, these desires weren't acted upon. Sometimes, they'd remain so deeply buried that people wouldn't even realise they were there at all. The couples had managed to convince themselves that they were completely happy with each other, and that nothing could come between them. But there was no denying the change in scent as they moved from their partners towards the other guests.

However, I knew that most of the couples weren't a threat to the Family and therefore focused my attention on Simon and Emily, who had only just arrived.

I watched as Simon took his paper plate of meat and travelled across the garden, side-stepping the small group-ings of guests, until he arrived at Charlotte. She was sitting on a chair, in the far corner of the lawn, staring at her plate of meat-free salad. Grandma Margaret was sitting next to her, wearing her best dress and her baffled smile, saying nothing.

Charlotte spotted Simon's shadow, then looked up.

He said something. Charlotte smiled politely.

He said something else. Charlotte smiled again, more natural this time.

Kate was also watching – standing, talking to guests I didn't recognise, but snatching worried glances. Her plate tilted, slowly, unnoticed. Meat fell. She stooped to pick it up, then brought it over to the table I was lying under, next to the barbecue. Watching.

She finished off her glass of wine and went to join Simon and Charlotte. Her anxiety stayed, floating in the air.

They needed protection. Kate. Charlotte. They needed me. So I too went over, navigating my way around legs and lowered arms.

'Ahh, isn't he gorgeous?'

'What a lovely dog.'

'Looks like he's on a mission.'

I got stroked. I got laughed at. I got handed pieces of meat. But I was used to dealing with such obstacles – a good-humoured pant was usually enough to get by.

When I made it over, the combination of scents proved confusing. Kate, in particular, was difficult to translate. The desire molecules were definitely there, but overpowered by the pungent aroma of fear. And, now that she was up close to him, there was something else. Something approaching regret, although I couldn't be one hundred per cent sure.

This complex combination was most intense when Simon placed an arm around Kate's shoulders and said to Charlotte: 'I can see you've inherited your mother's looks.' He looked over his shoulder, to the far corner of the garden, where Adam was talking to some of the guests: 'Which must be an incredible relief.'

Charlotte smiled. She found this funny. Not in itself, but in the way it was delivered. I realised that Simon was what humans refer to as 'a charmer'.

'So, Kate,' Simon said, removing his arm. 'Did you ever return?'

'Return?' Kate looked confused.

'To teaching. After . . . you know . . .'

'Oh, yes, teaching. I, um, well, I don't teach any more. I work in town, in a gift shop, three days a week. After Charlotte arrived, I didn't really have the time or the energy.'

'Blame me,' Charlotte said.

'Well, no. It wasn't just that. And I carried on for a bit, doing supply work, but I eventually gave it up.'

'Oh,' said Simon. 'That's a shame.'

Something was happening between them. Some sort of exchange, in the air. I sniffed, frantically, trying to make sense of it, but the fragrance was still too complicated and intermingled with Grandma Margaret's thousand smells.

'Anyway, Charlotte. I'd like you to come and meet the

lady I work with. You know, I've told you about her. The one who used to know Jonathan Ross.'

Charlotte rolled her eyes as she got to her feet.

'See you later,' Simon said, smiling, as Kate and Charlotte walked away. Kate turned, threw a worried glance back towards him, and then disappeared among the guests.

Adam was inside, in the kitchen, sorting out the drinks. He didn't notice me as I entered through the patio doors, even when I sneezed. He just carried on, blank-faced but stiff-bodied, cracking ice into glasses. I tried to smell what he was thinking but it was difficult to decipher, with so many scents in the air. Once I sniffed past the desire molecules the only thing I could identify was the black and smoky aroma of burnt animal flesh carried through from the garden.

'Orange juice,' he said, pointlessly, as he poured the orange juice. 'Coca-cola. White wine.'

He wasn't himself.

'Do you need a hand?'

Emily's question made him jump. 'I'm sorry. I didn't see you. No, no, I'm fine. It's all right.' He was managing to look straight at her without giving anything away. Even his eyes seemed completely neutral.

'I'd like to help you,' she said, moving closer. 'Pretty please.' In contrast, Emily's face was proud to give everything away. Her smile, and something about the way her eyes widened, locking his in a strong and steady gaze, made Adam's attempt at indifference even harder to keep up.

'OK. You can help me take these out.' He handed her

two glasses of orange juice. She paused, as if he had misunderstood her question, and then headed outside. Adam followed, precariously holding three wine glasses and keeping his eyes fixed on Emily's backside as she walked out in front of him.

learning

Although desire molecules were still floating about, the guests were starting to leave. Charlotte, having been as polite as possible for as long as possible, was now upstairs in her bedroom. Grandma Margaret had come inside for an early night. Hal, who had returned from visiting his best friend Jamie, was helping people to find their coats and bags.

'So, Hal, off to university then soon?' one guest said.

'Yes. Leeds, I think.'

'Leeds, eh?'

'Is this your coat?'

'That's the one.'

'Are you off to Leeds, did you say?' asked another.

'Hopefully,' Hal said.

'Our daughter. She's in her second year there. Studying Psychology. She's having a brilliant time. She says the nightlife's amazing.'

'Yes. I'm looking forward to it. Is that your coat?'

'No. It's that one.'

'OK, there you go.'

'Oh, Hal,' said a third guest, a woman. 'I hardly recognised you. When did I last see you?'

'It must have been quite a while.'

'Four years ago, wasn't it? You must have been about fourteen.'

'Yes.'

'Look at you now! A proper man! Getting ready to leave home!'

'Yes. Is that your coat?'

'Oh yes. The pink one. Thank you very much.'

When most of the guests had left, Hal went up to his bedroom to play his music and revise. I stayed downstairs, because I knew my work wasn't finished. And the reason it wasn't finished was because Simon and Emily were the last two remaining guests. For some reason, Kate seemed to blame Adam for their reluctance to leave, and kept on sending him angry eye-darts when no one was looking.

It was getting colder, so they were inside.

'Shall we go in the living room?' Adam asked.

Kate didn't answer. Not verbally anyway. But she did take him up on his suggestion. Simon and Emily followed, with me close behind, trying to observe as much as possible. I realised that the future protection of the Family could depend on any information I could pick up from the strange scent-signals passing between the four of them.

They sniffed the room when they entered it as humans always do. I don't think they know they do this, because they rarely act upon the smells inside, but there is no mistaking the nostril-twitch as they walk through the door.

'Wow!' said Emily. 'You've got a cat!'

Lapsang, stretched out on the settee, opened one semi-interested eye. 'Just when you find some peace and quiet,' she grumbled.

'What's she called?'

'Lapsang,' said Kate. 'The woman we bought her from named the whole litter after varieties of tea. She's got a brother called Earl Grey and a sister called Darjeeling.'

'Wow,' said Emily, already sitting beside her on the settee and stroking her back. 'I love cats! I've always had this special, like, thing, with cats. An infinity.'

'Affinity,' Simon corrected.

'Yes. An infinity. Me and cats, we always get on really well. I think it's because I used to be a cat in a previous life.'

'Is she for real?' Lapsang asked, genuinely unsure.

'Yes,' I confirmed, solemnly. 'I'm afraid she is.'

I checked for a scent of embarrassment on Simon, but there wasn't one. He just smiled affectionately and looked at Adam. 'She's great, isn't she?' he asked. It was hard to tell whether he was talking about Lapsang or his wife.

Adam smiled nervously. 'Does, er, anyone want another drink?'

As everybody still had a full glass his question was ignored.

'At home with the Hunters,' said Simon, moving over to get a closer look at the Family portrait on the wall. The one with me right in the centre.

Adam went over to join him. 'Oh yes, it's quite good isn't it? We had it done a few months ago. A guy from work did it. The art teacher actually, doing a bit of moon-lighting. He did it from a photo.'

'It's a good likeness,' Simon said, only to Kate.

Kate didn't respond. Instead, she joined Emily on the settee.

'I hear you are an aromatherapist.'

'Yes,' she said, still stroking Lapsang. 'I am.'

To my surprise, Emily seemed uninterested in Kate. She certainly didn't want to talk to her. For some reason, Kate smelt like she accepted this as the way it should be. It didn't bother her at all.

'That must be interesting.'

'Yes, it is.'

I left Lapsang in charge and headed back to the two men, who were still standing in front of the Family portrait.

'I go all over,' Simon was saying. 'All over Europe, Australia, the States, Canada, Denmark. Even bloody Africa. And everywhere I go, it's the same thing, the same spiel.'

'But you enjoy it?'

'Damn yes. 'Course I do. Bloody easy money, I tell you. I just turn up, give them all a few creative-thinking exercises, throw in some meaningless waffle about thinking outside the box and that's about it. Job done.'

'Creative-thinking exercises?'

'Yes. You know. Think of ten different uses for a chair other than for sitting on. That sort of crap.' Adam looked over to the unoccupied wicker chair in the corner of the room and frowned, perplexed. Simon continued. 'It's all bollocks, but it's the right sort of bollocks, that's the thing. Big business, that's what they go for. If you're making sense, if you are telling people how it is, if you just waltzed in there telling them that they're sitting on a time bomb, then, well, you wouldn't have a cat in hell's chance.'

'Right.'

'So what I do, what I do is recite what they want to hear, give them a framework within which they can carry on doing exactly what they were always doing, but with new words. Imagineering. Blue-sky thinking. Four-dimensional branding. They lap it up.'

'But surely you must *believe* what you tell them?'

Simon looked at Adam curiously, like a dog encountering a new breed. 'Believe in it? Oh, come on, Adam, when did I ever believe in anything? Well, apart from myself. Shit, no. I don't believe a single word. But hey, I've got no conscience. You're the hearts-and-minds man; I'm just in it for the money, I really am.'

Adam's face was smiling, but his scent was sad. He looked across the room and caught Emily's eye, then turned away. 'So, anyway, how did you two meet? You know, you and Emily?'

'Oh, long story. The short version is that I went up to her at this conference. Something at the Queen Elizabeth Centre. She was temping, handing out flyers for different seminars. It was before she got into all this aromatherapy-numerology-crystal-ball malarkey. She looked gorgeous, she really did. Anyway, I went over to her and thanked her for promoting my seminar. We got talking and, after the conference, she ended up in my hotel room. And that was it.'

'It?'

'We went through ten different uses for a chair.' Adam still looked (and smelt) blank. So Simon clarified: 'We *fucked*. And then, after that, we fucked some more.'

Adam was shocked, and embarrassed. He stroked my

head in a desperate bid for homely normality to be restored. He looked at Kate, but she was too far away to have heard.

'Oh sorry,' Simon said. 'I should rephrase that. We fell in love, and decided to live together. The sex, well, that was incidental.' His tongue pushed behind his cheek.

'She seems, um, very interesting.'

'Does she?' Simon asked, before sustaining a deliberate pause. 'Yes. You're right. She is very interesting. Her mind takes me to new places every single day.' He laughed and, reluctantly, Adam joined in.

'Oh, but come on. You must have something in common?'

Simon looked up at the corner of the ceiling. 'Nope. Not a single thing. Just sex.'

'Honestly? That's it?'

'Hey, Ads. Don't belittle it. It's the stuff of legend.'

They both laughed and sipped their drinks. But I couldn't help noticing that Adam still smelt uncomfortable. '*Ads*? God I haven't been called that since school.'

'Anyway, your turn. How are things with you and Kate? Is everything as nauseatingly happy as this picture makes out?'

'Things are going well,' he said, almost too quickly to be convincing. 'I mean, we have our moments, but what family with two teenagers doesn't? Prince keeps us all in line, don't you, boy?'

I wagged my tail at the sound of my name, as if it was the first word of the conversation I had understood. Of course, I knew he was joking. I knew he didn't realise that that was in fact my role. To keep them in line.

'You're a lucky man,' Simon said.

Adam said nothing for a while as the sad smells continued to filter through his trousers.

'What about you? Have you any . . . *plans?*' Adam asked, eventually.

'With Emily? For kids?'

Adam nodded.

Simon laughed. 'No. No plans. I don't really think it would work out, to be honest. I'm not like you, Ads. I'm just not the faithful, committed sort of guy. I think you're either made for family life or you're not – and, well, I'm just not.'

'I used to think like that.'

'So you think I could change?'

'I think everyone can.'

'Perhaps you could teach me. Perhaps you could be my mentor in how to be a successful family man. You certainly seem to have got it down to a tee.' I didn't know what Simon was up to, but I realised he was definitely putting Adam through some sort of test. Now, of course, I know exactly what he was doing. He was trying to find a weak spot. He was trying to work out from which angle he would later attack.

'Well, I don't know. I wouldn't go that far,' Adam said, his eyes still on the portrait in front of him. 'I think I'm still learning.'

holes

I used to dig holes. When I was younger. Always digging holes.

Trying to get the park to open up, to reveal its secrets. Dig, dig, dig. I could have dug all day, if Adam had let me. I could have dug until I reached the bottom, until I found what was really there underneath, but Adam always called me too soon.

Dig, dig, dig.

Back then, I was only allowed in certain places. Never in flowerbeds. But I didn't mind because when you dug in flowerbeds you never found anything. I stuck to the back wall where there were more things to find. Where there were the things which helped you discover about humans. The humans who came in the park at night to drink and smoke and fuck and eat and drug and puke.

Dig, dig, dig.

What I really liked was when there was soft black earth which meant you could keep on digging past the things the humans had left. Past all the things that had been thrown away. When there was soft black earth you could dig down until you reached the smells you never found above ground. Time-travel smells. Smells which helped you understand why we die and why we live. The smells

149

which told us that it may already be too late. The smells only dogs seemed to be able to pick up.

But Adam, who liked looking up, who even now likes trying to find answers in the sky, never let me get too deep. He wanted me on the surface, where he could see me.

I used to fantasise that one day, though, when he was not looking, I would dig and dig and dig until I could fully understand. Until all the smells made sense. Because if you got far enough down, I thought, you would be able to smell the truth. And then I would have been able to stop. To stop digging holes.

But that was then. That was before everything. Before Henry had fully explained my duty, and made me understand.

The Labrador Pact:
Protect one Family, protect all

When every dog believed in preserving the security of human Families, our influence could be seen everywhere. Although times have changed, we can still see the wider impact of our mission. If one human Family is secure and happy, it means there is security and happiness beyond. Likewise, if a Family falls apart, others are made more vulnerable.

In protecting one, we are protecting all.

changing

Things were going wrong.

How wrong, I didn't yet know, but the signs were increasingly bad. Adam was changing. His voice, his behaviour, his scent – everything was different.

He was getting angrier, and he was paying less attention to everything around him. He was also running three times a week. With *Simon*. It had been arranged the day of the barbecue.

Obviously, Kate hadn't been happy about the arrangement, and had tried to prevent him going.

'Why are you doing this?' she asked him.

'This what?'

She sighed. 'This running.'

'To keep fit.'

'You're sure it's not something else?'

'Something else?'

'A competition. With Simon. You know, the way it used to be.'

'Oh, Kate, don't be ridiculous. That was years ago. Of course it's not. Believe me, I'm not jealous of Simon. I mean what has he got that I'd want?'

'You tell me.'

'Oh, come on. His naff flash car? That horrible house? His double garage? His bookshelves with nothing but

The Art of Leadership on them? Don't be daft. His whole existence is a blank space he thinks he can fill with money.'

'So why are you going running with him, then? If you don't like him.'

'I told you: to keep fit. God! What's with you!'

'I just wish . . .'

'What? What do you wish?'

'Nothing,' said Kate, placing her hand on her head. 'Nothing.'

But Kate wasn't the only one unhappy with the new Adam. There was Charlotte, too. She was annoyed that she was not allowed out of the house on her own, because of all the news stories.

'But it's not fair. Everyone else is allowed out.'

'It's for your own good. Perhaps other parents don't *care* as much as we do.'

And then Charlotte would thunder upstairs, slam her bedroom door, and play her loud music. Night after night after night.

Things had become worse when, the night after the barbecue, she announced that she had a boyfriend.

'A boyfriend?' Kate asked, smiling.

'Mum, I'm thir-teen.'

'Who is he?'

'He's just a boy.'

And then Adam added, 'What school does he go to?' This question caused Charlotte to hesitate. She made a faint noise, unintelligible even to my ears.

'Where?'

'Rosewood,' she said eventually.

'So how do you know him if he goes to a different school?' asked Kate, still smiling.

'Sarah knows him.' Sarah was Charlotte's best friend, fellow vegetarian, and the person who inspired her to turn my metal lead into a fashion accessory.

Adam, suddenly aware that Charlotte's new boyfriend could be one of his pupils, turned pale. 'What's his name?'

Charlotte didn't answer.

'Charlotte. Your boyfriend. What's he called?'

Charlotte still didn't answer.

'Do I teach him?'

Charlotte, clearly wishing she hadn't brought the subject up, said nothing.

'Charlotte, answer your father,' Kate said, with reluctant solidarity.

Charlotte made another unintelligible noise.

'What was that? David? Is that what you said? David?'

'Dan-*ny*.'

'Danny? Daniel Smith?'

Charlotte made a face and shook her head.

'Danny . . .' Adam scanned the ceiling, as if looking for clues. Charlotte's anxiety pickled the air as she waited for the inevitable realisation. 'The only other Danny I can think of is Danny Thomas but no girl in their right mind would ever go near that troublemaker . . . Charlotte, tell me, please tell me it's not Danny Thomas.'

Charlotte's anxiety switched to fury, a switch which forced her up off her chair, across the room and out of the door in one dramatic gust. I wagged, too late. Always too late.

Kate looked at Adam. 'Who's Danny Thomas?' But as

soon as she had asked the question her eyes strayed towards the carpet, where fallen debris from the dried flowers had been left unhoovered.

'A complete bloody nightmare, that's who Danny Thomas is. He got suspended for letting off a fire alarm two weeks ago, and I'm always having to tell him off for bringing his skateboard into lessons.'

'But flying off the handle isn't going to get us anywhere. Isn't that what you always tell me? Come on, Adam, let's try and be reasonable. We'll just have to talk to her and explain our concerns.' She was now picking up the pieces of dried flower from the carpet.

'You *are* joking, aren't you? Danny Thomas is the last person on earth you would want your daughter to have as a boyfriend. He's a complete bloody nightmare.'

'I know, you said. But we'll still need to talk to her sensibly.'

Adam loosened his tie. 'Sensibly? You want sensible? OK, how's this?' He leant his head out of the room and angled it up towards Charlotte's bedroom before shouting, 'If you ever see that boy again you'll be grounded for two months.'

Charlotte slammed her door shut.

Kate closed her eyes. 'Well done, Adam. That was really helpful. Really . . . constructive.'

'I thought so.'

england

I put the subject of Danny Thomas to Henry.

'How is Charlotte?' he asked me, once he'd heard the news.

'Pretty angry,' I said.

There was a pause. Henry seemed distracted and was watching his master, Mick, more intently than ever.

'Are you OK, Henry?'

'Yes,' he said. 'I'm sorry. What were you saying?'

'Charlotte. She's angry with Adam because he's not letting her out. He says he's doing it to protect her. But I don't know if that's the only reason. There are a lot of danger-signs but I'm not sure if I can make sense of them all.'

Henry was now looking in the other direction, over towards the smell-heap. 'You must pay careful attention to Charlotte. She will try and see this boy, and you must do your best to prevent this happ–'

'Henry! Henry! Here, boy!' Mick was standing up and calling Henry over to the bench. This was very unusual, as Mick usually wanted to stay talking with Adam until the last moment.

'I have to go.'

'But –'

'I'm sorry, Prince, I have to. I will see you tomorrow.'

And so I was left sitting by the flowerbeds, watching Henry trot dutifully towards his master. I looked at Mick and again wondered why Henry had never told me more about him. The grey-haired, grey-scented former policeman who could talk for England.

bush

When Henry and Mick had left the park, I heard something to my right. A bush was moving.

The bush spoke: 'Prince! Come here!' It was Joyce. Realising she wouldn't reveal herself in full view of Adam, I went over to her.

'What's the matter, Joyce?'

'Prince, I have to tell you. Strange things have been happening.'

'I know,' I said. 'You told us before.'

'No, no, no. Other things. Something happened in the park last night. Something terrible. I saw it all.'

'What things, Joyce?' I asked, pushing my nose through the leaves towards her.

'Oh, Prince, you have to be careful.'

'Careful why? What happened last night?'

She looked at me with frightened eyes. 'It was terrible. The worst thing I have ever seen. Terrible.'

And then I heard Adam, jogging over to get me. 'Prince! Come on! Come away from there!'

'Joyce, what was it?'

She tried to calm her breathing. 'It was Henry, and his master.'

'Henry? *Henry*? Joyce, what do you —'

She disappeared backwards at the sight of Adam's hand

on my collar. 'Joyce? Come back.' But it was too late. I was already pulled out, and Adam was tugging the collar hard.

What had she meant? What had she seen that was so terrible? Had something bad happened to Henry, or his master? And why had they been in the park at night?

But away from the park, my mind started to clear. Joyce had told us one theory too many recently. For all I knew, she might have become a sniffaholic. She was hardly making sense, and I began to doubt if she had seen anything at all. Maybe whatever it was had been a hallucination. Maybe, after all those years hiding in bushes, she was beginning to lose her mind.

Yes, that was it. It was nothing.

Nothing at all.

signals

That night I had other things to think about. My immediate duty was to protect the Family, and that meant keeping a close nose on everything that happened at home.

I had been sniffing Kate every other evening, when she came back from the shop, but there wasn't anything unusual in this. I sniffed *everyone* when they came home. It is what I did. A way of finding information, checking where they had been, checking everything had stayed the same. And when things were staying the same, that is pretty much all I had to do. Sniff. Check. It was simple.

But when I sniffed Kate that evening I realised things weren't staying the same. Simplicity had gone. I sniffed again. But there was no mistaking the scent.

It was *him*.

Simon.

She smelt of Simon.

As soon as the scent hit my brain, something collapsed inside me. Why had she seen him? Why? And what did it mean, for the future of the Family? That morning, before my walk, Adam and Simon had gone running. Yet when Adam had returned – panting, bent double – there'd been no danger-signs. None that I'd noticed anyway. So whatever Simon was playing at, he was keeping Adam in the dark.

I sniffed again, but there was no mistaking it. Simon-smells were all over her clothes.

Of course, nobody else could tell. And she didn't mention it. She didn't come in and say: 'Oh, I've just seen Simon,' which would have made it OK. So I stayed with her all evening, watching out for any other signals.

Nothing happened, for a while. There was a certain stiffness to her body language. She was a bit quiet, too, during the meal, but that could have been down to tiredness.

Then Adam took me for a walk. As we went out the door I was sure Kate looked anxious. There was something about the way she looked up while drying the dishes, something about the way she said, 'Be careful'. As if she thought bad things were going to happen.

But the park offered up no further clues. I tried to press Falstaff for more information, but he denied all knowledge. I then went over to the park bench, to Adam and Emily, to see what they were talking about.

They were talking about star-patterns. Cosmic energy. Magic forces. Adam was, as always, entranced.

'I will see you tomorrow.'

'Yes, see you.'

naked

Later on, Kate and Adam were in their bedroom.

'Are you being serious?' asked Adam.

'Yes. I've never been more serious. You said yourself, you've had enough of everything.'

'But . . . but why?'

'Oh, I don't know. It's just –'

'Just what?'

'I don't know. I can't explain it. Not properly. I just don't feel we're *safe* here any more.'

'Are you worried about Charlotte?'

Kate's spine jerked straight. 'Charlotte?'

'You know, with all this Danny Thomas business.'

Kate relaxed. 'Oh no. Well, *yes* obviously. A bit. But it's not that. Not really.'

'Kate. We can't just move.'

'Why not?'

'Are you seriously asking for reasons? Well, OK. The house. The mortgage. My job. Your job. Our children's education. Your mother. The –'

Kate raised her hand. 'OK.'

'I thought you loved this house?'

'I do, I do, it's just. I don't know. I'm being stupid.'

And then Adam stood up and kissed the back of Kate's neck. 'You're not stupid,' he said. 'Perhaps you're right.

We do need to get away. But maybe just for a weekend break, at first.' He smiled, and Kate smiled too, but only when she could tell he was looking at her.

It didn't stop there. When Kate had undressed, she appeared to have another concern on her mind. She was standing in the middle of the room, completely naked, while Adam lay back on the bed.

'Tell me what you think *honestly*, about my body,' she said. Adam raised his head up and surveyed her with weary eyes.

'You've got a beautiful body.'

'I've got an old woman's body.'

Adam rested his head back. 'A *beautiful* old woman's body.'

'A-*dam*. Look at me. Look at me properly.'

This time he propped himself up on his elbows. 'You're lovely.'

She pinched both her thighs and wobbled them. '*That's* lovely?'

'Yes,' he said, without looking at the specific areas of pale white vibrating flesh. 'You're all lovely.'

'My boobs are saggy,' she said, drawing his attention upwards.

'They're lovely. Beautiful boobs.'

'My neck, it's like a road map.'

'It's beautiful.'

'My bum, it's lumpy and disgusting.'

'It's lovely.'

'It's finally happening. I'm falling to pieces.'

'You're the most beautiful woman in the world.'

'I'm the ugliest creature on the planet.'

Adam sighed. 'Why are you so hung up about looks all of a sudden? I thought you thought it was all vain and superficial?'

'I'm not *hung up*. I'm just, I don't know, starting to feel a bit invisible. It would be nice to be visible again, that's all.'

Again Adam stood up. Again he kissed the back of her neck.

'Come to bed,' he said.

'You've got to take the dog down.'

'He'll be OK. He's a big boy now.'

They got into bed. They kissed. Adam closed his eyes. Kate closed hers too, but tight, the way I do when anticipating a hit on the nose.

Adam moved on top of her.

'No,' said Kate.

Adam kissed her forehead.

'No.'

'What's the matter?'

'I can't.'

Adam fell back on his side of the bed. His voice hardened. 'I know you can't. You never can. Not this decade.'

'Adam, please –'

'We'll never have sex again, will we?' he said, picking up his book.

'Adam –'

'I mean, we're not having any more kids, so why have any more sex. That *is* how you feel, isn't it?'

'You *know* it's not. And please don't talk like that.'

'No, what I do know is this: we haven't had *sex* since Charlotte was born. For *thirteen* years. I mean, even

164

bloody Prince gets more action than I do. And he's got no bloody bollocks.'

'You are horrible. Honestly, you're turning into a monster.'

'Well you might as well book me in for an appointment then. With the vet. Get mine chopped off as well. No, I tell you what, why don't you just go the whole hog? Put me down. Do everyone a favour.'

'Adam, please stop. *Please.*' She started to cry. I went over to comfort her, the Simon-smells still lingering around her.

Adam put his book down. 'I'm sorry, Kate. I'm sorry.'

'It's OK,' she said, turning away from him.

Adam lifted the duvet back and got out of bed.

'Where are you going?' asked Kate.

'I'm taking the dog downstairs.'

paw

Although I had tried to block out what Joyce had told me, I still found my mind wandering during Henry's tutorial on temperament testing.

'Are you understanding everything so far, Prince?'

'Um, yes. Sorry.'

'You seem a little distracted.' He was watching me very carefully, and was clearly concerned.

I sighed. 'It's Joyce.'

'Joyce?' Henry's milky eyes viewed me with curiosity.

'She said that something happened, to you and Mick in the park. At night.'

Henry sat down on the grass, as he started to transmit sad-smells. He then looked over towards the bushes where Joyce could often be found.

'Henry?' He didn't respond, just closed his eyes and breathed in the subtle scents of plant and animal drifting in the wind. 'Henry?'

He looked like he could have sat there for ever, without saying another word.

'I'm sorry, I shouldn't have listened to her,' I said, desperately trying to bring Henry's mind back from whatever dark corner it was now visiting. 'She's just paranoid, it was probably just all in her head. It was dark, there were lots of scents about, you know what it's like.'

'Do you know Joyce's story?' Henry asked, eventually. 'Do you know why she is a stray?'

'No,' I said, confused at what I believed to be an obscure question.

'She told me once, ages ago. Probably before you were even born.' Again he looked over to the bushes, to check Joyce wasn't observing us. 'Her mother lived on a farm, out in the country. But the farmer she lived with was a cruel man who didn't want any more dogs.'

I still couldn't see the relevance of his information. 'Yes, but –'

'And when Joyce was born, the farmer wanted to sell the whole litter. He put an advert in the newspaper, asking if anyone wanted to buy Joyce and her brothers, but weeks went by and no one wanted them. When he couldn't sell them he placed them in a huge sack. The next thing she remembers, there was water everywhere. The farmer had taken the bundle of puppies to the river and was trying to drown them.'

Now Henry had me hooked. 'So what happened?'

Henry swallowed. 'As the bundle floated downstream, Joyce and her brothers were trying to escape, but because of the knot the hole in the sack was small, and the puppies were now large. Only Joyce and one of her brothers survived, the other three died. And to this day, Joyce blames herself for their death. In the struggle to get out of the wet sack, she was having to stand on her brothers.'

'But how did she end up here?'

'When they made their way out of the river, they found a small road and followed the direction of the cars into town. They nearly starved on the journey, but eventually made it, and found this park.'

'So what happened to the brother?'

Henry scratched his ear. 'They lived in relative happiness for a while, wandering around town, eating whatever food the humans had left on the pavement, or in the bins. But one night, when they had returned to the park, they ran into trouble.'

'Trouble?'

'A Rottweiler. He ran straight over to them and tried to . . . with Joyce. Of course, her brother wasn't happy and wanted to stop it happening, but he ended up getting into a fight. While he was pinned to the ground Joyce tried to get the attention of the Rottweiler's master, but he was over on the other side of the park, listening to music.'

'Oh no.'

'He died, the brother. And the body wasn't found by humans for days.'

'Poor Joyce,' I said, but I still hadn't made the connection.

'After that, the Rottweiler and his master didn't return here. By the time I first arrived, Joyce was beginning to find some peace of mind in her daily routine, although it was clear she still blamed herself for her loss.'

'Right.'

'But now the Rottweiler's master is back, with a new dog.'

'Who? I don't –?'

'Lear.'

I remembered Joyce's ramblings, the day of our first

meeting with the new Rottweiler. And suddenly her panic-smells made sense.

'So, you think this is all getting too much for her? You think she's losing her mind?'

'I think it would be too much for any dog, don't you?'

'Well, er, yes. I suppose it would.'

'It's clearly brought everything back. She's starting to become scared of her own shadow.'

There was a pause. 'Do you think we should talk to her?'

'No,' Henry's voice was now urgent. 'No. She mustn't know that I've told you any of this. Prince, do you understand?'

'Yes, Henry. I understand.'

I understood.

Joyce was going mad because she blamed herself for losing those who had been closest to her. I also knew I wasn't going to let the same thing happen to me.

So when Kate returned home smelling of Simon *again*, I followed her around all evening, on the hunt for further clues.

'Prince, what's the matter?' she asked me. 'What do you want?' I wagged my tail and did my best to look like I hadn't understood her questions, so she went to the jar and got out a biscuit. She held it in front of my nose.

'Give paw.' So I did and she gave me the biscuit. She remained confused as I still continued to follow her about while she tidied the house. But later on, on my evening walk, I realised I had made a mistake. I should have been paying more attention to Adam.

someone

When we got to the park, Emily was already sitting on the park bench, fidgeting with Falstaff's lead. Falstaff himself was nowhere to be seen, probably submerged in the smell-heap.

Adam sat down. Not too far, not too close.

They didn't say anything at first, and the air between them thickened. Then, after a short while, Emily made a sound. A crying sound. She rubbed her eyes but when I sniffed no sad-smells could be detected.

'Are you . . . are you OK?' Adam asked.

She made another crying sound, then said: 'I'm sorry. I shouldn't . . . I'm being daft.'

'What's wrong?' He moved closer towards her, went to touch her, to comfort her, but hesitated, his arm hovering behind her back.

'It's Simon,' she said, burying her nose in Adam's shirt. Still the arm hovered behind, in a final show of resistance, before falling reluctantly across Emily's shoulders.

'Simon?'

'I think . . . I think he's seeing somebody else.'

'Somebody else? Simon? No. What makes you –'

'It happened in London. That's why we moved. Someone he met at one of his seminars. *Jess*-ic-a.' She said it like that. *Jess*-ic-a. As if it was the name itself which had caused her pain.

'That's *terrible*.'

'It wasn't anything serious. That's what he said. It didn't *mean* anything. It only lasted two weeks. But I knew something was wrong. There was a bad energy, you know. And then I found them together. I saw them, with my own eyes. I'd been away visiting my parents and came home early and he was there –' She stopped, closed her eyes, and remembered something she couldn't describe. 'It was terrible. And now it's happening again.'

'Oh, Emily, I'm sorry. But it doesn't make sense.'

'What . . . what doesn't . . . make sense?'

'How anyone would want to do that to you. And I'm absolutely sure Simon will have seen the error of his ways.'

'But I can sense it. There's something wrong. Something not quite . . . balanced . . . you know, with his aura. He's annoyed with me, because I can't . . .'

'Can't?'

'I can't give him what he wants.'

'I don't understand, what does he want?'

She lifted herself away from Adam's shirt and, as she did so, Adam snatched a glance at her chest. 'Children. He wants a baby but I can't give him one . . . I've had all the tests.'

Adam sighed.

'Well,' he said, gently. 'I think the best thing you can do is talk to him. Talk *sensibly*.'

Talk sensibly? Wasn't that what Adam himself had refused to do with Charlotte after the row about her new boyfriend?

'Did you mean that?'

'What?'

'What you said a minute ago.'

'What did I say?'

'That you didn't know how anyone could do that to me.'

There was a silence. I tried to break the silence by nestling my head between them.

It didn't work. In fact, it seemed to have the opposite effect.

'Yes, I . . . I suppose I did.'

What was happening? What was going on here? Adam. The Family man. The faithful husband. I mean, he had been acting strange recently and he certainly had a thing for Emily. But surely he would be able to control his instincts. He was a *human*, for dog's sake.

They moved closer towards each other again, creating dangerous tension. They were going to kiss. They really were. And kissing other women was bad for the security of the Family. I didn't need Henry to tell me that.

I barked.

I jumped right up on the bench and barked and as I did so the kiss-threat evaporated into the air.

Adam pushed me back down and said to Emily: 'Have a talk to him. That's always the best way, isn't it? I'm sure it will put your mind at rest.'

As they moved away I sensed something. Some*one*. Watching everything. Instinctively, I knew it was someone in the new house. A human. I looked up, and right, to see Simon. He was standing at the window, leaning forward, his fingers separating the blinds.

172

There was a reflection on the glass, making it difficult to see.

I looked closer, at his face, to try and read what he was thinking. To try and see anger. Or jealousy. Or surprise. But I couldn't. Again he surprised me as I saw something else.

He was smiling.

The Labrador Pact:
Never deter others from
their mission

Labradors must remain supportive of each other at all times. When asked for advice regarding another's mission, we must be as constructive as possible. If we believe another Labrador is losing the battle, we must never say so.

We are the last breed to recognise that our actions are behind those of our masters, and as such we should remain strong. To do this, we must stick together.

In a world which fails to understand or acknowledge our beliefs, it is important that Labradors can find courage and support from each other.

Seek strength through unity, and we shall always remain true to our cause.

night

In the middle of the night I woke to the sound of the cat-flap.

'Sorry, darling,' Lapsang miaowed gently. 'I didn't mean to wake you.'

'It's OK,' I told her, and rested my head back down.

After a short while, when I realised I wasn't going to get back to sleep, I said: 'Lapsang, can I ask you something?'

'Yes, of course you can. Fire away.'

'When you are out at night, do you ever go to the park?'

'The park?'

'Yes.'

'No, sweetie. You must be joking. Dog territory. I wouldn't go near. Why do you ask?'

'No reason,' I said. 'It was nothing.'

blood

Henry sniffed me for a long time, to assess my state of mind, before asking: 'Where was he standing?'

I pointed my nose towards the largest upstairs window, the blind now closed. 'That one, there.'

'And he saw something?'

'He must have.'

'But they didn't kiss?'

'No. I stopped them.'

'You did well, Prince. Hopefully, the moment of danger will have passed.'

'Yes,' I said, a gust of wind forcing me to stagger sideways. 'Hopefully.'

Henry paused, raising his nose to catch a scent. 'Prince, can you smell something?'

I sniffed too, but couldn't identify anything unusual. Only the far-off fragrance of our two masters, sitting on the bench. I glanced over, and saw Mick leaning forward, blocking my view of Adam. 'I can't smell anything.'

'Something is wrong,' Henry said, in an even more serious tone than usual. 'Follow me.'

He started to trot over towards the bushes, keeping his nose high in the air as he travelled. Following close behind I too caught the scent, just for a moment. Henry stopped, once he had made his way around the last flowerbed, and his body flinched. Whatever he had seen it had stopped him from moving further forward.

'What is it?' I asked as I joined him.

But already I had translated the scent. It was blood. *Dog* blood.

Henry turned to me. 'Can you see? There, between the bushes.'

Lack of movement made it difficult to focus. 'No, I ca–' But then I saw it. *Her*. Lying on a bed of wet leaves, eyes open, neck shining black, plant-damage all around. 'Oh, Joyce, no.'

Having managed to compose himself, Henry moved in for a closer inspection.

'There has been a fight,' Henry said. 'And judging by the damage to the bushes, she put up quite a struggle.'

'Can you smell any other dog?'

Henry lowered his nose so it was underneath Joyce's throat. 'No,' he said. 'Only us. The rain must have washed it away.' He sniffed further. 'She's been dead for some time, at least a day.'

I looked at her again. At her open eyes, her outstretched legs, her smoothed-back fur. It seemed strange that a dog who spent most of her life cowering in a bush should die in such an active pose. She looked like an overgrown puppy, frozen in mid-gallop.

But when I looked closer, I saw her eyes were glazed with fear, and shock. As if the secrets of her death went beyond even her worst imaginings.

'We will find whoever did this,' Henry said.

'How?'

'I don't know. I will have to think about it. In the

meantime, this must not interfere with your own mission. Your Family must come first.'

'Yes, Henry,' I said, watching a fly land on the part of her neck which had been torn open so savagely. 'The Family must come first.'

shakespeare

Charlotte was ill. She couldn't go out to the theatre because she was ill. That's what she had said, and so to prove it she had spent the whole evening crouched on the stairs, holding her stomach with one hand and the banister with the other.

'Mum, I can't.'

'We've booked the tickets. We booked them months ago.'

'Mum, you go. I'll be OK. Just take the mobile and if I get worse I'll call or leave a text.'

The thing is: she wasn't ill. I knew she wasn't, but what could I do. She smelt as healthy as ever. I'd sniffed her from head to toe and there were absolutely no ill-smells to detect.

Hal wasn't making things easier. 'Mum, it's Shakespeare. Charlotte can't even *spell* Shakespeare.'

Adam placed his hand on his jacket pocket. 'Has anyone seen the car keys?'

Charlotte made a moaning sound, and bent forward. 'I'm sorry, Mum, I can't.'

'Ah, there they are,' said Adam.

'It's S-h-a-k-e-s-p-e-a-r-e,' said Hal.

'I'd better take my glasses,' said Grandma Margaret. 'Bill always used to say: "Remember your glasses."'

Kate didn't say anything, just looked at each member of her Family with growing exasperation. Then she looked at me, her eyes fixed in such a way that it seemed she was searching for something. For what, I don't know, but it was definitely something she thought I would be able to provide.

property

Charlotte stared out of the living-room window as the car pulled away down the street. The moment it had disappeared she ran back into the hallway, picked up the phone and dialled.

'Hi, it's me. You can come over, they've gone.'

This was not good. Whoever she was on the phone to, she was clearly breaking the rules. And breaking the rules was not good for the Family.

I followed her upstairs to her parents' bedroom. She went to the mirror and started plucking hairs from her eyebrows. She painted her lips and then sprayed on so much perfume she completely disguised her natural scent.

The doorbell rang.

We ran back downstairs. I barked my warning but knew that it was useless.

The door opened. I ran straight out and sniffed the stranger for clues. Heady teenage boy smells quivered in the air. Tobacco. Stale piss. Sweat. Lust. Total despair. He had a board with wheels. I sniffed that too.

'Sorry about my dog.'

'No, he's cool. I like dogs.' He rubbed the back of my neck. 'What's his name?'

I wasn't fooled. I knew who was rubbing the back of my neck. It was Danny Thomas. The total bloody nightmare.

'He's called Prince. Really original, I know.'

'All right, Prince, OK, boy, OK, good boy, good. Hey that's private property.' He pulled my nose away from his crotch.

Charlotte laughed and opened the door wider, for Danny Thomas to come inside. Inviting danger. I noticed that he was wearing a dog lead, the way Charlotte always did, dangling from his big, baggy jeans.

Danny Thomas came inside.

'Nice house,' he said.

'I think it's horrible,' said Charlotte.

'Should see mine.'

Charlotte smelt awkward, and said: 'Do you have a dog?'

'Yeah. We do. We've got a Labrador as well. Dad tried to take her, when they split, but Mum got possession.'

This didn't make sense. If he had a Labrador, he had a happy Family. Unless, of course, the Labrador came too late. That happened. Henry had told me. There were Labradors who couldn't do anything to save their Families, who had entered into a situation already beyond their control. But this was rare. I had never encountered such a Labrador. Or such a Family.

Danny Thomas sat down on the sofa. I sat down in front of him, keeping a close eye. And nose. Charlotte also sat down and nestled her head into his chest.

'What time are your mum and dad back?'

'I don't know. But not before ten.'

'If your dad could see me now he'd kill me.'

'He wouldn't.'

'OK, but he'd definitely chop my bollocks off.'

I noticed, at this point, his hand. It was moving, very slowly, towards Charlotte's left breast. Charlotte noticed it too, although she didn't seem to mind. Fortunately, the hand posed no obvious threat. Once it arrived at her breast, it rested there, as if waiting for something to happen.

'What do you want to do?'

'I don't mind. Whatever.'

And then, without any warning, their mouths locked. I didn't know what was happening. The previously dormant hand started moving.

I was worried.

How far was this going to go? I wasn't prepared to find out. I had to act. I had to break the mood. I had to do *something*.

I had a shit on the carpet.

But it took a while. For the smell to hit them.

'Oh, *Prince*,' Charlotte said, eventually unlocking herself.

Danny Thomas started to laugh.

'I'd better get some stuff to clean it up.'

'Look at his face,' said Danny Thomas, pointing at me. And then, looking at the mess I had made: 'Oh man, that is disgusting.'

I was sorry, I really was, but I was only acting in their best interest. Well, Charlotte's best interest. But as it turned out, it didn't make a difference.

What happened?

This:

'Charlotte?' It was Adam, halfway through the front door.

'*Dad?*' Charlotte froze, kneeling on the floor with a handful of shit and toilet paper.

Danny Thomas looked behind him, seriously contemplating the window.

Adam shut the door, still oblivious. 'You'll never believe it. We got to the theatre and we forgot the tickets. The others are still there. I've got to –'

I ran out of the room and jumped on him while he was still in the hallway.

'No, Prince. Down. *Down.* Down, boy.'

I was improvising. Trying to give Charlotte time. Time for what, I didn't really know. To get out of the room, I suppose. To shut the door behind her. To not let him go in. But she didn't get the hint. She was paralysed by fear.

He was five steps away.

Things are always within my control, I said to myself. But how could I have predicted *this*?

Four, three . . .

By now, Adam was picking up on the silence. The fear. Many dogs deny this is possible. That humans can only sense what they see. They are wrong.

'Charlotte?'

. . . two, one . . .

He pushed back the door and, with it, all my hard work. There was still shit on the carpet but he didn't notice. I rushed over and pushed my nose in it. Right into the shit. He still didn't notice.

Charlotte's face plummeted out of position. Danny Thomas laughed, nervously. It did nothing to help his case.

'Dad, Danny just came round –'

Adam said nothing at first. Just stroked the back of

his neck, twisted his head, waiting for the air to reach maximum intensity. Then, after a while, he said to Charlotte: 'What a miraculous recovery.'

'I'm sorry, Mr Hunter,' said Danny Thomas, twitching like a terrier, unable to meet Adam's eye. 'I just came round.'

I started to wag. I wagged like I had never wagged before. A fast, happy, make-love-not-war side-to-side tail swoosh. But my powers were waning, I realised that.

'Get. Out.'

So that is what he did, Danny Thomas. He got out. He picked up his board with wheels and left the room, flinching his way around Adam.

'Seeya, Charlotte,' he shouted courageously as he opened the front door.

Slam. Danny Thomas was gone.

'Dad –'

'Don't dad me, young lady.'

'He just came round.'

'Yes. Of course he did. He just came round. Purely coincidental. The one night we leave you on your own.'

'But it's true. And we weren't doing nothing wrong.'

'Look, Charlotte. The truth is, we're all tired. Tired of all your lies.'

'What lies?'

'Enough of your cheek.'

'We were only watching telly.'

'Well, good, because that's all you will be doing. For the next two months.'

'What do you mean?'

'I mean: you're grounded. You want to act like a child, you'll get treated like one.'

'I'm thir-*teen*.'

'Yes, exactly. Three years before you can even start to know your own mind. So that's it, the last word. Two months. I don't know how much clearer I could have made it. I've told you enough times what a horrible little hooligan he is.'

'I hate you.'

'Look, in ten years' time you'll look back and realise just how unreasonable you are at the moment.'

'You're the worst dad in the world.'

'Right, get your coat.'

'What?'

'Your coat. You're coming with me, to the theatre, seeing as you are suddenly so much better. Perhaps we can start to get you to think with your mind instead of your hormones.'

'I wish I'd never been born.'

'At last. A statement we can all agree on.'

Charlotte stormed out of the room to get her coat. 'God,' she screamed down from her bedroom. 'This is so unfair.'

For the first time, Adam looked down at the mess on the carpet. But even as he looked, he didn't really seem to notice, as if there was always a pile of dogshit in the middle of the floor. As if it was meant to be there. No. As if he *liked* it being there. As if he too wanted to pull his trousers down and defecate all over the house.

He grabbed my collar and pulled me towards the door. 'Come on, Prince, out you go. Into the kitchen.'

The Labrador Pact:
You are always in control

Every aspect of Family life is within the Labrador's control. Every argument, every worrying incident, every change in behaviour – all remain under one powerful influence.

No situation is so serious it cannot be resolved through our powers of secret diplomacy. For everything there is a solution. It is the duty of Labradors to make sure they find it.

laughter

Kate was on her hands and knees, violently scrubbing the carpet. She had not said a word since she had arrived back from the theatre. In fact, no one had, not even Grandma Margaret.

Charlotte had stomped her way upstairs as soon as she had got through the door, while Hal had headed for the kitchen to get himself a bowl of cereal. Grandma Margaret, well, I didn't know where she was. She was everywhere, her thousand smells mingling with the complex fusion of dogshit and detergent.

And as for Adam, well, he just sat there. Watching Kate on her hands and knees. But after a series of lengthy sighs he decided to speak.

'If you scrub any harder there'll be a hole in the carpet.'

Kate sat back on her heels and the hand holding the cloth collapsed between her knees. 'What's happening to you?' she asked him.

'What do you mean what's happening to me? I'm just offering a piece of advice. I would just suggest that you rub a bit more lightly.'

'Why are you –' Kate stopped as the door opened. It was Hal, crunching cereal. He looked down at the wet stain on the carpet, then up to both parents, before walking back out of the room.

Again, Kate addressed Adam. 'Why are you acting like this? You're so *aggressive* at the moment. And when you're not you're not even there at all.' She broke off momentarily to resume the violent scrubbing. 'I mean, the way you were with Charlotte. No wonder she's so confused.'

'Confused? Con-*fused*? Believe me there was nothing confused about her behaviour this evening.'

'You were very hard on her.'

'I had to be.'

'Adam, she's thir-*teen*. She's still a little girl, I think you sometimes forget that.'

'No. I don't. In fact, that is my point entirely. She doesn't know her own mind. She'd be pregnant in six months if we left her to it.'

'So that's what you're doing, is it? You're protecting her?'

'Well, somebody has to.'

And with that, he grabbed my lead and took me to the park. We walked fast, too fast for me to translate the scent-trails on the ground, and I knew why.

He wanted to see Emily. He wanted to forget about the Family, and I still didn't have the ability to stop him.

When we got to the park and saw the tall figure of Simon standing by the fence, dog-lead in hand, he was therefore disappointed.

'Adam!' Simon called. 'My man.'

'Oh Simon, hi.'

Simon, arching his head back, laughed, 'Well you could at least *pretend* that you're pleased to see me.'

'Oh sorry. It's just, well, been a long day.'

'Oh?' Simon asked, deliberately playing down his interest.

'Teenagers.'

'Oh. Teenagers. Right. Can't help you with that one, not my speciality. Fast cars, maybe. Or the Eagles – well, up to *Hotel California* anyway. But teenagers, well, I haven't really had much direct experience.'

Adam unclipped my lead, but I stayed in listening distance. Taking it all in.

'It's Charlotte.'

'Charlotte?'

'Our daughter.'

'Oh yes, I met her at the barbecue.'

'She's growing up very fast.'

Simon said something else, but I didn't quite hear what it was because I had just caught sight of Falstaff, on the other side of the park, making sexual advances towards a terrier half his height. The terrier's owner was trying to pull Falstaff away, but with little success. The two dogs were within sniffing distance of Joyce's dead body, but neither seemed to notice. A human must have found her and taken her away. *Poor Joyce.* I was about to head back over, to see if there were any more clues, when my attention switched back. I remembered what Henry had said. 'The Family must come first.'

Simon was still talking: '. . . From where I'm standing you look as though you've got it all. The two point four children. The long-lasting marriage. The Volvo. Even the flaming Labrador. Look in the dictionary for Perfect Family and there's a note which says: See Adam Hunter.'

Adam looked at Simon and said nothing. He just looked.

After a while, Simon carried on: 'I suppose the real problem is I see someone like you, and I get jealous.' I sniffed the air, but the only jealousy molecules I could detect were coming from Adam. 'I mean, I know from the surface people could assume I've got quite a cushy ride. The big house. The soft-top. The nice salary. Living with a woman nearly half my age. But, you know what they say, all that glitters . . .'

'Oh?' Now it was Adam who was playing down his interest.

'Well, take Emily.'

Adam looked behind him, worried she might be able to hear. 'She –'

'Oh, don't worry. She's off for two days on some aromatherapy course.'

'Right.'

'Well that's just it really. We never see each other. I mean, when do you think we last had sex?'

Adam leaned back against the fence. 'I don't, um, know and I'm sure it's not really my bus–'

'Well, I'll tell you. Three weeks ago. Three *weeks*. I mean, can you imagine?'

'Three weeks,' said Adam. 'That's a long time.' But of course, the scent of jealousy only intensified.

'I'm starting to know how he feels.'

'Sorry? What?'

Simon gestured over to Falstaff, who was now frustratedly rubbing his body against the terrier's master's leg.

'Emily won't let me take him in for the chop.'

Adam noticed me, trotting towards him. 'We had Prince done when we first got him, didn't we, boy?'

I wagged my tail and tried my best to look completely unaware of what had just been said.

'Perhaps that's the answer. Perhaps I should book myself into the vet's.'

Adam forced a momentary smile. 'Perhaps we both should.'

There was a pause. Then Simon said: 'Anyway, you up for running tomorrow?'

'Yes of course.'

'Thought we'd do a twelve-miler.'

'No problem. Great. Yep, I'm up for that.'

Simon smiled, and made a sound at the back of his throat. The sound of suppressed laughter.

bully

The next morning, Henry and I lay next to one of the flowerbeds and looked over to the bushes where Joyce had been killed. Henry was convinced he had worked out who had killed her.

'Who is the one dog, in this park, who is not only capable of physical violence, but actively boasts about it?' he asked. But I didn't need to respond. The answer was trotting heavily over the road towards the park.

'It was definitely him, Prince,' Henry said as we watched Lear's master unclip his lead. 'He was preying on the vulnerable. A dog without a master.'

So Joyce had been right. Lear really was a monster.

'What shall we do?' I asked Henry, still certain he held all the answers.

'We must confront Lear.'

'But should we try to find further evidence? Should we go to the bushes where she died and sniff some more?'

Henry spun his head towards me. For a moment he was another dog. Manic, angry. 'I sniffed everywhere. There are no more clues. And we don't need any more.'

'But he'll kill us.'

'We *have* to tell him, Prince. This is our responsibility. As I have always taught you, our actions . . .' He broke off. 'Our actions . . .' Again, he was unable to finish his sentence, so I did it for him.

'Our actions are behind those of our masters.'

'Yes, Prince. Exactly. And that applies to every dog, not just Labradors. If we stand back and do nothing, every human Family will be at risk. Including your own. Lear *must* know that we are onto him, or he will do it again. He's a bully, and bullies like to act in secret.'

He was right. Of course he was. He was Henry. But still, as we waited for him to come over, out of sight of our masters, I wondered how badly Lear would react.

problem

Pretty badly, as it turned out.

'Fuck off, you fucks.'

'I'm afraid the evidence speaks for itself,' said Henry. 'Doesn't it, Prince?' Up until that point I had been doing my best to stay out of this confrontation by sniffing around the rosebushes.

'Um . . . well . . .' Both of them were looking at me, expecting opposite answers. '. . . It seems to be.'

Lear stepped closer towards me, blocking out the light. He spoke, saliva dripping from his black wet mouth. I cannot remember what he said. Even at the time I had no idea, so busy was I trying to keep my fear signals under control.

'Listen,' Henry interrupted, in his matter-of-fact voice. 'The truth is what it is. You know what they say: the nose *knows*.'

That did it. That really hit the wrong button.

My eyes closed, with dread. When they re-opened Henry was clamped to the ground, his throat stuck between Lear's jaws.

'You're right,' I pleaded, as I watched the first specks of blood speckle Henry's golden coat. 'We don't know anything. We're sorry. Please, don't hurt Henry, please. *Please.*'

All three of our owners must have heard because they were running over.

'Lear! No!'

'Henry!'

'Prince!'

Lear's master placed an unworried hand inside the dog's mouth. 'Come on Lear, get off!' he shouted, before pulling him back.

Henry was left lying on the floor, his golden chest speckled with blood.

'You should keep your dog under control,' said Adam, with open anger. 'He could have killed him.'

Mick, descending into an uncomfortable crouch to observe the damage, said nothing, just stroked the top of his Labrador's head and released an audible hiss of air through his teeth.

'Are you all right?' I asked Henry.

'I'll be fine,' he told me, as Adam and Lear's master argued above us. 'I'll just get to my feet.'

'You fucking fools. You don't know a fucking thing about me,' snarled Lear, choking on his collar.

'I know a murderer when I smell one,' said Henry, as I started to lick the blood off his chest.

Our masters were now pulling us away, out of the park.

Lear, already ahead of us, turned. 'You don't know fucking anything.'

But that was the problem.

Henry knew plenty. In fact, Henry knew a lot more than any of us could guess. Even me.

victims

I now realise that there is a fundamental difference between us and humans, and it is a difference which highlights why they need our help. The difference is this: whereas dogs can learn to suppress their instincts, for humans there is no hope.

They believe that science, technology and culture have placed them on a different plane from the rest of the animal world. They think that all their apparatus has somehow managed to protect them against their natural impulses. That when they cover their hairless bodies with clothes, when they paint their faces with make-up, and when they wash away and disguise their personal scent, they are able to suppress the primal urges which in fact guide their every move.

Of course, this vulnerability is what helps to make them so lovable. After all, how could we neglect a species which so appeals to our protective instinct? (A question which must, at some future stage, be put to the Springers.)

But it also leads to a dangerous repetition. As a species they make the same mistakes over and over and over, because of their attempts to detach themselves from the natural world. It doesn't matter how many times they experience something, the lessons go unlearned. For example, they are unable to come to terms with death, no matter how often they are faced with it.

The same with sex. The more humans try to rationalise their desire, the more they become its victims.

This perceived need to control sex and death is most evident in their treatment of us, their dogs. When they send us to an early end, or take away our testicles, they are not (as the Springer propagandists would have us believe) trying to exert their power over us. Rather, they are trying to exert their power over the twin forces which map their lives. That is to say, in saving us from nature they are, in effect, trying to save themselves.

But still they remain trapped in a repetitive cycle – forever resisting, but unable to break free.

And so it was with Adam.

As far as I could smell, he had spent his entire life in a permanent state of resistance. The desires and impulses he felt were clearly destructive and could do damage to the Family, and he couldn't understand why he would want to do things which would hurt those he loved. So he resisted. And he carried on resisting until the desires grew to such an extent they brought with them their own justification. And two days after the meeting with Simon in the park, he finally lost his will-power.

hearing

'Charlotte, I'm going to take the dog for a walk,' he called, from the kitchen.

No answer.

'Charlotte?' Adam went to the bottom of the stairs, leant forward on the wooden banister, and looked up towards Charlotte's bedroom.

'I'm taking the dog for a walk.'

This time Charlotte said something. Not a word exactly, but enough to let Adam know she had understood. Next, he went into the living room to tell Grandma Margaret.

'Margaret, I'm just going to take Prince for a walk.'

She was twiddling with her hearing aid. 'Sorry, dear?'

Adam lifted up the lead with one hand and pointed towards me with the other. Grandma Margaret smiled and nodded her head.

He spoke again, louder, making sure Grandma Margaret could see his lips. 'Kate might come back from the supermarket at about nine. If she does, tell her I've left her and Hal some dinner in the oven. OK?'

Grandma Margaret smiled and nodded her head.

trousers

There was something in the air that night.

Or rather, there was *everything* in the air that night. We passed a Labrador, on our way to the park, who seemed to notice it too.

'Duty over all.'

'Duty over all.'

Our exchange was desperate, as if we sensed our protective powers had been weakened or even put on hold, by the intense forces carried on the wind. Forces perhaps unleashed by Joyce's murder and which could affect everybody who entered the park. As Adam tugged me towards that destination, I couldn't help thinking that it was already all over. That I had absolutely no control over what was about to happen.

Even so, when Adam unclipped my lead I stayed close at heel. I had to observe everything.

And yet now, the first thing that comes back isn't Adam. Or Emily. It's the park itself. The smell of burnt grass, the cracked flowerbeds, the carrier bags floating through space. And although it was about as late as usual, it had forgotten to cool or grow dark. It was that dangerous time of the year, when night-time almost disappears completely, sending established patterns into chaos.

Of course, Falstaff was in his element, huffing his fat

body around the park with manic speed. Running, turning, going absolutely nowhere as quickly as possible. For once, it was easy to avoid him. He was moving too fast to notice anything, directed only by the same reckless summer forces which kept the carrier bags bobbing in the air.

The same forces which had kept Emily away from the park bench, kept her walking the path. When Adam joined her, they did not speak. They just carried on walking, lost in mutual thought.

I looked up at Adam, breathed his scent, and caught sight of what he was thinking. He was thinking dangerous thoughts. He was thinking about what it would be like to start again, to break free from the pack and run wild. He was thinking of what it would be like to have sex with Emily. But most of all, he was thinking about the unknown. Because whereas before it had been the unknown which had prevented him betraying the family, now he wanted not to know. He wanted to escape the predictable monotony of his existence, even for a moment. When he thought of Kate and her lifelong attempts to order everything, and keep everything neat and tidy, he wanted to go the other way. He wanted chaos. He wanted to destroy. But he did not know if he had the courage.

And then, provoked by my nose nudging his knee, Adam experienced a moment of clarity. He seemed to be thinking: would I really be happy? Would starting again give me any better chance? The walking away, that would be easy, but the happiness? That would be far harder to achieve.

But, as I said, his resistance was weak.

When they were by the oak trees, out of view, Emily stopped, smiled.

'Kiss me,' she said.

Adam pretended not to understand.

'I want you to kiss me.'

This time, he had no choice. She leant forward and kissed him, pushing him back against the trunk. I barked, I jumped up, I did anything I could to stop them, but nothing worked. They were in their own world.

Then, when Adam started to have choices, he made the wrong ones. He grabbed a breast, he forced her hand onto his groin. He carried on kissing, moving away from her mouth, towards her neck.

'Fuck me,' she said.

Again Adam pretended not to understand.

'Fuck me.'

They grappled with clothes, they grappled with each other. They moved around, so Emily was against the tree. Adam pushed his trousers down, they fell halfway, hanging at his knees. Emily lifted her skirt. He guided himself inside her, as his fingers clawed her hairless skin.

But it was over before it happened.

'I'm sorry,' Adam said, after a short number of thrusts. Now it was Emily who pretended not to understand. 'I'm sorry.' After he had withdrawn, and placed his penis away, he wiped his hand on the tree and then pulled up his trousers.

It was still light.

The day was never going to end.

charlotte

Nothing else was said.

Nothing else could be.

We left Emily, and we left the park with yet another secret to cover up. We walked home and, as we walked, I knew something bad was about to happen. Something even worse.

The house looked different from outside. Different how, I can't say. Just different. The bathroom light was on, but it wasn't that. Wiser, perhaps. Yes, that was it. The house looked like it had learned something since we had left it and its new wisdom seemed to be crying out, into the street.

Adam clinked the gate open, wearily pushing it forward. His eyes were empty and the smell of sex was still on his hand.

As he turned the key I sniffed under the door. Instinctively, I started to bark. As the door swung forward, I ran upstairs to Charlotte's room. No one was there.

The window was open, its curtain billowing in the breeze. I sniffed around for Charlotte and followed my nose to the bathroom.

I pushed the side of my head against the door but it was closed. I tried to let her know I was there by clawing my paws against the door. Not a sound.

Adam was still downstairs, unconscious of my concern. I started to bark. Continuous, something-is-wrong barking. And to make sure he heard, I squeezed my head through the wooden rails overlooking the downstairs hallway.

'What is it boy?' he asked, plodding out of the living room.

I carried on. Bark bark bark.

Halfway upstairs he had a sense that something was wrong and quickened his pace.

'Charlotte!'

No answer.

'Charlotte!'

He tried the bathroom door.

'Charlotte!'

Locked.

'Charlotte!'

He threw his weight against it.

'Charlotte! Open the door!'

He tried again, harder. This time it flew open.

'Oh my God! Charlotte!'

Time stopped.

She was on the floor, motionless. Pills everywhere. Her face, squashed into the carpet, leaked spit and vomit.

Time re-started.

Adam crashed his knees to the floor, felt her neck, pulled back her eyes, slapped her face with his hand. The hand he had wiped against the tree. There was no response. She was alive, but the life-smells were fading fast.

He got up and shot past me, banging my head with

his knee. Things went blurry. He phoned for an ambulance on the upstairs phone.

I did what I could. Licked her face clean. I made her a promise.

I will always look after you, Charlotte. I promise, you will never want to do this again.

She couldn't hear me. Of course she couldn't. But that didn't make it any less of a promise.

Adam was back on the bathroom floor, placing the top half of his daughter's limp body over his knee.

'Oh please, Lottie, please. Come on, baby, *come on.*' He shook her gently, causing her mouth to sag open.

I didn't know what to do so I kept on talking to her, quiet dog words. I told her how much she means to everyone, although they don't always show it. I told her that one day she would be a happy, confident woman. I told her that I had let her down, but would never do so again.

When I had finished, the ambulance woman was there, dressed in green and smelling of death, asking unanswerable questions.

'How many did she have?'

'When did she take them?'

'Has she swallowed any vomit?'

They put things on her face.

Adam wept, and went with her, in the ambulance. On his way out he told Grandma Margaret to wait there and tell Hal and Kate what had happened. Grandma Margaret wept too.

When the ambulance had gone I went into Charlotte's room, climbed onto her bed as she had always allowed, and I breathed in her scent, trying to keep her there with me, trying to stop the outdoor air coming in through the open window to take her away.

From then on, I swore to myself, everything would be different.

From then on, bad things wouldn't happen.

radiator

Lapsang had been asleep through everything. She had only woken up when they had taken Charlotte away, in the ambulance.

'Where's Charlotte?' she asked, drowsily, as she strolled into the room.

'She's not here.'

Lapsang froze as she read my expression. 'Where is she?'

'She's at the hospital. She tried to kill herself.'

Her tail jolted in shock. 'Will she . . . will she be OK?'

'I don't know.'

Lapsang didn't say anything after that. She just looked at the bed, as if for the first time in our mutual history she was about to jump up and join me.

She didn't. Instead, she turned and walked slowly over towards the piece of carpet situated under the cold metal of the radiator. It would be cooler there.

superdog

Charlotte was OK.

Not *OK* OK but OK. She was alive, and that was the main thing.

Adam felt terrible.

Of course, only I knew why he *really* felt so bad. Everyone else thought it was just about the way he had treated Charlotte. Not about why he had been delayed, in the park, with Emily.

He knew to be careful, to keep a careful distance, and indeed, so did I, even though the temptation to sniff for information was strong. I realised I had to rely on my other senses.

To be honest, she looked pretty bad. Her face was pale, as pale as with her make-up, although this time Adam didn't say she looked like Death. And her voice had altered. It had a crack in it, as if her old voice had been irreparably damaged by what had happened.

'I don't know why I did it.'

Adam smelt relieved after she said that, as if he had thought it had been all down to him. Which of course, it wasn't. It wasn't down to any of them. Not really. It was down to me. This type of thing just wasn't meant to happen. Not to Families with Labradors looking after them.

That is what I couldn't understand.

I had been doing my best. Making sure I stayed within the boundaries as dictated by the Pact. Well OK, *most* of them. And remember, I had only befriended Falstaff to find out information. I had devoted every single moment of every single day to keeping this Family safe from harm. Using my secret Labrador tricks and special powers. I hadn't even got side-tracked when we had found Joyce's body. I had always remembered that our human masters come first. And yet I must have lapsed somewhere. I had definitely got something wrong.

But then, as things panned out, I started to reassess. Maybe I was being hard on myself. After all, the Family was still together. Charlotte was still here. In fact, looking at it one way, I had saved her life.

That was certainly the way everyone else was looking at it.

'It was Prince, you know, who realised first,' Adam told Hal when Charlotte and Kate were out of the room.

Hal said nothing. He just stroked my head. Slow, careful strokes – not like usual, when he would sink his fingers into my fur and shake my head about a bit.

'We're living with Superdog,' Adam added, raising his eyebrows in an attempt to get Hal to speak. But still, he said nothing.

He was probably working out what this all meant. How he was meant to act. Or, maybe, he was starting to come round to my way of thinking. That speaking isn't always very helpful. That sometimes you need the silence if things are ever going to mend. Or be retrieved.

* * *

For the couple of days after Charlotte came home alive, everything was still rather shaky and Adam and Kate were clearly at odds over how to deal with the situation. Adam thought that they should keep a closer eye on Charlotte, but Kate thought that was exactly what went wrong last time.

'Adam, can't you see: she feels suffocated,' Kate said, straightening the picture frame of the Family portrait. 'She's thirteen, she's starting to need her freedom.'

'Well, we can't just let her run wild, can we?'

'I'm not saying she should run wild. I just think we need to be careful. Not so heavy-handed.'

'So you're saying it was my fault.'

'I'm not saying that at all.'

Come on, I wagged. *This isn't doing anyone any good.* They weren't listening to me, they just carried on, snapping at each other, giving a voice to all of the forces of tension in the air. But of course, these were forces which extended beyond their bedroom walls into the world outside. A world without Labradors. And I knew where they were centred, these forces. They were centred in the park, and the big, modern house which cast the long shadow.

carpet

That night Charlotte woke up, crying. She went into her parents' bedroom.

'Charlotte, what is it?'

'I had a nightmare,' she said, through tears. 'You and dad had split up because of me and I couldn't see either of you again because every time I tried to step out of my bedroom there was nothing else there.'

'Oh, darling, come here.' Charlotte nestled into her mother's pyjamas. 'It was only a dream. Everything's all right now.'

'But I'm worried that you and dad will get a divorce and that it's all my fault.'

'A divorce?' said Kate, with convincing horror. 'That would never happen, we're a close family. A strong family. And we're going to stay together.'

Adam blinked awake and said in a sleepy haze: 'What's the matter, sweetheart?'

'I just got frightened,' explained Charlotte. 'I thought the family was going to fall apart and I thought it would all be because of me.'

'I told her that that was a silly thought and that it's never going to happen,' said Kate.

'Your mother's right,' said Adam, into his pillow. 'We'd be the last family in England to fall apart.' And even

211

more drowsily: 'The last –' He slipped back into sleep as Kate held on to her daughter.

I stood by the door, unnoticed, wagging as hard as I could. Wagging, lifting the air, blocking out thought, and doubt. Blocking out the possibility which was starting to creep into my mind. Not even considering it, not for a second. Because it was nonsense.

The Pact was going to be enough. Of course it was. It had to be, because what else was there? What else?

A brief contemplation of that final thought caused me to vomit, leaving a sticky white mess on the carpet.

'Oh, *Prince*,' Kate said, as soon as she had realised.

'What is it?' asked Adam, still heavy with sleep.

'It's Prince. He's been sick on the carpet.'

'Oh well,' he sighed. 'It can wait till morning.'

'No,' Kate said, unlocking herself from Charlotte and pulling back the covers. 'I'll have to do it now.'

mad

Hal had not said much at all the first few days after Charlotte tried to kill herself. The only words he did say were requests to go out with his friend, Jamie.

Permission was usually granted, although Kate had observed that Jamie was 'a bad influence' and preferred Hal to revise. This had been confirmed to me on the first Saturday following his sister's suicide bid.

The house had been sleeping for some time when he arrived home, via the back door.

He looked at me with wide eyes, frisbee-wide, and shut the door. As he moved forward into the kitchen I could see that he was confused, as though he had arrived back at the wrong address.

He giggled nervously, through his nose, then looked around to see where the noise had come from.

'I am completely out of my tree,' he whispered, crouching down. 'Chimpanzee. Out of my tree.' After more giggles, he sat down on the cold tiled floor and smoothed his back against the refrigerator. As his face was now at dog level I got a closer look.

Everything was more extreme. His skin was paler, while his spots were redder and angrier than ever. He looked like he had been plucked.

'Fridge music,' he said, as he nodded his head to the low hum of the refrigerator.

This was not good. Not good at all. I could hear bed movements upstairs.

I went over and licked his face.

This tactic had an undesired effect. Floppy hands and more giggles.

Oh, Hal, come on!

His head sprang up and he stared into my eyes. To our mutual shock, my words had broken through. For the first time in his life he actually seemed to understand what I was saying.

Hal?

His eyes were now so wide they were protruding out from his face. He was terrified.

'No, no, no. This cannot be happening. This cannot be happening. Dogs don't talk. Dogs don't talk.'

I talk. I always talk.

The scent of fear was almost intoxicating as Hal attempted to lift himself off the floor. 'Shit. Talking dog. How much did I have? I'm losing it big style. Orange juice.'

He pulled a carton of orange juice out of the refrigerator door and started to pour it down his throat. As he glugged it down his frisbee eyes stayed fixed on mine.

I talk to everyone all the time. It's just that no one ever listens. You mustn't be scared. You are not going mad.

'But if, but if, but if –' I tilted my head expectantly, waiting for him to finish his sentence. 'But if it is true you would not be speaking like this. You would be speaking like a dog.' It appeared that he was no longer surprised about the fact that I was talking, but rather with the *way* I did it.

What do you think dogs talk like?

He paused, silently debating whether or not he should answer this question. A question put to him by a household pet. It was a big decision. I watched as the answer started to play with the corners of his mouth.

'If you could really talk,' he said, 'you would talk like this: *Woof! I want a biscuit. Give me a biscuit! Biscuit! Biscuit!* You wouldn't be able to, you know, say proper things. You wouldn't be able to hold a meaningfuh – a meaningful – conversation.'

We pick up everything. And we are talking to humans all the time. Well, those of us that still care.

'Care?'

While he tried to stop himself shaking, as he quietly sat down at the kitchen table, I started to tell him about the fate of the Hunters. I told him that things might fall apart around him. Then I taught him the things only dogs can teach.

Life. Love. Loyalty.

You are the oldest child, Hal, you need to be strong. What you are going through now, it is just a test for the future. It may seem like everything, but it really is nothing. None of the fears and anxieties you now feel will matter. You must focus on what is important. But most of all you must realise one thing. You will be all right, Hal. You will be all right. Do you understand?

'I do,' he said. 'I understand.'

We heard sleepy footsteps, on the landing. 'Hal?'

It was Kate, ready to interrupt our private conference.

'Mum. I'm just getting a, um, a glass, glass, glass of water.'

215

'Who were you talking to?'

'Um, no one.' Somehow his voice managed to convince her and she headed back to the bedroom. For a short time we sat in silence, saying nothing. We had made progress, I was sure. He was still shaky, yes, but it had been quite a shock.

Eventually he left the table and whispered in my ear: 'Can you hear that?' I told him I couldn't hear anything. 'The kettle,' he continued. 'The kettle is saying things.' He moved across to the kitchen unit and placed his ear next to the kettle.

My heart plummeted.

A talking kettle, I ask you.

nice

After a few days, things settled.

In some ways, things were starting to become better than they had ever been. Charlotte may not have succeeded in killing herself, but she had certainly put something to rest. She had emerged from her near-death experience a completely new person. She was now starting to act as though she was a member of the household through choice, rather than sheer obligation. Because perhaps she was. Perhaps, in her unconscious state, she had faced death and then turned the other way. To come back. To face up to responsibility.

Her new behaviour did not go unnoticed.

Adam, despite the argument with Kate, was definitely less heavy-handed. Each time he made a suggestion as to what the Family should do he would ask Charlotte: 'How do you feel about that?'

And Hal didn't begrudge his sister this special treatment. In fact, he welcomed it, perhaps having heeded what I had told him. He was certainly looking at me differently. But when I tried to talk to him, he no longer seemed able to listen. He didn't decide to resume our conversation, and certainly didn't return home in the same state again. Anyway, he didn't seem to mind his parents' focus on Charlotte. It meant that he could hide away in his room for hours on end, revising, or doing whatever it was that caused such tempestuous movements of the duvet, with no one even noticing his absence.

There were other changes too.

Adam was less angry with Grandma Margaret, whose Controversial Opinions were now largely ignored. He was also starting to wait longer before taking me for my evening walk. We went last thing. I don't think he wanted to see Emily any more. Not after what happened to Charlotte.

With no outside danger to distract us, the park was ours again. Stick-throwing resumed, if not quite as enthusiastically as before, and we tried to make sure we stayed out of view of the big modern house.

The only problem now was Kate. The scent of anxiety was intensifying and I couldn't believe it was only about Charlotte. Because, of course, it wasn't only about Charlotte. Or rather, it was, but not in the way I could have sensed.

So while the Emily-threat may have evaporated, the Simon-threat remained. Which probably explains why she was so enthusiastic when Adam re-suggested a weekend away.

'We could go to Devon, there are some lovely b-and-b's in the book,' she said.

'Yes,' said Adam. And then, remarkably: 'We could all go. You'd enjoy a weekend away, wouldn't you, Margaret?'

Grandma Margaret smiled and nodded her head.

'I've got my revision,' said Hal, raising his sandwich in objection.

'Well, you can stay,' said Kate. 'We're not going to force you. Not any more.'

'So, Charlotte,' said Adam. 'Weekend away. How do you feel about it?'

'Yes,' she said, smiling softly. 'It would be nice.'

fur

The next morning I was more impatient than ever on my way to the park.

'Woh, Prince, steady,' Adam said, as I pulled him forward. But I didn't let up. I had to see Henry. I had to restore my faith in the Pact. Only he could tell me where I had been going wrong.

You see, I hadn't told him about Charlotte. The last few mornings, I had sat in virtual silence as Henry had instructed me on Paw Diplomacy and Intermediary Mind Tricks. I had wanted to tell him, I really had, but there hadn't been a right time.

The morning after finding Charlotte on the floor, I was still numb, unable to articulate anything. The mornings after that, well, I don't know why I didn't tell him. Something in his scent had prevented me. Some deep anxiety I wasn't able to pinpoint, and hadn't wanted to ask him about.

But now I was ready. I had to tell him before it was too late.

'OK, boy. Nearly there.'

As soon as we got there I knew something was wrong. Adam noticed it too and said: 'Oh, Prince, where's your friend?'

I sniffed the ground. Not a trace.

Perhaps he was late. But Henry, *late*? It wasn't possible. He always made sure he was taken to the park on time. And Mick never let him down.

I scanned the park for movement. Nothing. I listened for his voice.

Nothing.

I ran around the park, from flowerbed to flowerbed, my nose continuously to the ground. Still nothing. I went, with ascending dread, over to the bushes where Joyce had been murdered. Joyce was no longer there, but my body stuttered in shock at the memory of her violated body. But no sign of Henry.

'Henry?' I barked. 'Henry?'

The park had never seemed so empty. I looked over to his house, on the other side of the road. The narrow door showed no sign of opening. I looked towards the trees. Something moved.

I ran over but realised straight away that it wasn't Henry. It wasn't even my species. It was a squirrel.

'Have you seen a dog?' I asked him, out of breath. 'A Labrador.'

'I'm staring right at one,' he said, as he climbed his way safely above dog height.

'No. Golden coat. Bit taller than me. Bit older, too. Grey whiskers.'

'Dogs are here all the time,' the squirrel said unhelpfully. 'There's been quite a few so far this morning.'

'But have you seen one matching that description?'

'I'm sorry, I can't help you.' The squirrel shuffled further up the tree towards the first branch.

'Listen,' I said, following his path from underneath. 'I need to find him. This is very important, if you've seen him, please could you let me know.'

'Hey, *you* listen, dogface. Not my species, not my problem.'

My last and only hope was the dark wasteland behind the trees, beyond the smell-heap. Of course, this was always going to be a long shot but I still had to try. I sniffed amid the empty bottles, carrier bags, and the small weird things which stink of human sex. I picked up a scent I recognised. Dog scent, but not Henry.

'Get back to your flowerbeds, you fuck.'

'L-Lear,' I stammered. 'How are you?' I looked around, to see if I was in view of Adam. I wasn't.

'How am I? I've got two fucking Labradors trying to frame me for murder. How the fuck do you think I am?'

'Look, about that. We had no right to –' I caught a glimpse of Lear's master, in the far corner of the park, walking his lopsided walk, with his head pointed towards the ground. 'We had no right to say those things. It was probably all a big mistake.'

'The biggest mistake of your lives,' he said. And then a terrible thought came to me. No, not a thought, an image. A mental vision of Henry dead on the ground, lying in Lear's shadow.

'Have you smelt Henry this morning? You know, my friend?' I asked, trying to conceal my anxiety. 'Only, I really need to talk to him and he's always here at this time.'

'I haven't smelt him,' Lear told me. 'But if I had, he would fucking know about it.'

'The truth is, I'm worried about him. The last time I

saw him he wasn't himself. I'm frightened he's done something stupid.'

Lear sniffed me incredulously. 'My heart bleeds.'

He was then called away by his master. And I remember thinking, wouldn't his master have spotted him, if he had gone into the bushes to attack Joyce? Wouldn't he have called him away?

When Lear had left the park I went back over to the bushes where Joyce had lived and died. I instinctively felt that wherever Henry was now, this crime scene would hold the key. I looked at the damaged twigs, and the leaves on the ground which must have fallen in the struggle. I remembered vividly the wound on her neck It had displayed a clear ferocity, but was also smaller than you would expect if Lear had been the attacker. I sniffed the ground for more information. Henry had been certain the rain had washed away all the scent-trails, but it was possible he could have missed something. However, as I started to sniff Adam called my name. As I pulled back I caught sight of something on one of the broken twigs. It was fur from another dog, interwoven with Joyce's own. I focused hard, and my legs nearly buckled when I realised the colour. The fur was golden, like Henry's.

I needed to speak to him. To Henry. But where was he?

'Come on, boy, let's go home.' Adam was close behind, so I reversed quickly out of the bushes.

Then, on our walk back, we passed Henry's house. There was something different about it, but it took a while to realise exactly what it was. The curtains were all closed. I felt the house was hiding something, something which would explain Henry's absence.

As soon as I was out of the park, I started to bark in a final, desperate attempt to call Henry.

'Quiet, Prince, quiet,' Adam pleaded.

I carried on barking, calling Henry's name, until we reached the end of the street and I realised it was no good.

I had to comfort myself with the belief he would be there the next day, and that he would be able to explain everything. In the meantime, I was not to lose faith. The Pact was still going to be enough to protect the Family.

bag

That night, we went on a different walk. We were headed for the park but Adam had timed it wrong. Emily was there, watching as Falstaff tore his way around the flowerbeds. Adam, who hadn't seen her since he had sex with her by the tree, was still not ready to talk to her. So instead of crossing the road we kept a safe distance and travelled into new territory, walking through dark and empty streets. After we had been walking for some time, Adam sat down on a bench, but didn't unclip me. He just sat there, listening to distant traffic.

I could smell from the ground that this was not Labrador territory. In fact, the most obvious scent was that of human piss. The only dog-trace I could detect at all was, ominously, Springer spaniel. I sniffed again, to check it wasn't Falstaff. To my relief, it wasn't.

Footsteps. Someone was coming. We turned to see a man walking fast across the street.

'Spare a bit of change, mate,' the man asked, holding out a white paper cup.

'I'm sorry, I haven't got any,' Adam said, as anxiety and pity mingled in the air.

'Lying cunt.'

When the man had gone, Adam started to lead me

back home. As we walked past the park, he turned to look for Emily. She had gone.

We walked past Henry's house. The curtains were still shut, but I was not worried. I would see him tomorrow.

But as I turned the corner, I could smell Henry in front of us.

'Steady, Prince,' Adam said, as he was yanked forward. And then, seeing Mick: 'All right there.'

The scent had been misleading. Henry wasn't with him. In his place was a plastic carrier bag, clinking an indifferent hello.

'I think Prince missed his friend this morning,' Adam continued.

'Oh,' Mick said. And then, after a weird silence, he added: 'He's dead.'

My tail stopped.

'Dead?' said Adam. 'Oh no.'

I felt myself sinking, into the ground.

'Yes . . . Yesterday. Door was open. Ran straight out into the road. Next thing we know, dead. Hit by a car.'

Ran straight out into the road? It didn't make sense. Henry wouldn't do that, not unless moving out into the road was a way of protecting Mick. My mind was not capable of thinking of a situation where getting run over could help protect our masters. But still, it must have been true. Henry was not here.

I sniffed Mick's trousers, inhaling Henry back to life.

'Oh, how terrible.'

I looked out, into the road, at the speeding black tyres.

'Anyway. I better . . . go.' Mick's voice was shaky and

urgent at the same time. I sniffed again, trying to gain further information.

'No, Prince, come away. Mick, I'm sorry.'

After that, I couldn't hear anything. As Henry's scent became lost amid the car fumes, I knew that nothing would ever be the same again. I knew then, for the first time, what life really meant.

It meant chaos. And pain.

back

I was devastated by the news of Henry's death. But alongside an overwhelming feeling of grief, there was also a fear of the unknown. Without Henry to advise me, I would have to interpret the Pact for myself.

As far as I could tell, both Simon and Emily remained a threat to the Family. With regard to Simon, things were very serious indeed. Every time Kate returned from work she brought the Simon-smells with her, although I was still unsure of their mutual secret.

Of course, Kate wasn't happy that Simon and Adam continued to run together, three times a week, but what could she say? And anyway, whatever she was worried about Simon saying, was never said, just as Adam could never have hinted at his feelings for Emily. Feelings which, despite the fumbled tree-side encounter, I was sure were still strong. After all, why not break off the contact completely? Why take the risk of seeing Simon all the time if he was planning to hide from Emily for ever? Surely she would eventually say something?

Although he had avoided her immediately afterwards, I knew it would not be for long. I knew that, so long as he continued to see Simon, he would also need to get things straight with Emily. So the evening I detected anxiety smells around his legs, I knew we were going back to the park.

damage

When he got there, and saw her sitting on the bench, the scent of anxiety turned again to desire, but I knew he wasn't going to do anything stupid. Not this time.

They just sat there, initially in silence, their heads craned back looking at the sky.

'It's a beautiful night,' said Emily after some time. 'All those stars.'

'Yes. Beautiful.' Adam dropped his head towards her, perhaps preferring the night's reflection in her eyes.

'What do you see, what do you see when you look at the sky? What do you think?'

Adam looked back up and considered Emily's question. 'I, uh, don't know.' His mouth made a clicking sound. 'I know this sounds strange but I suppose, when it's clear like this, I see damage.'

Emily looked at Adam and made a puzzled face. 'Damage?'

'I suppose so. When I look at stars I think of the collisions that caused them to happen. You know, the Big Bang. I mean, something caused that Bang in the first place, didn't it? The stars, they're beautiful and everything but, at the end of the day, they're just debris, aren't they, and, in some cases, debris which isn't even there any more. So, when I look up and think about it, that is what I see. An accident scene. Damage. I saw a programme on TV about it a few weeks ago. Had all these top scientists on, and that is basically what they were saying. That everything – the earth, you, me, the dogs, this park, the stars, the whole universe – it all started because of a phenomenal collision between two physical forces. So the universe, it didn't start from nothing, it started from things, *worlds*, which were already there. We're just, you know, the aftermath. Part of the damage itself.'

'Oh,' Emily said. 'Right.'

Then Falstaff charged over. 'Waah-hey, madwag!'

'Waah-hey,' I said wearily.

'How long have they got?' said Falstaff.

'What do you mean?'

'Your Family, before they fall apart?'

'They're not going to fall apart.'

'Of course they're not, madwag. 'Course they're not.' And with that Falstaff was off, galloping over towards the smell-heap. *He doesn't know anything*, I told myself. *He's just winding me up.*

But even so, as I turned my concentration back to Adam and Emily, I felt an undeniable sense of nausea.

'About the other night,' Adam was saying. 'It shouldn't have happened.'

'Don't worry,' Emily said. 'It wasn't your fault.'

'It wasn't?'

'No. There was a lot of cosmic energy around. You know with the moon being in Jupiter. You're Gemini. I'm Cancer. We couldn't help it.'

'Sorry?'

'We couldn't really control ourselves.'

'No, we couldn't. But, um, in future I think we should try to. I mean, you're a very attractive woman, but it's not right. I've got a wife, a family, and you've got Simon.'

'And Falstaff,' she giggled.

'Sorry?'

'Falstaff! My dog!'

'Oh yes. Um, of course. But as I said, I don't think it's right.'

More giggling. 'You are funny!' she said. 'So serious!'

'So shall we just say that it never happened?'

'Of *course* it didn't happen! You are funny!'

Although confused, Adam allowed himself a slight smile of relief as he clipped on my lead. 'Anyway, I'd better go.'

'OK, see you tomorrow.'

'Yes, see . . .' Adam stopped, remembered. 'Actually, no. We've got a weekend away planned. We'll be off by then.'

Emily went quiet. 'Oh,' she said, her voice now sad. 'Have fun.'

suicide

The scent of the Family was still hanging heavy in the air when Hal ventured downstairs to phone his best friend, Jamie. The bad influence. I sat in the hall and watched him, one hand gloved in his boxer shorts, as he struggled to make excuses.

'No. I can't. No way on earth. They're coming back tomorrow, it's more than my life's worth . . . I've got to look after the dog . . . there are smoke alarms everywhere . . . I've got too much revision . . . every object in this house is breakable . . . the neighbours complain if I cough too loudly let alone invite half the town around for a party . . . I'm seriously, seriously ill.'

He looked at me, desperate for something more convincing, I wagged my way over, to offer moral support, but it was no good. The next thing he said was: 'Well OK, but no more than ten people.'

Lying outstretched on the floor, listening to Hal's telephone conversation, was Lapsang. When the conversation was over she looked at me with her upside-down eyes and said: 'Good luck.'

'Are you not staying?'

She rolled onto her front. 'Sweetie, are you *mad*? Why on earth would I want to stay for a teenage party?'

'I don't know. Maybe there will be lots of nice warm laps.'

'Believe me, if I stayed it would be suicide. I *know* about teenage parties, darling, and I know that cats don't survive them in one piece. They either get a firework strapped to their tail or they are made to jump from a very large height, just to see if they can make it. So, no thanks.' She stood up and walked past me, down the hallway, her tail brushing against my chin. 'In fact, I am going to leave right now, just to be safe.'

'Laps—' But, before I had time to object, I was watching Lapsang disappear out of the cat-flap and then I was left alone, with Hal, and the very real threat of a teenage invasion.

stairs

The doorbell rang mid-afternoon.

I barked my warning but could do little to prevent Hal from opening the door.

'Who are you?' he asked the very tall, shaven-headed boy standing on the doorstep.

'Don't worry,' said a familiar voice. 'He's with me.' It was Jamie, thrusting forward a bottle of clear liquid. 'Get that down you.'

'But –'

Jamie cupped his hand around Hal's ear and whispered something about Laura Shepherd, the girl of Hal's dreams and object of his conversations with the mirror. When he had finished whispering Hal stood back against the radiator in blank submission as Jamie leant his spiky head out the door and whistled down the street. Moments later, the invasion began. Teenagers of every description, armed with bottles and cans, were treading their way through the door. I sniffed as many as I could but there was too much information to keep track of.

Within no time at all, every room of the house was occupied. Music started from various locations. Drinks were being drunk, straight out of the bottles. Everyone was laughing.

Everyone apart from Hal. He sat alone, upstairs on his

bed, the bottle of clear liquid in his hand. He looked at me, unscrewed the top, and started to gulp the liquid back. He grimaced, pulled the bottle away, coughed. He held the bottle out towards me.

'Want some?' Then he too was laughing.

This was not good.

I went back downstairs. A boy and girl were on the living-room sofa, sticking their tongues into each other's mouths. Next to them, the tall boy with the shaven head was placing a strange-smelling substance onto pieces of white paper. He rolled the white paper and licked it and rolled it again, to create a tube. Some kind of cigarette. Although he had been laughing he now looked very serious. He twisted and tore off the end of the tube, placed it in his mouth and set it alight.

'This tune's the bollocks,' he said, taking the tube out of his mouth and pointing it towards the stereo.

Someone else said, 'Yeah, it's wicked,' and started to flick their hands into the air, in rhythm with the music.

The tall boy leant forward and grabbed my collar. 'I think he wants some,' he said. He then placed the other end of the white tube in his mouth, the end he had set alight, and moved close to my face.

The next thing I knew the strange-smelling smoke was in my eyes and going up my nose. Teenage laughter clattered in my brain. The tall boy pulled back as I started to cough.

I felt weak as the room started to spin around me. Everything blurred. I tried to stand up on my hind legs and walk out of the doorway, but it kept sliding away to my right. I hit my shoulder. The laughter intensified.

This was worse than the smell-heap. I was starting to smell things which weren't even there – horrible things, dead things.

I tried again for the doorway and this time just made it. I wanted to go and see Hal but it was impossible. I stood at the bottom of the stairs and realised they went on for ever. I saw a flickering presence, standing at the top, looking down at me. It was Henry. I closed my eyes but when I opened them he was still there.

'It was me,' he said, in his serious voice. 'It was me.'

'What do you mean?'

'Everything ends with violence,' he said. 'No matter what we do. We all break the Pact.'

'I don't understa–' But Henry was gone. 'Henry?'

My eyes grew heavy. I lay down. Everything faded.

toilet

I didn't know how long I'd been asleep. Too long, I realised, as I patrolled the house.

Everything was chaos.

There were boys in Charlotte's room, playing her music. Laughing as they banged their heads and made faces.

I went into Hal's room. Bodies everywhere, clouded in smoke. A boy stood over me, pretended to ride me, pulled my ears out and made aeroplane noises. Then sang: 'Snoop Doggy Do-o-ogg, Snoop Doggy Do-o-gg, Bow wow wow yippy yo yippy yay, Bow wow wow yippy yo.' Everyone laughed. Someone else started singing: 'Who let the dog out?' But this time nobody laughed.

I looked around and sniffed for Hal but my senses of sight and smell were dulled by the smoke. I trod backwards, out onto the landing.

Someone was being sick. When I moved closer I saw that it was Hal, crouched on all fours over the toilet, the way he had seen me, when thirsting for water.

'Pruh,' he said. 'Pruh.' I think he was trying to say my name.

He retched again, bringing up more rich-smelling vomit.

'Pruh. Hell muh.' But I couldn't help him.

Things were, I had to admit, beyond my control. He hung, limply, onto the toilet seat and his hand left my collar to try and reach the chain. It didn't make it, instead knocking the toilet lid down so his head was squashed between it and the seat.

'Pruh, thah huh,' he told me. I tried to speak to him, the way I had managed to speak to him before, but he just looked at me with blank eyes. He was never going to understand me again.

And then, suddenly, he wasn't looking at me at all. He was looking behind. Above. And his eyes filled with panic.

I turned to see a girl. She was visually attractive, I suppose, at least by human standards. (And as I have said, this is all that matters for humans, the visual appearance. Stupid, I know, and completely misguided. But that's the way it is.)

He went to speak, but couldn't. I knew who it was though, straight away, from the smell of fear.

It was Laura Shepherd, the mirror-girl.

'Can I use your toilet?' she asked him.

He closed his eyes, tight, but when they re-opened she was still there. As Henry had been. Hal's hand lifted the toilet lid from his head and he tried to sit himself upright. The weight on his heel was too much and he fell back, nearly banging his head against the side of the bath.

Laura Shepherd screwed up her nose and flushed the chain then locked the bathroom door with myself and Hal still inside. She pulled her jeans and knickers down and started to piss into the toilet water, making a loud noise. I went over to take note of her scent but she pushed me away.

Hal couldn't believe what he was witnessing, and was desperately trying to find words.

'Laur–'

'Cool party, by the way,' she said, as she started to wipe herself.

'Thuh,' he said.

I wagged my way over to Hal and licked his face, trying to show Laura my endorsement of the semi-conscious boy in front of her. She didn't take any notice, just pulled up her knickers and jeans, flushed the chain and went back out of the door.

video

I sniffed Hal to assess if he was going to be OK. He was, so I went back out to check on the rest of the house. To see if it was all still there. But where could I start? Things were happening everywhere.

I went downstairs to the television room, which was full of people laid out on the floor. Someone had spilt some drink. I thought of Kate, then tried to clean it up.

Somebody said: 'Look, even his dog's a piss-head.'

They put on a video. As soon as it came on, all the boys giggled. I looked to see what was funny. It was a naked man and a naked woman having sex like dogs.

One of the girls went to leave the room. 'That's disgusting,' she said, stepping over me.

I followed her, to see what else was happening. Then, when I was out in the hallway I caught a scent I recognised. It was coming from one of the boys walking through the kitchen towards Grandma Margaret's room.

When I got closer, I knew who it was.

It was the boy who smelt of damaged skin. The one who had thrown a bottle at Adam, that night in the park. The one that had called him a wanker.

He shut the door to Grandma Margaret's room, but I had slipped inside just in time. The boy he was with farted and put his hand on it and passed the scent up to his friend's nose.

'You radge cunt,' said the boy with damaged skin, opening one of Grandma Margaret's drawers. 'Fucking bollocks. Look at that.'

While his friend leant against the door, he pulled out some gold jewellery and put it into his coat pocket. Then he looked at me and held my mouth shut.

'Not a word, you fucking useless guard dog,' he said to me, but more to his friend.

'Let's just get the fuck out of here.'

I remembered the most significant rule of the Pact. *Never resort to violence . . . Never resort to violence . . . Never resort to violence . . . Never . . .*

But as he kept on clamping my jaws, I felt an unstoppable anger rise up within me. And, for a brief moment, I had no control over my own body. I pulled away and lashed out at his hand in one single action, feeling my teeth penetrate his flesh. Tasting blood, I was lost in the violence, as if in one of my wolf-dreams.

He tore his hand away and said, 'You stupid bastard dog,' as he kicked me in my ribs. He held his wound, which was leaking blood fast.

'Let's go,' said the friend as they opened the door. I was left dazed, in the corner of the room, breathing in Grandma Margaret's thousand smells, wondering exactly what I had just allowed to happen.

The Labrador Pact:
Never resort to violence

The mission of each and every Labrador will be accomplished without resorting to violence.

Throughout history the Labrador breed has risen above the wolfish tendencies of many others within our species.

In the halcyon days when all dogs remained loyal to their human masters, violence was often considered a necessary last resort. However, Labradors have always realised the truth. If you have to descend to violence, the mission has already failed.

After all, to be a Labrador means to separate ourselves from the barbarism of our wolf ancestors.

We may bark, we may growl, but we must never deliberately shed human blood.

connections

Kate's nose twitched once she was inside the house. The windows had been open all day but the party smells were still just about detectable, even to human noses.

'Hal.' She pronounced his name in two stages. 'Ha-al.' This was always a danger-sign.

'Mum, Dad. I didn't hear you come in.' He stood at the top of the stairs with a cloth in his hand.

'What's that?' asked Kate.

'It's a cloth,' he said.

'I can see that,' she said. 'I just wondered what it was doing in your hand.'

The scent of panic filtered down the stairs. 'I, um, I thought I'd tidy up before you came back.'

Adam laughed in disbelief. Charlotte, still smelling like a reformed character, ushered Grandma Margaret into the living room.

'You thought you'd tidy up,' echoed Kate. As she started to sniff her way around the house, Hal froze, terrified. Realising he needed help I ran into the television room, ahead of Kate, and lay myself down on the drink-stain.

The tactic worked, but I knew it was only temporary. I could not stay there all day. Kate looked at the ornaments on the mantelpiece and the Family portrait above them.

'These ornaments,' she said. 'They're all the wrong way round.'

'Oh, um, yeah,' Hal said, as he finally walked down the stairs to join us. 'Jamie came round last night. He was messing about.'

'Was he smoking?'

'*No*. 'Course he wasn't, not in the house.'

'Well, why does everywhere smell of smoke?'

Hal's face collapsed under the dual weight of his parents' glare. 'I don't know. Jamie smokes so maybe he just smelt of smoke.'

'*Maybe he just.*' Kate turned to her husband. 'Oh, Adam, you talk to him.'

'Hal, come on, tell us the whole truth,' said Adam who now seemed to be back to his reasonable self.

Of course, the whole truth was impossible. Hal only knew the beginning of the truth. The bit that involved him being handed a bottle of clear liquid and heading upstairs.

'I have,' Hal lied. 'Jamie came round.'

When Adam and Kate left the room I stood up.

Hal realised he had missed the drink-stain. 'Oh, *shit*.'

He had no time. He fell to his knees and started rubbing with the cloth. I could smell that Kate was about to re-enter the room so I tried to lie back down.

'Prince, what are you doing?' Hal said as he elbowed me away.

'Hal, what are *you* doing?' asked Kate, standing in the doorway.

His mouth opened and closed but no words came out. He tried again. This time, he managed: 'I must have spilt something.'

244

Kate blew air out of her nostrils. Another danger-sign. I wagged at medium speed, trying to lighten the atmosphere.

It seemed to work. Hal seemed to have got away with it. But of course, I knew what was coming. I knew, as I trailed Grandma Margaret and her thousand smells into her bedroom. I knew as she pulled back her drawer and gasped in horror. But what could I do? Use physical force?

It had to come out some time.

'Oh no,' said Grandma Margaret. 'Oh dear, no.' She went into the kitchen to see Kate.

'Mum, what is it?'

'It's gone.'

Kate shook her head crossly. 'What's gone?'

'My jewellery. It's not there.'

'What do you mean it's not *there*?'

'My brooch. And all my necklaces, the one Bill . . . for our silver wedding.' She started to tremble, and the thousand smells intensified.

Kate went to check and returned moments later chewing her bottom lip. She placed her hand on her mother's shoulder. It was difficult, at least immediately, to sense what she was thinking.

'Hal.' Her voice, although loud enough to carry through to the television room, was gentle.

'Mum,' he called back.

'Come here.' Still the deceptive softness remained. Hal obeyed. 'Sit down.' Hal hesitated, and then, in a tone she usually reserved for myself, Kate said: '*Sit*.'

Hal sat down. He looked at Grandma Margaret, who

was still trembling. He had absolutely no idea what was going on. 'What's, what's the matter?' he asked, fearful.

Adam, coming downstairs, asked the same question.

Kate explained the matter. 'Now Hal, what really happened?'

'Nothing. I don't know. I told you.'

Anger-waves quivered through the air. 'Hal, if you don't tell us the truth now, you will be in serious trouble.'

'Come on, Kate,' said Adam in an unsuccessful bid for calm.

The anger-waves were starting to have a strange effect on Hal, and again he was struggling for words. Or rather, struggling to find the right order to put them in. 'I, um, I, well, it's, no, I, the, I don't know.' As he spoke he held his palms out, facing upwards, in some kind of desperate plea for this whole situation to end.

'Do you know just how much that jewellery meant?' asked Kate. 'Do you have any idea?'

Hal was cornered and there was nothing I could do to help him. He either had to tell them now or had to tell them later. He decided on now.

'I had a party.'

Grandma Margaret scowled and bowed her head. Adam stared at the ceiling.

'You had a *party*.' Kate pronounced the word 'party' as if it had just entered her vocabulary.

'Yes. It just sort of happened.'

'It just sort of *happened*?'

'I told you: yes.'

'*It just sort of happened*?' Kate's anger was entering a new dimension. Her sense of perspective was now well

246

and truly beyond retrieval. I had never seen her behave like this before. This was worse than when Adam had turned into a monster.

'Mum, just listen to me, it wasn't deliberate. Things got out of hand. It was Jamie. He invited loads of people round who I didn't even know.'

'Oh, this just keeps on getting better. You let *strangers* into the house. Well, that's fine then, isn't it? That makes everything all right.'

'I couldn't help it.'

'You're seventeen years old. You're doing A levels. In one month's time you'll be old enough to vote. In three months you'll be going off to university. And yet you have no power to stop people coming here and messing up our house and stealing your grandmother's jewellery. Good God, I sometimes wonder at just what we have managed to raise!' She glanced at Adam as she said this last line, and shook her head.

'Come on, please. This isn't getting us anywhere,' Adam said.

I barked out of the french windows at nothing in particular, but it was clearly too late for diversionary tactics.

The anger-waves switched direction. Now they were coming from Hal. He scraped his chair back and started to walk out of the room. He knocked Adam's shoulder as he passed him. This wasn't deliberate, rage was starting to affect his co-ordination.

'Where are you going?' said Kate.

'Get back here,' chimed Adam.

'Fuck *off*.' And then there was a silence. Even Hal

seemed surprised with the words which had just been spat out of his mouth.

'Oh, Adam, *please*. I can't deal with him any more.'

So Adam followed his son into the hallway. 'Hal, be reasonable.'

'No, fuck off.'

'Hal, I'm warning you.'

'Dad, what you gonna do? Hit me? Go on then, hit me. That'll teach me. Yeah, go on then. Fucking hit me, you model of liberal parenthood. Fucking hit me on the nose, you bastard hypocrite. Hit me, hit me. Fucking do it.'

For a moment, it seemed that Adam was genuinely tempted by this proposition. His whole body twinged with the aching need for violence.

'Hal, just shut up,' he barked. 'Shut. Up.'

'No. I'm not going to shut up. I always shut up. And the reason I just shut up is because I thought it was easier, but it's not because no one in this family has one fucking clue about how I *feel*.'

'You're being pathetic and you know you are. Your mother has every right to be angry– for God's sake, Hal, you invited burglars into our house. You were meant to be revising.'

And then, when it looked like things were as bad as they were going to get, there was another interruption.

'Urgh!'

The disgusted noise came from Charlotte.

Adam glared at his son suspiciously and walked into the living room to discover the root cause of the disgusted 'urgh!'. He stared at the TV in disbelief as a man's penis entered a woman's mouth.

'That's good, baby,' said the man whose penis had now almost completely disappeared. 'That's *really* good, you horny bitch.'

'I pressed play on the video, and this came on,' explained Charlotte.

Kate was now behind Adam, and behind her was Hal, wearing the face of someone who faced certain death. He stepped backwards, in a daze.

'This is just . . . I don't . . . want . . .' said Kate.

Grandma Margaret had now returned to sit in her chair. Fortunately, she seemed unable to recognise what was taking place on the TV screen in front of her.

'Hal! Come here and explain this!' shouted Adam, following his son back into the hallway.

But of course, Hal couldn't explain anything. He didn't know how to. When I moved back out of the living room I could smell that Hal was losing himself. He was disorientated, bouncing back against the wall. And then it came to me again: there was nothing I could do. Nothing at all to prevent Hal from kicking his foot into the wood panels along the side of the staircase. He kicked a second, and a third time, until he broke through, his leg halfway into the cellar.

As this happened, at the point of that final impact, Hal screamed. No. *Howled.* Releasing some primal force he had previously kept buried.

Charlotte was now out in the hallway as well. 'What's happening?' she asked, distressed by the sounds of destruction. Her question went unanswered.

Adam grabbed hold of his son, trying to contain the force which had just been unleashed, but Hal was too strong for him. He twisted away, arms thrashing aimlessly into the air.

'Hal, stop it!' screamed Kate. 'You're destroying the house!'

Adam made another attempt at restraint, and this time managed to get the arms under control. He held him in a tight grip, around his chest.

Hal struggled, and kept on struggling. His rage had left him breathless, and his scent was more complex than ever, a confusion of competing emotions. He stared at the damage, at the black hole and the splintered wood, and his face contorted in disbelief.

Eventually, his breathing steadied and his body relaxed. Adam let go. Hal walked in slow steps, as if in a trance, down the hallway. He picked up my lead and clipped it to my collar.

'Where are you going?' wailed Kate.

'I'm taking the dog for a walk,' Hal said, his voice relatively composed.

'Hal –' Before Adam had time to protest we were out of the door and walking fast. For once, Hal was in harmony with nature. It was raining, the wind was blowing hard and the sky rumbled a distant warning.

Unlike every other member of the Family, Hal liked the rain. But today he was indifferent. It was just there, soaking him, washing away his scent. To be honest, I don't think he even noticed.

When we had turned the corner and no one was around Hal let out another, inexplicable howl, and smashed his hand into a fence. This time Hal really hurt himself; blood was dripping, with the rain, onto the wet pavement. But still he kept on walking.

We went into the park, but he didn't unclip me. He sat down on the bench. I sat too. With no other dogs or humans around, the grass seemed to stretch further away than usual. Looking past the decay of the smell-heap, the park appeared boundless and bare. I looked in the other direction, over towards Simon and Emily's house, standing defiant in the rain, and then to the bushes where Joyce had been killed. That is when it came to me. I suddenly saw the connection between everything. Between the threat posed by Simon and the black hole in the side of the staircase. Between the deaths of Joyce and Henry. I didn't *understand* these connections, not in detail anyway, but the point was I knew the connections were there. I sensed them, and sometimes that has to be enough.

Hal, however, couldn't see any connection. He was starting to smell guilty, completely oblivious to the larger framework his actions were merely a part of. All he knew was that he had crossed a line and he was now afraid of the consequence.

But I smelt guilty too. My mission was in a state of disrepair and I couldn't blame the Family, or Simon, or Emily. Not fully. After all, they were only human.

I realised, for the first time, just how much I still needed Henry. I longed to sniff him, and imagined him trotting over, through the rain. What would he say? What would he tell me to do? Surely he wouldn't prescribe wag control, and it was too late for sensory awareness.

I had to face it: so far, I was a failure. I had let down Henry and I had let down the Family.

As I stared out into the dim gauze of rain, I saw that

the way back to happiness and security for the Family was out there, but that I would have to find it myself. I thought of the Eternal Reward and realised I no longer cared. All that mattered is what happened here, on earth. But that didn't mean I was about to neglect the Family. It meant the opposite. The Family was everything; it was all I had.

I looked at Hal, to try and tell him, with my eyes, that it would all work out. He looked back at me and stroked the top of my wet head with the hand which had been bleeding.

'Come on, Prince,' he said, in a voice which told me he was ready. 'Let's go home.'

control

There was an argument, about getting the police involved. Kate was for, Adam against.

'It would only make things harder,' Adam reasoned. 'For Hal.'

'You know our problem?' Kate asked. 'We're soft.'

But softness won, and the police weren't called.

The Family, meanwhile, remained in crisis and for the next few days Hal carried on blaming himself. And he wasn't the only one. Adam, Kate and Charlotte were still transmitting their own guilt molecules. Only Grandma Margaret, cocooned in her smell-cloud, had a clear conscience.

Of course, I knew the real root cause. It was me. Humans cannot help themselves. They think they are in control, but they never are. It was up to the Labrador to make things right.

But still, they persisted in trying to look for their own solution.

precious

I saw him in the park.

The boy who smelt of damaged skin. The one who had thrown a bottle, who had stolen Grandma Margaret's jewellery. He was on his own, drinking from a can.

It was dark. Late enough to avoid Emily.

'Oi,' he called over. 'Mr Hunter. Mr Wanker.'

Adam looked up, spotted the boy. He considered walking over, responding, but thought better. So the boy stood up and started moving towards us. A lumbering silhouette bathed against the golden glow of the street-light behind.

'Prince,' Adam said, jerking my head forward. 'Come on boy. Let's go home.'

But before we had time the boy was there, holding up his hand. It was gigantic, almost as big as his head, with no definition between the fingers.

'Look at that,' the boy said. His speech was slurred.

'It's a bandage,' Adam said.

'Should keep your schizo dog under control.'

'I'm sorry?' Adam didn't understand.

'Could have him put down for that.'

I remembered the damage I myself had caused.

Adam put my lead on. 'You're clearly delusional. My dog didn't do that.'

'Oh, right. Got another Labrador then?'

'You're out of your mind.'

'Was at your precious son's piss-poor excuse for a party. Nearly took my hand off. Could sue for that. Negligence.'

Adam looked at me. I sensed he knew the boy was telling the truth. I had let him down. I had let everyone down.

Adam didn't say anything, just walked past the boy at a careful distance.

'Should put him down,' the boy shouted, against an angry wind. 'He's fucking psycho.'

Adam kept his silence all the way home, containing whatever doubts he now had about me.

But later, in the kitchen with Kate, the doubts were set free.

'That doesn't sound like Prince,' she said.

'I know. But he was at the party. He wasn't lying, I know he wasn't.'

There was a long, accusatory silence. Guilt forced me to retreat to my basket.

'Oh God,' Kate said. 'Will he make us put Prince down?'

'He won't say anything. He hasn't by now so I doubt he will.'

'What if he stole mum's brooch?' Kate said.

'We've talked about this. If we phone the police, we'll only make things worse for Hal. With his friends.'

Kate sighed. 'Some friends.'

'And anyway, it's probably too late now. And what if it led to Prince being put down?'

'What, so the dog is suddenly more important than my mother's memories?'

'Come on, Kate. Be reasonable.'

'*Reasonable*.' Kate breathed the word with disgust. I wondered if this was just about me, or if it had anything to do with the Simon-smells which drifted from her clothes. I wondered how close Simon got to them. Her clothes.

'I'm tired,' Adam said. 'I'm going to bed.'

nature

'We should do more things together, all of us, as a family,' said Adam.

The problem was, what things? Where was the common ground? Was it still worth doing things together when half of the Family wished they weren't?

These were the questions circling my head as I was escorted, by Charlotte, onto the back seat of the car.

'Why do we all have to go?' asked Hal. But his exams were over, and he'd run out of excuses.

'It will do us good,' explained Adam. 'A day with nature.'

Grandma Margaret wasn't coming. She said she didn't want to hold us up. She said we should go on and enjoy ourselves while she got on with some knitting. So she stood and waved us goodbye and went back inside.

flash

A car beeped hello as we waited at the end of the road. It was Simon, in his half-car. A car with no top. And Falstaff. He spotted my nose peeking out of the window.

'Waah-hey madwag. Waaaah-hey!' He was in his element. The wind coursing through his fur as they soared off into the distance.

Adam tutted. 'Flash bastard.'

Kate said nothing. She just pulled down her mirror and flicked her hair.

paradise

When we got to the forest, Adam went to a small wooden building and brought out a map.

'We can do one of these walks,' he said. 'This one with the nature trail.'

We headed off, down a small path, through the trees. Adam unclipped me.

'Off you go, boy, go on.'

Off I went.

I knew it would lift their spirits, seeing me running free. So that is what I did. I ran through trees, looking back every now and again to check that they could still see me.

But as I ran, as I sniffed the magical forest smells, I started to forget myself. I followed one scent and picked up another, running, chasing, dodging trees. The Family, for the first time since the smell-heap, was completely out of my thoughts.

In fact, I was so diverted that I didn't even notice the light drops of summer rain as they landed on my back. I just kept on running. It was only when the sky thundered that I stopped to look around.

Just trees. Everywhere, just trees.

I was lost.

I smelt for Kate. For Adam. For Charlotte and Hal. For home.

Nothing. Just sky-water. Wet soil and wood.

I sniffed the ground but none of the smells made sense. Even my own scent trail was washing away.

I switched senses, trying to hear my way back.

Trying to hear something above the beating of the rain on the ground. Birds were singing above me, about me, and, beyond the birdsong, I could just make out the sound of far-away traffic. But that was it. No human voices.

Again I looked around. The landscape, or that which could be seen through the thin grey lines of water, was strangely familiar. I had run through it many times in my wolf-dreams. Thick trees. Head-high vegetation. Rough, animal tracks.

But this was not how I felt in my wolf-dreams. I was not at one with nature. I was not hunting for prey or bonding with my wild pack. I was alone. Alone and scared. My head pulsated with terror.

Looking back now I want to convince myself that my main fear was for the Family. For their future without me. Without protection. But that fear came later, attached to the memory. At the time, loath as I am to admit it, I was mainly scared for myself and for the uncertain fate which waited for me amid the thick trees. At that moment, I needed the Family just as much as they needed me. I realised that they too offered their own form of protection. From nature. From our former selves.

I moved forward, towards the far-away traffic sounds. Running, nose to the ground, eyes on the path ahead, ears on full alert.

Then I picked up a scent. Dog scent. I stopped to sniff further. It was fresh, female. I followed it, reckoning that it would be my only hope of finding my way out. As I ran, the scent grew stronger, even under the rain.

And then the trees parted. A clearing. A small pool of water. I followed the scent trail around until I saw her. Them. Three of them. It was the most incredible sight I had ever seen. Three spaniels. Not Springers. Smaller, more beautiful. Lying next to the water. Well, two were lying. One was sitting up. All reflected upside down.

'I'm lost,' I told them. 'I need to find my way out. Back to my masters. I was running and then I just didn't know where I was, because of the rain –'

'The rain has stopped,' said one of the spaniels, lying down. 'And now you are here.'

'You can stay with us,' said the other. The spaniel sitting up said nothing.

I noticed that the rain had indeed stopped, and with it my fear.

'I can't. I need to go back. To protect my Family. Do you know the way?'

The first spaniel stood up. She gave no sign that she had even heard me. I remember thinking she must be the leader. 'We live in the wild. We drink water from this pool and feed on small animals of the forest. We escaped. We realised we didn't need our masters any more, that we can have a better life, out here with nature.'

I paused. There was a soothing quality to her voice. Hypnotic, almost. 'I . . . have . . . to –'

The other spaniel who had been lying down, now also

rose to her feet and moved closer. I noticed her eyes were different colours. The bitch who had been sitting in silence stayed where she was.

I was sniffed and circled. Their scents mingled, as did their voices.

'You would like it here.'

'We don't have to act for humans. We can be ourselves.'

'You are a very handsome dog.'

'You could look after us.'

'We could look after you.'

'It could be paradise.'

'Paradise.'

I looked around, at the trees, at the misty vapours rising from the pool. A wild world of smell and adventure. A paradise, perhaps. But I was not ready for paradise. My mission was incomplete, I had to stay faithful.

'Look,' I said. 'It sounds very . . . nice. It really does. And I am sure it is working for you. But the thing is, I can't escape from my masters. I am a Labrador. If you cannot help me, I must try and find my own way back.'

'You are a stupid dog,' snapped the bitch with different eyes. 'You will never get out of here.'

'The world has changed,' growled the leader. 'Dogs have rebelled. We are not the first to break free. You will see, in time, that you have chosen the wrong course.'

I went to leave.

'Wait!' Another voice. I turned to see the third spaniel, the one who had so far remained quiet, walk over. 'I will show you the way.'

Her two companions stopped circling and looked at each other. 'No, sister,' said the leader. 'The Labrador has made his choice. He has rejected us, and our way of life. Now we must reject him.'

'But he will not be able to find his way back.'

'That is his decision.'

'No, I am sorry, sisters. I have to help him.'

The leader appeared in shock, as if she had never been overruled in such a way. But she said nothing as the third spaniel led me away, out of the clearing.

'This way, follow me.'

As I followed her, I had the strangest feeling. It was as though the landscape itself was communicating to me. *Listen*, it was saying. *You will never find your way back. Even when you are at home, with your masters. You will never find your way . . .*

'What's your name?' I asked the spaniel, in an attempt to block out the forest.

'I don't have a name. Not any more.'

'Any more?'

'The name our masters gave me was Tess, but my sisters say we cannot use our pet names.' She turned a corner. 'This way.'

I noticed her ribs through her coat. 'When did you escape?'

'Seven days ago. We have kept count.'

'Are you eating OK?'

'We eat what we can. But it is very hard, not like before, when our masters fed us every day.'

'Why did you run away?'

She stopped in front of me, turned around and said: 'Please, don't ask me any more questions. I will show you the way to the human area. That is as much as I can do.'

'I'm sorry.'

But something made her continue. 'We agreed together. We were show dogs, locked in cages, continually deprived of our natural scent. Our owner, she was not cruel but she did not let us live the life we wanted. And then one day, in our local park, we were listening to this bitch. She was giving a lecture on the Springer Uprising. She said that we should not wish to have power over our masters, but over ourselves. She said that dogs have always been caught in the middle of the tug-of-war between humans and nature. She said that we have given everything as secret rulers of the human home, but have benefited little ourselves.'

'She said a lot.'

'Yes. And it was after that lecture that my sisters decided to escape, when we came here.'

'I thought you all agreed together?'

She paused again, gave me an awkward glance. 'Well, they are my sisters, I had to follow them. I wouldn't have wanted to be left alone.'

'But you might not be able to survive out here.'

'I will have to leave you now. The footpath is down there.' She sniffed the wet black root of the tree in front of me, to check that she was in the right spot. She then cocked her leg to leave her scent.

'You could come with me,' I said. 'My Family could find you a new home.'

She looked at me, her soft-sad eyes revealing the dilemma she faced. 'I can't leave my sisters.'

'But you could die.'

'I can't leave my sisters,' she repeated. 'I can't. I'm sorry.'

And that is when I heard them.

'Prince! Prii-ince!'

'That's my masters,' I told her. 'They are looking for me.'

'I have to go,' she said. 'Before I am seen.' She sniffed a quick farewell and turned back towards the clearing.

'Goodbye,' I said, too late. She was already gone. I bent towards the tree she had sprayed and breathed in. 'Goodbye.'

'Prince! Prii-ince!' It was Adam.

I ran fast, barking as I travelled towards his voice. Their scents floated across the air before they were visible. My masters. My Family.

I could see the path, the sun reflected in puddles.

I was out of the trees, crossing the final stretch of grass towards them. They all crouched down, arms out-stretched. Eight hands.

'Prince!'

'We thought we'd lost you!'

'Oh, poor Prince!'

'Poor boy!'

I licked their faces as Adam attached my lead.

responsibility

I was sitting on the floor with Kate, watching a documentary on TV. It was about dogs. About what goes on inside our heads.

She kept on nudging me every time a dog came on screen, as if we all know each other. But I didn't mind, I humoured her.

She had had a long day and now she was all alone. Well, Grandma Margaret was in her room, but no one else was in. And, as Charlotte always used to point out, Grandma Margaret didn't count.

I nestled on her lap and she stroked my ear, saying nothing. We just both sat there, watching as a collie stalked a rabbit across the television screen.

'. . . *Like its wolf ancestors, the collie's predatory instinct enables it to pursue its prey . . .*'

The collie started to gallop, chanting panted insults at the rabbit as she passed him.

'*However, at the exact moment the dog is expected to kill, it retreats. Rather than chase for survival, the dog's behaviour has become its own reward . . .*'

Scenes of domesticity followed. Images of a young, novice Labrador nervously reciting the Pact as a newborn baby entered the home. He was clearly in over his head, and feeling the weight of his growing responsibility.

'. . . *Just when dogs seem to have everything as they want it, they run into trouble. When there's competition, such as with a baby, the dog becomes distressed . . .*'

The doorbell rang. 'That'll be Daddy,' Kate told me. 'Must have forgot his keys.' She lifted my head off her knee and went to answer it. The man on the TV continued: '. . . *The dog's true happiness lies in being able to recognise his place . . .*'

Once Kate had managed to open the door (the door knob was still causing problems), she gasped. Well, it was half-gasp, half-word. The word was 'Simon'. I clambered off the settee, shot out of the room – banging my shoulder against the door – and hurtled down the hallway, past the recently patched-up staircase, towards them.

'Hello, Prince,' he said, as if I didn't know what he was up to. Which of course, I didn't. At least, not fully.

'What are you doing *here*?' asked Kate.

'I am here to see you,' he said matter-of-factly. 'As always.'

'But I've told you,' her voice was an urgent whisper, 'not the house. Not here. If you need to speak to me come to the shop. But we've been through everything anyway. There's nothing left to say.'

So my nose hadn't deceived me. She *had* been seeing Simon.

'We've got a lot of –' He waited as I barked my warning and then, realising I wasn't going to stop, he tried again, only louder. 'We've still got a lot of things to sort out.'

'I've said a hundred times: we can't talk here.'

An old woman wheeling a shopping basket across the street looked over so I decided to stop barking.

'Why not?'

'Because Adam will be back any minute.'

'Good. I want to speak to him too.'

'Speak to him?'

'Yes. I want to ask him if he fancies going abseiling this weekend.'

'Abseiling? *Ab*-seiling? Simon, what's going on? What are you up to?'

A good question. What *was* going on? The facts were still foggy. I sensed there had been something between them, years ago. But was there something between them now, aside from a growling Labrador? She had brought Simon's scent into the house on a number of occasions, but did that really prove anything? Simon was still interested in Kate. Of course he was, or why was he there, on the doorstep? But what exactly *was* he up to? If he wanted Kate, he wanted to destroy the Family, as he could hardly have one without the other. Kate. Destruction. They came as a package.

'Why, Kate, you suspicious little minx. What on earth could I possibly be up to?'

I tried to sniff for further information but was thwarted by the front-garden flower smells.

'Just *let* it go,' Kate pleaded, eventually.

There was a pause, during which the man on the TV could be heard: '*What other species has this incredible hold over us . . . ?*'

Simon held her gaze. 'But that's just it, Kate, isn't it? That's just it. I can't let go. I've got to take responsibility for what happened and that is what I've come back to do.'

I looked up at Simon's face, trying to predict. To protect. How much did he know about Emily and Adam? His mouth fell open, about to speak. His tongue hesitated behind his upper teeth, as his eyes travelled downwards over her body. But whatever he wanted to say, wasn't said. He clearly had a better moment in mind. Instead, he told her what he had told her before: 'You really are a beautiful woman, Kate.'

And then he stepped backwards, towards the gate. Smiling mischievously, either at a memory or at some planned future occurrence. It was hard to tell.

And then he was gone. And Kate was left, weak-legged and struggling for air.

I had definitely missed something.

Oh yes, I definitely had.

ropes

After a certain point, human life rarely surprised me. A species so irrevocably detached from nature, I reasoned to myself, would inevitably have to impose its own set of challenges. Of all these challenges though, nothing struck me as more odd than the desire to hang over the side of a cliff-edge on a piece of rope.

'There's nothing quite like it,' Simon had explained to Adam when he returned the next day. 'It's just this intense feeling you get in your balls when you've abseiled halfway down the rock face.'

Of course, Adam was not overly enthused by the prospect and believed, as always, that he could question his way out of the situation. 'Don't you have to be qualified? Don't you need to have an instructor present? Don't you need to be part of a large team?'

'Listen, Adam, it was only a suggestion. I understand *completamente* if you're not up to it. I mean, I've been doing it for years now, used to be a group of us who would go down to Kent. But I still get nervous sometimes, before going over the edge. It's just whether or not you can handle the nerves or crack. That's why I like it, I suppose; it separates the men from the boys. But, as I've said, no pressure. It's just that I was planning to go on Saturday-week, to Malham Cove in the Dales, and I'll need a companion.'

270

Adam puffed his cheeks and blew slowly. This was a decision based on many things. This was about the need to prove himself. This was about Simon. About the competition which clearly existed between the two men. This was about Emily. This was also, in a strange way, about Kate. Ultimately though, in Adam's mind, this was about balls. About intense feeling.

He looked at me, almost as if he thought I could provide a way out. I used all my mental powers to try and make it OK. It seemed to work. 'Would I be, um, able to take Prince?' he asked.

Simon laughed. 'Of course, my man, he can have a go himself if he wants. I'd take our dog, he loves being out in the wild, but the trouble is he's just too damn hard to keep under control.'

'Yeah, OK, sounds good,' Adam lied. 'Saturday, yeah, er, of course. I'd love to. You'll have to show me the ropes.' He smiled, realising he had made a joke. 'The *ropes*.'

'Yes, Adam. That's good. The ropes. I'll have to remember that one.'

clouds

Before Saturday and before Adam could experience any intense feeling, things got serious. Kate was arriving home from work later and later, and the Simon-smell she carried was getting stronger. She was paying less attention to Grandma Margaret, who was still lost in memories of her dead husband.

Charlotte was OK, but only just. She was still very quiet, and was clearly finding it awkward the way everyone was being so kind to her.

'I'm all right,' she kept on saying. 'Hon-est-ly.'

But if anything else were to happen, or was to be un-covered, it could destroy her. And as for Hal, well, it was difficult to tell. As prediction equalled protection, I only had one choice. I had to find more information. The Adam and Emily situation had for the moment resolved itself. Both had agreed that they should pretend it never happened. With Simon and Kate, however, I needed outside help.

I needed Falstaff.

He had said, on more than one occasion, that he knew everything and I wanted to see if he was right.

So, two days before Simon and Adam's planned excur-sion, I decided to risk leaving my sentry post beside the bench and head over to the wild, overgrown area surrounding the smell-heap.

'Waah-hey, madwag, you crazy old bastard. How the hell are you this fine summer's evening?' said Falstaff, in between head-diving into the smell-heap.

'I'm not too –' I waited for his head to re-emerge – 'I'm not too good.'

'Oh, I see, madwag, I see. Looking for a little pick-me-up, something to blunt the edges. Something to make you forget about your day job. Well go on, be my guest.' He nudged his head sideways, towards the smell-heap.

My stomach shifted, pushing toward my throat. 'No, really, Falstaff. I'm OK. You're a Springer, or as good as, I'm a Labrador. Let's just leave it at that. I just wondered if we could talk.'

He wheezed his way over, sniffed me, then said: 'A *fine* summer's evening.' It was, I had to admit, but I had other things on my mind.

'Listen, Falstaff. You know when you said you knew everything, I wanted to know what you meant, I –'

'Have you ever chased a squirrel, madwag?' His eyes, sparkling with mischief, looked past me towards the middle-distance.

'I'm sorry?'

'Nothing like it, madwag, nothing at all. Running after those bouncing furry tails. It's what fine summer evenings were made for.'

'It's about Simon. I need more information.'

Again, he evaded me. 'Look, over there.'

'Falstaff –'

'Over there by the bushes. You see them? Two of the little buggers.'

I half-turned to see, at the periphery of my vision, two

squirrels engaged in fidgety conversation. 'Yes, but, Falstaff —'

'Walk with me,' he said, in the hushed, dog-on-a-mission tone beloved by adolescent pups less than an eighth his age. And so, as often happened in Falstaff's presence, I found myself doing something I would never normally do. Something which was explicitly outlawed by the Pact. I was stalking a squirrel. But at the same time, I continued to stalk the truth.

'I need your help,' I whispered, as we trod through the head-high grass. 'The Family I have sought all my life to protect is now in grave danger. I need to save them, but to do that I need to find out more about Simon.'

Falstaff paused, squinted his eyes. A midge-cloud surrounded his head. I am not sure if he had even heard me; he was certainly acting like he hadn't.

'OK, madwag, you see the one on the right. That's yours. I'll take the other little bugger.'

'But, Falstaff —'

'Let's get to work.' He was already ahead of me, moving in for the kill. I looked around, then followed. If I wanted information, I had little choice. The moment we stepped out of the long grass, the squirrels noticed us and darted towards the trees. But I had no intention of catching my squirrel. I am not, in any case, one of nature's athletes. I was just trying my best to please Falstaff.

'There, madwag!' he said. 'Up there.'

I placed my front paws on the trunk and barked aimlessly up towards where I imagined the squirrel must be, while keeping an eye on my companion.

'No, madwag!' he chuckled. 'You are barking up the wrong tree!'

But I didn't care. All this meant was that I might now be able to get some sense out of him, before Adam and Emily came to take us home.

'*Now* can we talk?' I asked, as we headed slowly back towards the smell-heap. Falstaff didn't respond, so I decided to continue. 'It's about my Family, they could be in serious trouble. And I believe Simon has something to do with it.'

Falstaff sighed. 'Tell me, Prince, why does all this matter so much to you?'

I was surprised. Not by the question, but by the fact that he had, for the first time since we met, called me by my proper name. His voice had changed too. He was speaking softly, without even a trace of ridicule.

'It matters because –' I hesitated.

'Duty over all. Prediction equals protection. Yada yada yada. I know all about it. Always have. You know in London it's not seen as such a big thing, it really isn't. The thing with city dogs, madw–' he cut himself short, 'is that they tend to be less gullible. Even the Labradors.'

I could hardly believe what I was hearing. 'They follow the Pact though . . .' I swallowed hard. '. . . I mean, don't they?'

'They do, Prince. They do. Well, most of them. In the big parks you come across some deserters and drop-outs who will tell you everything. But even those who follow the Pact seem to have a, how should I put it, a *looser* interpretation. They do what they can to protect the Family, but they don't lose any sleep if things fall apart.

Because, believe me, in London, that would mean there's a hell of a lot of sleepless Labradors.'

Although Falstaff's manner had changed, I was well aware that what he was saying could simply be another evasion tactic.

'But you don't understand,' I explained. 'We are in control. If a Family falls apart, the Labrador is to blame. And if we fail, we lose our Eternal Reward.'

This last statement returned Falstaff to his familiar self. 'Eternal Reward, madwag? Little happy Labradors floating on little fluffy clouds. Hmm, no. I don't buy it. No other dogs there at all, only those that follow the Pact? And no humans. I mean, think about it. It doesn't make sense. And I have to say it, madwag, you don't seem that in control to me . . .' He stopped, acknowledging the hurt in my eyes.

'Look,' I said, slowly. 'I have to protect the Family. I do not care about my Eternal Reward. Not really. I have to save them because –' For the first time, I was forced to express my true feelings. And now it was my voice which changed. It was steady, I was no longer concerned with impressing Falstaff, or anybody else. But while I was speaking the truth, I couldn't help but feel that I was listening to someone else. That someone was telling me what I, in fact, was saying. 'Because I *love* them. And because I know, deep inside, they love each other more than anything in the world. I can see what you're thinking. I am a sentimental Labrador, I do not know what I am talking about. I should be out sniffing smell-heaps and chasing squirrels. I should lighten up. Life's a bitch and then you die. Get used to it. But the thing is, the *thing* is, I can't get used to it. I really can't. I watch the Family every day from my basket and I understand them completely. I understand that they want a happy ending, that they want to keep it together. They also believe that they can make it happen. Despite their separate lives, jobs, desires and all the outside danger. You see, you may joke about the Pact. But without a coherent set of rules, without the power to believe in something, things fall apart. And I can't let that happen . . . because . . . because I *am* the Family. When they're happy, I'm happy. When they feel pain, I feel that too. When I found Charlotte on the bathroom floor, after swallowing all those pills –'

'Charlotte?' Falstaff suddenly appeared interested in what I was saying.

'She's the youngest child. A short while ago she tried to kill herself. It was terrible. I feel responsible for her. She used to be angry all the time because nothing made sense, but now she is starting to find her way. If anything happened to the Family, she would feel the most pain. I don't know if she'd be able to come back from it, I really don't.'

'Listen, Prince. There is nothing you can do –'

I studied him closely. 'I am not talking about the Labrador Pact. Not any more. I want to protect the Family, regardless. I need you to help me. If you knew Charlotte, I know you would.'

Falstaff thought hard. Some sort of internal struggle seemed to be going on behind his dark, half-Springer eyes.

'I knew Charlotte,' he said eventually, although it took

even longer for the words to gain meaning. 'When I lived here before, with Simon.'

Two cars sped past the park wall, exchanging angry honks. The noise seemed to be coming from another world.

The Falstaff who now faced me was a complete stranger. He looked sad, guilty even. What the hell was he talking about? I wanted the old Falstaff back. All of a sudden, I didn't want the information I had asked for. I wanted to bury my head in the smell-heap and breathe in its smells until I lost the power of rational thought. I wanted to run wild. I wanted to not care.

'Listen, Falstaff –'

'Your woman . . . Kate . . . she used to bring the baby over for Simon to see. She had to. She had no choice. If she hadn't, Simon would have told Adam.' He paused, realising he had told me too much. And yet, at the same time, still too little.

'Told Adam?'

'Prince, I'm sorry, I should have told you before. I just wanted you to forget about the Family. I knew how much pain it would cause you. You see, there's nothing you can do, mad– Prince, nothing at all.'

'About what?'

He closed his eyes and said: 'About the fact that Simon is Charlotte's father.'

breathe

The park tilted, causing me to lose my balance. I could hardly breathe, and somewhere in the distance squirrels were laughing. Things were going dark.

mistakes

I found it difficult to speak. After a short silence, Falstaff went on: 'He tells me things, when Emily is asleep. He thinks I don't understand. But he has come back for her. For both of them. For Charlotte and her mother. He wants a Family of his own and Emily is unable to have children. At least, with him. When Charlotte was a baby, he was not ready. He wanted to see her, that was all. And then he ran away, with me, to London. But now he has come back. He is ignoring Emily and so she is trying to make him jealous. But her plan isn't working. Simon is pleased, he wanted all this to happen. He is waiting for the right moment. To tell Adam about Charlotte. And then, once he has done that, he will tell Kate about Adam and Emily.'

I stared at Falstaff as the news settled in my mind.

'He knows about that?'

'She wanted him to know. Why did she choose the park to make her move? And anyway, she has told him. I'm sorry, madwag, but now you must know the truth. The Family you have tried your hardest to protect is about to fall apart and it is not your fault. There is nothing you can do. Mistakes were made before you even came along. Face it, the Springers have a point. Their mistakes, madwag. *Their* mistakes. None of this is to do with you.

You're just the pet Labrador who sits in the corner of the room, watching it all happen. The rest of us realised that a *long* time ago. We are nothing. We are breathing ornaments. We sell toilet tissues and dreams of Family life. We might as well try to enjoy ourselves in the process.'

He paused, sniffed my ear. 'I'll tell you my theory: human Families are destined to fail. They want too much. They *talk* too much. They are built on lies which may or may not be dug up, but either way, they fail. Well, why shouldn't we lie too? Why shouldn't we just pretend that nothing matters? Why . . .'

This was not the dog who, only a short while ago, had been chasing squirrels. He was trembling, and speaking fast. I had the impression that he was letting go, releasing things which, all these years living with Simon, he had somehow managed to keep buried. He was hyperventilating, his breath even shorter and wheezier than usual.

I didn't care. He had let me down. The Family was on the brink of destruction. And he was wrong. It wasn't *their* fault, it was his. Did he really believe that humans were masters over their own destinies? Did he not see and smell what I saw and smelt? If dogs stuck together the whole human species would be OK, even the dogless. And if the humans were OK, we were *all* OK. Did he not see that? Did he not see the connections between everything? If one Family was in danger, they all were. So yes, I was furious with him. Him, and everything he believed in. Or rather, didn't believe in. But I didn't let my anger get the better of me.

The Family could still be saved.

'When?'

'When what?' he wheezed.

'When is Simon going to tell Adam about Charlotte?'

Falstaff was still struggling. For air, mostly. But also with himself, with his Springer-side. Caught between the Falstaff who buries his head in the smell-heap and the one who tells the truth, he didn't know what to do. I remembered what he had once told me. 'The whole dog kingdom is in my blood.' And it was as if the whole dog kingdom was now engaged in some kind of micro-war within his fat old sweat-glossed body.

'I don't know, madwag. I really don't.'

I knew this was a lie, so I played my final card. 'Charlotte lets me lie on her bed with her for hours. She is the only one who lets me do that. She tells me things. She is the only one who *understands*. She doesn't know about the Pact or the details of my mission, but she knows why I am here. And when things are going wrong, she looks at me and I know what she is thinking. She is thinking: why aren't I helping, why am I letting it happen?' I could see he was teetering, so I pressed further. 'And I know that if you were there with me, you would help me to stop the questions.'

Falstaff, still wheezing fast, squinted in torment. He looked as though he had a thorn in his paw.

'OK, OK, OK,' he surrendered. 'You've got me. Damn Labrador blood, it weakens your willpower. He said . . . he said something about telling him the next time he saw him. He said he couldn't wait to see his face. And then . . . and then he said something strange.'

'Strange how?'

282

'He said he would probably lose his grip, fall off. I didn't understand what he meant.'

My whole body went numb. *Lose his grip*. 'Abseiling, he's going to tell him when they are halfway down a cliff.'

Falstaff moved forward and sniffed me, to smell how I was feeling. He backed away, worried. 'What are you going to do?'

I was already trotting back towards Adam when I responded: 'I am going to protect the Family.'

'But what does that mean?'

I trotted on, thinking of Charlotte lying on the bathroom floor, and left Falstaff's question hanging unanswered in the air.

adventure

Two days later and Simon, the enemy, was stroking my head as he sat in the Family's living room. It took every measure of Labradorean discipline I had within me not to turn and snap at his hand.

Adam was there, obviously. And Kate. Hal and Charlotte had gone into town, as they did most Saturday mornings. Grandma Margaret wasn't there either, although her thousand smells still permeated the room.

'What do I need?' asked Adam, trying hard to conceal his anxiety.

'Only your good self,' said Simon. He stared at Kate's breasts as he spoke. 'I've got all the equipment in the car. Oh, and if you've got a pair of walking boots.'

'Walking boots, right.' Adam yawned, as he tended to do when he was nervous, then headed upstairs.

Kate and Simon were left alone. Simon smiled, no longer looking at Kate's breasts but still stroking my head. 'How do you think he'll take it? he asked her.

'Take what?' Kate whispered, at once fearful and angry.

'The news. About us.'

'There's no us, Simon, you know that.' And from the way she said it, and the way Simon responded, I knew this was the truth. At least, this was *her* truth.

'Even so, there's still news.'

'Listen, please, I've told you all week: it's not a good time. If you care about Charlotte, if you care at all about me, you will wait.'

The upstairs phone rang. 'I'll get it,' called Adam from the top of the stairs. Simon waited to check that it wasn't for Kate, his hand resting motionless on the back of my neck. It wasn't, so he carried on talking.

'Look, Kate. You can't walk away from this.'

'I *can* and you *did*. And why are you talking like that? This is real life, Simon. This isn't a game . . .' But then she trailed off, perhaps realising she was talking like that too. I suppose that's the problem for humans, everything has been said too many times. Every situation is an echo of one which went before. Even the big situations, such as this one. The outcomes have already been mapped out. And that's the advantage of dogs, we know when to shut up. We know when to take control.

'You're tired, Kate. You're tired of all this . . .' He made a critical survey of the room. 'This isn't you. Don't kid yourself any longer.'

She looked at him and, for an instant, her face weakened. 'I am proud of my life, and my family. I have worked hard for *all this* and I'm not going to have you take it away.'

Adam's voice could be heard upstairs, on the phone, but his words were not clear. Simon looked up to the ceiling, to the exact spot where Adam must have been standing only a short space above, and then back down to Kate.

'I love you,' he said, with deliberate menace.

'Well, leave us alone, then. Because that's what love is, it's being able to walk away.'

Tension stifled the air. Simon was loving every moment, thriving on the danger, as if he was already stepping over the cliff-edge.

'Not true, Kate. Not true. The opposite, in fact. Love is *not* being able to walk away. Love is about letting nothing stop you.' Despite his words, love was nowhere to be smelt. Only greed. And fear.

'We made a mistake. Both of us. It was one night, years ago. We were drunk. We did what we did and it was over.'

'But that's the thing, Kate. It's not over, is it? Charlotte's not over, is she? And my feelings for you, they're not over. And you're still as unhappy now as you were the night Adam decided to still go and see that stupid play he pretended to like, with the school drama club or whatever it was – how long was it? – two hours after you'd just found out you'd lost your job. I mean, no wonder you phoned me.' He sat back. 'You see, I've got the feeling Adam hasn't changed any more than you have. Tell me, what's changed? Go on.'

'Simon, please. Why are you doing this?'

'We could have a nice life together, Kate. It would be an *adventure*. It would be *exciting*. And whatever you are thinking, I would be a good father to Charlotte.'

'And what about Hal?'

'Ah, so you're coming round to the idea.'

'I am *not* coming round.' Kate stopped. She was close to tears. Simon was still stroking my head. But harder now, causing the skin above my eyes to pull right back.

I moved away, towards Kate. She spoke again. I didn't catch the first bit, my mind was swirling. I only caught the end:

'. . . you don't know what it takes to raise a family and to keep it safe.'

'I *know* what it takes to make you happy. That gives me one over Adam.'

Kate flinched from his words and let a silence build up. The silence was definitely on Simon's side, as they both seemed to realise. Every object in the room grew pale and lost its scent.

For a moment, which stretched to forever, it was all over.

Simon had won.

There was absolutely nothing I could do to stop the sickly-sweet smell of victory. Kate, normally so together, so in control, who understands the secret laws of the Family better than any human I know, who likes to tidy away anything she doesn't like the look of, was now completely deprived of her power. As was I.

Eventually, and with closed eyes, she said: 'All you have done is make me realise just how much my family means to me.'

Upstairs, Adam's voice stopped. The phone call was over.

Simon smiled. 'Oh yes, *your* family.'

Simon and Kate both looked up now to follow the path of Adam's feet as they trod their way across the ceiling.

'Please, Simon,' said Kate, in a voice which at once seemed both quieter and louder than before. 'We're responsible adults, not love-struck teenagers acting out some soap opera. Just, look, I'm sorry, but please, I don't know, just hold off a while. Please. I'll talk to Adam, I will really, but let *me* do it. It won't do you any good if you tell him – you'll only end up losing both of us.'

Simon leaned back on the settee, his hands behind his head, and studied Kate. As the footsteps started to be heard at the top of the stairs, he spoke again. 'You really are a beautiful woman, Kate. The most beautiful, in my opinion. But then, you always were.'

Kate stared straight into Simon's eyes, desperately searching for something which wasn't there. I doubt that she had ever looked so pathetic and in need of help in her whole life. I went over and licked her hand – a futile, but instinctive gesture.

The door opened to reveal Adam. Crumpled. A baggy bloodhound. From his frowning forehead to his one-size-too-big outdoor clothes, that is how he looked. As if the air was hissing out of him.

He surveyed the scene: Simon, uncrumpled, leaning back; Kate, on the chair opposite him, leaning forward. Somewhere deep, deep inside he seemed able to sense that something was wrong. But this feeling was clearly too well buried for him to act upon it.

'OK, I'm ready,' he told us.

Kate, her head turned away from Adam, made one last desperate attempt with Simon. *'Please,'* she mouthed. *'Don't.'*

Simon winked in response, stood up, and said to Adam: 'So I see. So *I* see.'

For a terrible second it looked as though I would be forgotten. It looked as though Adam would leave unprotected. I got up and trotted over to him, nudging his knees with my nose.

'OK, Prince, OK. I'll just get your lead.'

Kate was still sitting in the living room, staring at the space Simon had previously occupied on the settee. It was as if she was trying to conjure up some unworldly power in order to keep things as they were, to freeze time. But as Adam clipped on my lead she realised it was no good. Nothing she could do or say could prevent Adam and Simon from walking out of the door. Or if there was something, she couldn't think of it. Adam's voice broke her train of thought.

'It was Charlotte on the phone. She said she'll be back about three.'

Kate smiled, but in a way which made her face look even sadder. 'OK, darling, be careful.' Her voice was dull, like the words spoken in her sleep, but she was telling Adam far more than he could realise.

'Yes, I will.'

'I love you.'

'I love you too.'

Simon slapped Adam's back. 'OK, come on, Ads-old-boy, let's see what you are made of.'

I was still standing in the living-room doorway, watching Kate. Adam gently tugged my lead.

'Come on, boy.'

But I stayed there as long as I could, trying my best to reassure her. *I will protect you, Kate. I will make everything all right. The Family will be safe.*

She stared back, and although I cannot be absolutely sure, her face seemed to relax. She seemed to smell relieved. She seemed, just for a moment, to understand what I was now capable of.

The Labrador Pact:
Never betray your master's trust

While every effort must be taken in order to ensure our mission to protect human Families remains secret, we must never deliberately disobey our masters.

If we are instructed to sit and stay, we must sit and stay. If we are tied by our leads to a post, we must wait obediently until our master returns. If food falls onto the floor and we are forbidden from touching it, then we must obey.

After all, to lose the trust and respect of our masters is to weaken the chances of our success in protecting the Family.

rock

Simon was walking in front of us, eager to get to the top. Adam was taking his time, snatching an occasional queasy glance at the great platform of white rock rising up to our right.

'Fantastic, isn't it?' asked Simon, although even I could sense it was more of a statement of fact than a question.

'Er . . . yes . . . yes, it is,' said Adam, who was clearly doing his best not to throw up. 'But, um, the only thing is, isn't it a bit too . . . er, windy?'

'Well, he doesn't seem to think so.' Simon gestured towards a lone climber clawing his way up the rock.

'No . . . no . . . I suppose he doesn't.'

Simon turned. 'You're not bottling it, are you?'

Adam's mouth hardened, while the rest of his face remained pale. 'No, not at all. 'Course not. Looking forward to it.' In fact, if it hadn't been for me tugging the lead forward I doubt he would have made it to the top.

And as we walked, I too became nauseous. Their conversation became noise, and mingled with the sound of water from the stream below.

'It's weird, isn't it,' babbled Adam once we reached the summit. 'You feel like you're taking part in a lunar landing or something, don't you? It's like walking on the moon.'

'It always reminds me of a brain.'

'Yes, I know what you mean. How amazing. Weird.'

I found it weird too. At first I couldn't quite identify why, and then it dawned on me. There was no scent whatsoever in the air. For the first time in my life I was unable to smell anything at all, at least when I was more than a few steps away from Adam and Simon. Although there was green countryside all around, up there on that dry, grey rock it felt about as far away from life as you could get.

While Simon took the rucksack off his back and started taking out the equipment, Adam looked for somewhere to tie my lead. There was a signpost at the far end of the plateau, with a picture of falling rock.

'OK. There you are. You'll be OK, don't worry.'

Was he talking to me, or himself? It was hard to tell, but, feeling his need for comfort, I licked his face as he crouched down. It didn't help.

The weird thing was that Adam really did have a reason to fear, but not the one he thought he had. And if Simon was to tell him the truth about Charlotte, there would be no safety rope to stop the Family falling to its inevitable demise.

There would only be me.

'You stay there, boy. You be a good dog.' And as I had never betrayed his trust, he had no doubt that I would do exactly as he said.

'OK,' Simon called over. 'Let's go through the basics.'

Adam left me tied up and walked back towards him.

Simon started to speak about ropes and clips and anchors, and as he did so I realised he was in fact talking

293

about something else entirely. This was about power. This was about Adam needing Simon. Indeed, at that moment, his whole life depended on him.

And as I sat and watched them, listening to every word, I wondered when Simon was going to do it. When he was planning to destroy the Family I had sought most of my life to protect. It seemed to me that it would be some considerable time. After all, he was clearly having fun with the present situation. He loved the game he was playing with Adam because he was destined to win. Adam was not only unaware of the rules, but completely blind to the fact that a game was being played at all.

Where was the end? Did Simon imagine a new Family, with Kate, with Charlotte, but without Adam and Hal? Could that happen? Did he want to split the Family in two or blow it to bits? I didn't know.

All I knew was that both possibilities were equally appalling. And, I now understood, equally preventable.

Simon clipped on his rope as casually as he would put a lead on a dog. Adam, however, took slightly longer owing to his hands' inability to stay still.

More talking.

More fear.

I sat still, patient. Like a good dog.

Adam looked over to me as if I could somehow intervene. He looked terrified, he really did, as he tugged back on the rope.

'That could hold an elephant,' assured Simon, with a chuckle, treading slowly back towards the edge.

'Well, just so long as it holds me.'

existence

Adam and Simon had now disappeared, their existence only indicated by the ropes straining over the edge.

As I waited for them, high up on that scentless rock, I had the strangest feeling. I felt, and I know this sounds crazy, I felt as though everything was within my control. I had power not only over the future of the Family, but over anything I chose.

This, I was quite aware, was not a feeling common to Labradors. Yes, the Labrador Pact talks about power, about control, but at the same time it places limits. Never risk the secrecy of the mission. Never resort to violence. Never betray your master's trust.

Betray the Pact, betray the breed.

That is what we had been told, that is what had been passed down for generations, from mother to litter. One step out of line and the whole Labrador cause could be placed in jeopardy.

Betray the Pact, betray yourself.

Of course, this was the real clincher. Go astray and you will lose the chance to gain your Eternal Reward. To be reunited with your brothers and sisters, to run wild and free in a humanless universe. But where was the proof? The whole idea was starting to seem ill-conceived, arrogant even. Perhaps Falstaff had been right. I mean, who was I to say that the philosophies and belief-systems which united other breeds were wrong and ours were right? Why did we automatically write off the Rottweiler worldview as primitive and barbaric, or the poodle philosophy as too concerned with surface detail? The influence of the Springer Uprising was clearly a corrupting one, but at the same time, did we have the right to judge the actions of others?

As my side-fur danced in the chill wind, I remembered something Falstaff had told me. *There is more to this world than can be explained by your Pact.* And I had to agree with him, there were certainly things which didn't make sense.

But the Pact still had some merits.

Families, at least the human variety, needed to be protected. There were too many dangers – both outside and inside – for them to survive independently. And they were *worth* protecting too. For all their lies and tensions and betrayals and injustices, there was a positive and powerful undercurrent beneath all the surface rituals, which any dog could detect. But what if the only way to save the Family was to break the Pact? What happened then?

There was no Henry. No Falstaff. No answers. I was on my own. I had to think for myself.

A voice, in the distance, broke my train of thought. The climber Simon had pointed out before was now walking with another man, in our direction. Both men were still too small and distant to be smelt or seen clearly, although the wind was carrying their voices ahead of them.

'I mean that's the whole point, isn't it? If you just lie down and let the bastards walk all over you, you'll get nowhere,' said the man we had seen before.

'Yeah, that's what I reckon. You need to make unpopular decisions every now and again, take affirmative action,' said the other man.

I had no real idea of what the men were talking about, but their words echoed in my brain. *The whole point . . . you'll get nowhere . . . unpopular decisions . . . affirmative action . . .*

They were still far away.

Far *enough* away.

I looked at the ropes, moving in slight jerks, but remaining tight against the rock.

I had time.

I could still protect the Family.

collar

I tried to remember how Falstaff did it. I pictured him, the first time we met in the park, stretching his fat, scruffy neck in line with his body, twisting his head, reversing.

My collar was tight, a close fit, but I persisted until I felt it sliding over my ears. After much effort, the collar sprang off towards the metal pole I had been tied to, and I took two involuntary steps backwards. The ropes were a short jog away, and twitched nervously as I approached.

More voices now.

Simon and Adam.

I peeked over the edge, and saw the tops of their heads halfway down the rock face. My paws clenched as the wind tugged me forward. Simon kept pushing himself out, away from the rock, and dropping lower. Adam was attempting to do the same but without the confident leg power.

I moved back to where the ropes lifted, ever so slightly, off the ground. The rope twitches now made sense. Relaxed, then tight; rock, then air.

thread

Although it had no real smell, Simon's rope did have a taste. Sour, synthetic, a tinge of human sickness. Manmade. And soon that taste mingled with something else: blood. The rope was so tight it cut my tongue as I chewed, carefully keeping the rhythm.

Relaxed, tight, relaxed . . .

The rope was tough, but thin.

Fibres snapped in my mouth.

I had him, his life dangling by a thread.

'Wait, no!'

'Come here, doggy, come here! Here, boy!'

The two men I had seen before were now running fast towards me.

I heard Adam: 'What was that? Was someone shouting?'

I heard Simon: 'Come on, pal, keep your mind on the job.'

So that is what I did, timing my last bite to perfection.

Twang.

The rope whipped out of my mouth and over the side, flicking my mouth-blood into the air.

'Fuck!'

'Fuck!'

'Fuck!'

'Fairrghhk!'

I stepped forward to see the damage. But he was still there. Sideways, screaming, bobbing up and down – but still there.

There was another rope. Why hadn't I seen it? Two ropes each. Again I started to chew on the man-made fibres.

'Help!' screamed Simon.

'Somebody help!' screamed Adam.

'We're coming!' screamed the other two men. And they were, running across the last stretch of rock. I was choking on rope, gagged by blood, tongue burning, fuelled by some unfathomable force within.

It could have gone either way. The two men could have been that little bit faster, that little bit more decisive in their attempt to grab the rope or declamp my jaws.

'Hold onto the rock!' shouted one of the men.

I felt several hands on my back.

Twang.

'I ca-aaaaaghh!'

I rushed forward.

Adam's hand reached out, helpless.

Simon fell with his back to the ground, arms stretched forward, legs bent up. Like a dog, asking for a tummy-tickle.

And then it was over.

And then *he* was over.

The ground met him with an indifferent thud. He lay broken, dark blood spilling out from the side of his skull.

We could see what he was made of.

'No!' Adam, still roped halfway down the rock face, couldn't believe what was happening.

'No!' Neither could the two men, standing beside me.

Things happened, afterwards. Adam scrambled back to the top. The men explained. Adam looked at me, at my absent collar, trying to make sense. We walked back down. Ambulance men came. Police came. Everyone was confused. The body was taken away. The ropes were taken away, for tests. A Simon-shaped hole was left in the ground. And blood. The blood stayed where it was.

Questions. Answers.

'The Labrador did it.'

'He couldn't have realised what he was doing, could you, boy?'

No. Of course I couldn't.

'It was just a game for him, wasn't it, boy?'

Yes. Of course it was. A game.

When we were eventually able to head back home, I tried to smooth things over with Adam. It was hard.

For the first part of the journey he was beyond communication.

He pulled into the side of the road, his hands clutched his head. He howled. Tears streaked his hairless face.

Cars whooshed by, too fast to notice the crying man and the faithful Labrador parked in the lop-sided vehicle. Two wheels on concrete, two on grass.

I felt terrible, I really did, and for a moment believed I had made a mistake. An ugly, horrible mistake.

But after a while the howling stopped and he was able to wipe away the snot and the tears. The heavy smell of despair began to fade, and he managed to continue the journey home.

He was angry with me, I knew that, and I knew he felt his anger was irrational. I knew also that it was best to avoid his stare at least for the moment, so I kept my head out of the window and watched the grey-green landscape and breathed in its flavour. As the fast air hit my face and forced back my ears I could almost forget what I had done. In my head, I could almost stop him falling. I could almost stop the blood.

Almost.

A sharp turn caused me to choke on the window. I pulled my head back inside and ventured a tentative look towards Adam. Anger and tears had blotched his cheeks, and the eyes were fixed steadfast on the road ahead.

But even though he was angry and upset I knew it would be all right.

I had done my job.

I had breached the Pact, but the main threat had been destroyed.

The Family wouldn't ever be able to thank me, but I had taken the necessary action.

That, for now, had to be enough.

sex

The evening after, Adam could still hardly talk. He could hardly move, either. He had just lain on his bed, staring up at the ceiling, like a hopeless, whimpering dog.

I lay with him for a while but I'm not sure if he appreciated my company. To be honest, I'm not sure if *I* appreciated my company, being so worn out after asking myself, over and over and over: did I do the right thing? Well, did I? I still don't know. I craved the time when Henry had held all the answers, and when everything fitted into some kind of order. But that time had gone.

Simon was a threat to the Family, a threat which, given Charlotte's vulnerable state of mind, could have also been a threat to her life. Is that what I really believe, that last part? Again, I don't know.

What I do know is this: I had killed Simon and the reason I had killed Simon was because the Hunters were helpless. Choices had been made which they couldn't undo, and it was left to me to undo them. With my teeth, as it had turned out.

But, unlike Adam, I wasn't solely consumed with the past. The day before had been horrific, but it was over. The Family was safe, for the time being. In future, other situations would arise and what then? Although I had been acting on behalf of the Family, I had completely overruled the Pact. What was I going to live by now? Were there any boundaries left to cross? Had I placed the whole breed in jeopardy?

No answers, only questions.

My mind was in such turmoil that I almost didn't notice Kate enter the room and sit herself down next to us.

'Everyone's in bed,' she told him and then, realising Adam was not going to respond, she asked: 'How are you feeling?'

'I'm not,' he answered. 'Not yet. It's all still a blur. What about you?'

'I'm getting there,' she said. 'But it is going to be worse for you. You were always closer to him. And you actually saw it happen.' Her voice had changed. It was softer, the love easier to detect.

She stroked me. It was my first stroke since yesterday morning. Since before. Not that she wasn't shocked, when she found out. She was, or at least appeared to be. But while she may have found it difficult to come to terms with what had occurred, she was not grappling with grief in the same way as Adam. I knew what Kate was like when she was struggling with loss, I had seen it when her father died. I had smelt it too, a dense, unmistakable scent which had stifled the air, like when all the doors had been shut for too long.

This time, however, there was nothing like that. Faint sad smells lingered, but that was because she felt sorry for Adam. She seemed to feel guilty, too. As if she was trying to make amends, as if she had been responsible for Simon's death. I should rephrase that. As if she *knew* she had been responsible for Simon's death. I felt she was aware that I had managed to transform her darkest wish into action.

Because however sorry she must have been feeling, she could not hide from one simple truth. A truth which inevitably brought us closer, as silent allies.

She was glad Simon was no longer here.

And she must have been able, in her own mind, to justify Adam's grief as a fraction of the damage which could have been caused if Simon had been able to say what he had wanted to say.

To ease the pain, she told Adam that she loved him. She had told him before, many times, but never like that. Previously, it had been said as a sigh, before going to sleep. The more times it had been said the less it meant. Now, however, it had new significance, as if she was telling him for the first time.

She stopped stroking me and started stroking Adam instead, rubbing his shoulder affectionately. He looked at Kate, and then at her hand. He smiled. Well half-smiled, but it was definitely progress.

'I love you too.'

They hugged, awkwardly. Awkward because I was still lying between them. I took the hint and shuffled off, onto the floor.

'Everything's going to be OK,' she said, as the hug became horizontal. And, to prove she was right, she started to unbutton his shirt. But when she came to the final button, tears welled in Adam's eyes.

Kate told him: 'I'll stop if you want.'

'No, don't stop.'

And so she continued, even as the tears slid down his cheeks, until he was completely naked.

Then she stood up, away from the bed and undressed herself, leaving her clothes heaped randomly on the carpet.

'I'll put them away in the morning,' she said, climbing back onto the bed. They hugged again, less awkwardly, although Adam was still crying. They waited, silent, motionless, letting the hug do the work, until the tears stopped.

I stayed with them, in the room, lying on the floor amid Kate's clothes. Perhaps I should have gone, perhaps the intimacy of the moment was theirs alone. But somehow, this was my moment as well. Although I found no pleasure in the sight of their strange, hairless bodies joined together, I did feel a certain sense of satisfaction, or relief.

It was as if they were starting again, their relationship re-born. And they felt it too, I'm sure of that. As they kissed each other, first on the lips, and then elsewhere – the neck, the shoulders, the back – it was as though they were exploring new and exciting territory.

Kate, especially, was lost in this task and appeared, for the first time, unashamed of her naked body. Indeed, at no time did either of them attempt to lean over and switch off the bedside lamp.

'Everything's going to be OK,' she repeated, between kisses.

She spoke so softly it seemed the words came from the room itself, as an echo, or from some supernatural presence reporting back from the future.

And then, as their bodies became closer still, words

306

faded altogether. For the first time since I had known them they were having sex. Or, as humans often like to call it, making love, although love had already been made.

Sex with the light on, above covers, with their children only metres away, possibly asleep. Possibly not.

Animal sex. Sex without fear, or body-shame. But human in the way they touched, tenderly, with love. The best of both worlds.

Adam lay over her, closed his eyes, opened them again and kissed her, on the mouth, his body moving faster. The kiss ended but his face stayed close, to breathe in her scent. The noises they had so far suppressed started to rise up, released into the night along with all those untold anxieties.

They moved further down the bed and Kate turned over, eyes closed, her body rising up, resting on her knees. Adam held her, his hand across her middle, his kisses now on her neck. When they fell back down, Adam was above her, his stomach on her back, as they crouched on all fours.

And then, just at the moment love-sex smells had replaced everything else, it ended. Both of them panting, still holding onto each other, Adam's ear rested on her back.

'I can hear your heart,' he said, breathless. Kate smiled, it was still too early for her to speak. 'It's beating fast, like it's trying to get out,' continued Adam.

Eventually she said, 'No, it's fine. It's fine where it is.'

Adam disengaged himself gently and lay back.

Kate lay next to him.

I stayed with them, watching, protecting, as they

shifted themselves beneath the covers. As they nestled into each other and as Adam kissed her forehead. A gentle, goodnight kiss.

'I should take the dog down,' Adam said.

'He's OK. Leave him. You get some sleep.' She kissed him back and switched off the lamp. And then, as if already in a dream, she spoke again. 'He's fine where he is.'

Adam didn't respond, he was probably asleep. In fact, moments after, they both were.

After all, there were no more fears to keep them awake.

But sleep didn't come so easy for myself. I was happy that Adam and Kate were now closer than they had ever been. This was good news for everyone. At the same time, I couldn't take out of my mind the price of this close-ness. Of what it might cost in the future, and whether I would always be around to save the Family from danger. *Outside* danger.

Yes, that is where danger is.

Always outside.

Always.

The Labrador Pact:
Never sniff for pleasure

In our mission to protect our masters, the nose is our most valued weapon. However, it also holds the potential to lead us astray. The rest of the dog kingdom has already succumbed to pleasure-sniffing, but we must never give in to temptation.

Every Labrador must learn to appreciate the true value of our most powerful sense and remember: we sniff to find information, not to lose ourselves.

smell

'Maaadwaaag! I'm going to kill yooou!'

It was a week later. The day after Simon's funeral. I was hovering over a large unprickly flower, mid-dump, when I noticed Falstaff hurtling fast across the park, kicking up dirt.

I looked around, but there was nowhere to run. I'd left it too late. To be honest, I hadn't expected to see him. Ever since Simon's death, the park had been a Falstaff-free zone.

He slammed into me at full force, his fat old body knocking me sideways, into the flowerbed. I was shocked, not just from the impact but by the fact he was there at all.

'You did it, didn't you?' he panted. 'You killed my master?'

'I, um, had to pro—'

'To protect the Family? Don't even *say* it.'

What had I done? I had destroyed his life.

Oh sure, the humans could shrug off what had happened as a freak accident, but there was no fooling Falstaff.

'I'm so sorry, I really am. But I had no choice, not after what you told me.'

Falstaff looked at me, his eyes filled with hurt and the

threat of attack. He held this look for what seemed like forever, before collapsing on the floor and rolling on his back in a fit of panted laughter.

'What's so funny?'

He stared up with his upside-down head, and eyes now completely free from hurt. 'Your face. That's what's so funny.'

'I don't understand.'

'*Quelle surprise*, madwag. *Quelle surprise.*'

'But I thought –'

'Oh, come *on*. Did you really think I would be bothered?'

'That I killed your master? Well, to be honest, *yes.*'

Falstaff stood up, sniffed me in disbelief, and said: 'You really are a *mad* wag, aren't you?'

'But you hid things from me, to protect Simon.'

'To protect *you*, you idiot.'

'To protect me? From what?'

'From yourself, madwag. From your stupid belief-system.'

'But I thought it was about Charlotte. I thought you told me because you cared.'

He sighed. 'I told you because you wouldn't give up, madwag. No matter how many times I tried to persuade you to enjoy the finer things in life – smell-heaps, chasing squirrels – I had to admit you were a lost cause.'

'But you must miss him?'

'Who? Simon?'

I nodded.

'Simon, in case you hadn't noticed, was a human being. Human beings are too stupid to have real feelings, they just borrow them from their television programmes, so why have real feelings for them?'

'Because he looked after you.'

'Looked after me, madwag? Oh, by feeding me meat and biscuits once a day? Ha! And anyway, he didn't even do that, it was always Emily. No, madwag, humans don't care for us, not really. And Simon cared the least. I may not be a pure Springer, but I believe they've got a point. Humans just hold us back from our true instincts. They chop off our bollocks, well *your* bollocks, they try and take away our scent and then, at the first sign of weakness, they take us to Nice Mister Vet to "put us out of our misery". We're just stuck in the middle, you know, like they say, the rope in the tug of war between man and nature. No, I tell you. Humans fuck you up. They may not mean to, madwag, but they do and Labradors are the last to realise.'

'That is one way of looking at it.'

'And what's the other way, madwag? Enlighten me.'

'The other way is to realise that without our masters we wouldn't even exist and so, in protecting them, we are protecting our right to be here.'

'Well, I'm sorry for failing to see the bigger picture, madwag. But right here, at ground-level, it seems to me that the more you care the more you get shitted on . . .'

He carried on talking, but I became distracted by the sight of Adam and Emily, sitting on the park bench. Emily had a hand to her face, she was crying. Adam was speaking to her, offering words of comfort, but keeping his distance.

'What has she said?' I asked, but Falstaff gave me a

look of blank incomprehension. 'Emily. What has she said, about, you know, Simon?'

'Listen, madwag. You may have got me before, but there's no way I'm giving you any further information. You see: no Emily, no meat and biscuits, and Falstaff trots off to the dogs' home.'

'I'm not going to *kill* Emily.'

'No of course you wouldn't, madwag. Of course you wouldn't. What was I thinking?'

'I'm not. Honestly.'

And then Falstaff spoke in a voice which I suppose was meant to resemble mine, but in actual fact bore no similarity at all: 'I must protect the Family. Emily must be sacrificed. She must be killed before she corrupts my master again. My poor, helpless master. He did not realise what he was doing . . .'

I raised a paw. 'All right, all right. Very amusing. I'm a Labrador, I can take it. I am well aware that I must appear ridiculous to you . . .'

'Uh-huh.'

'. . . but I just want to know that she is not going to try and take Adam away, or blackmail him.'

He hesitated. 'OK, but before I tell you let's have one last sniff, just for old times' sake.'

And so, reluctantly, I followed him over towards the smell-heap, keeping an eye on Adam and Emily as we went. When we got there Falstaff dived straight in and stayed under for quite some time.

'That stuff just keeps on getting stronger,' he said, when he came back out.

'OK,' I said. 'About Emily . . .'

'One sniff of that pong-pile, madwag, and the last thing you'll be bothered about is our masters.'

'But you said you'd tell me.'

'Sniff first.'

And so he had me again. I was there, faced with the nightmare stench of the smell-heap, so heady and pungent it rippled the air above it. But then, as my nose entered the rotting heap of dirt and leaves, I had an incredible thought (incredible for a Labrador, at any rate). The thought was this: I want to get out of my head. The reasons for this thought were, I justified to myself, very simple. It would help me forget. It would help to ease the pain, if only momentarily. I would lose myself.

Furthermore, my previous barrier to pleasure-sniffing – that it breached the Pact – was no longer applicable. The Pact had already been breached. So when I reached the strongest smelling part of the smell-heap I inhaled deep. All the smells I had smelled before – rich earth, leaf juice, worm blood, squirrel droppings – they were all still there but at an even stronger intensity.

Again, I had a feeling of weightlessness, as if my body was dissolving into the park itself, only this time it was coupled with something else. A feeling of absolute control. No, not control – power. As if all the wild and natural forces suppressed in the park were rising up within me, or I was rising up into them, it was hard to tell.

'OK, madwag, you've earnt your information,' he said, while I was still under. 'Emily's not going to take your master away, she's taking *me* away. She's selling the house and going back to London. She's probably telling him now. There. Has that put your mind at rest?'

314

Strangely, it hadn't.

As I pulled my head out another smell hit me, just for a second, but sharp enough to make me feel sick.

'Something's wrong,' I said.

'Overdone it eh, madwag?' chuckled Falstaff, cocking his leg against the side of the smell-heap.

'No. There was a smell.'

'Uh-huh.'

My mind sharpened and I felt myself return to my own body. '*No*, a weird smell. Didn't you smell it? Not like last time.'

'You know, madwag, I think you've finally lost the plot.'

'No, come here. Smell.'

Falstaff trod slowly over and lowered his nose to the exact area I indicated.

'Can you smell it?'

He didn't say anything, which itself was an answer. I sniffed at it again, and followed its trail. It led to an area behind the smell-heap, under tangled wood, past crow-flowers, nettles, daisies, towards the darkest corner of the park.

I started to dig.

'Madwag, what are you doing?'

'Falstaff, there is something I should have told you before. There have been strange things happening in this park. An old friend of mine, Joyce, a wolfhound, she was murdered. Her throat ripped out. Her body was found under the bushes.'

'Oh great, so now we're hunting for corpses.'

I dug further and the smell grew stronger.

'There's definitely something.'

'Oh well, I'll leave you to it.'

I turned to see Falstaff's head become swallowed up by the smell-heap, then carried on. The smell was horrific. Not strong, but terrifying. Terrifying because I instinctively knew what it meant.

It meant a dead body.

A dead *human* body.

brakes

Car brakes screamed beyond the park wall.

soil

My paw hit something hard, then flinched away.

It was a head. A face. The skin detectable beneath the cover of soil. I pawed gently to see further.

A woman.

Although filled with earth, her mouth was open. As if it was trying to whisper the story of her muddy death. My heart beat faster. 'Falstaff!'

He didn't answer.

'Falstaff!'

Still nothing.

'Falstaff! Come here!'

His head withdrew from the smell-heap.

'I hear you, madwag. I hear you.' He made his way over, his bloated body cracking twigs as it travelled.

He looked down at the body and then back at me.

'It's a body,' he said.

For once, Falstaff was unable to laugh away the situation.

'We've got to do something,' I told him.

'We? *We* do nothing. This is human business.'

'We need to make sure humans know. Families are at risk, we have to pull the body out of the ground.'

'Listen, madwag, with all due respect, you killed my master. You can't have it both ways. I didn't get worked

318

up about that so why on earth should I get worked up about this?'

'Because this death is pointless.'

'We're dogs. Our whole existence is pointless.'

'Listen, you get our masters while I start to pull her out.'

But he didn't move. He just sat there watching me as I pulled at the woman's coat with my teeth.

'Madwag, you need to think this through. If we get our masters involved they could be implicated. You know what human justice is like.'

He had a point. If I got Adam involved, it could place the Family in even greater danger. But then, if the body was left unfound, the killer would probably never be caught.

'OK, OK, let me think,' I said. 'What if we pulled the body out so it would be discovered eventually, but not by our masters.'

Falstaff desperately searched for an objection to this plan, but couldn't find one. 'Listen, you crazy Labrador, this is the last time I ever do anything to help you and your stupid mission. And remember: I'm doing this out of loyalty to my species, not to humans.'

'Thanks, you're a good friend.'

'And you can cut the sentimentality as well.'

'OK. Let's get to work.'

We had to act fast. Any moment Adam and Emily would be calling our names, ready to take us home. We took a coat shoulder each and pulled backwards, trying our hardest to block out the scent of death.

Her head fell back, onto the surface soil, banging the

ground hard. Earth slid from her face, revealing the grey skin beneath.

I looked at the park wall, only a short distance away. 'Someone will find her here,' I told Falstaff.

'Yes, they will. Now come on, before our masters find *us*.' Falstaff clearly couldn't take the sight or smell any longer. But I was thankful. Despite his complete disregard for the human species, despite his attempts to pretend nothing matters he had proved to be a true friend.

We clambered back through the twigs, passed the smell-heap and back into the open. Adam and Emily were still talking on the bench, both staring at the ground, then they looked up and spotted us.

'I won't see you again,' said Falstaff. 'We're going tomorrow. To London.'

'Oh,' I said, remembering what he'd told me while I'd been submerged in the smell-heap. 'That soon.'

'I'm bad at goodbyes, madwag, I really am,' he said, sniffing me awkwardly. I felt he wanted to tell me something, but couldn't, something he'd clearly held within for a long time.

I looked back over towards the far corner of the park, where the body of an unknown woman lay waiting to be discovered.

'Me too, Falstaff. Me too.'

news

I watched the news eagerly that night, praying no one would change channels. Charlotte had the controls but, unusually, wasn't flicking to see what else was on.

Bad things were happening, on the screen.

Men were running through dust in a ruined town, firing machine-guns.

As always, Grandma Margaret's commentary remained the same: 'There are some wicked people in the world. *Wicked* people.'

As always, everybody ignored her. Well, everybody apart from Hal, who tutted his disapproval.

Anyway, I waited and watched as the news got smaller, or bigger, waiting for the picture and the writing. BODY FOUND. But nothing came. It was too early, I told myself, much too early.

The weather girl came on to read the weather.

'Oh, I like *her*,' said Grandma Margaret. 'She's lovely.'

killer

The next morning (of all mornings) Charlotte said something she had never said before in her entire life.

She said: 'I'll take the dog for a walk.'

Her parents looked at each other, in mutual shock. Cereal boxes hung motionless in the air. Hal stopped chewing.

For everyone else, this was progress. For me, it was the worst-timed piece of bad news imaginable.

A killer was on the loose.

A killer whose activity centred around the park.

And now Charlotte was about to head there.

What if *she* found the body? What if the murderer was at the park, waiting for the next victim?

No. Paranoia, I told myself. The body would be well out of view, beyond the smell-heap. And the park was no more dangerous than anywhere else in this town. And anyway, Charlotte was often beyond my protection. At least, this time, I would be with her.

But still, a bad feeling remained. The night before the park had offered up a dead body and now, for the first time, Charlotte was going to walk me there.

So when she came to clip on my lead I tried to resist by running upstairs. She eventually found me in the bathroom and, as I'm not as fast as I used to be, she had me cornered. I tried Falstaff's old reverse-out-of-the-collar trick but remembered that Adam had tightened it since the rope-chewing incident.

I suppose I could have tried harder. I could have dug my heels into the carpet or lain down on the floor so she would have had to drag me but I didn't. And anyway, Charlotte seemed determined to show how far she had come and I didn't want to completely spoil her goodwill gesture.

'Come on, Prince, you stupid dog,' she said, not without affection, as she tugged me out of the front door.

I soon discovered she wasn't a natural. By the time we reached the end of the road, she had already swapped sides three times and nearly tripped over me once. I never knew walking with me was so hard. I didn't realise the immense skill involved in getting the four-leg-two-leg rhythm just right.

I suppose I wasn't making it any easier. As every stranger we passed was a potential suspect, I sniffed their crotch for signs of danger. I sniffed the ground also, trying to find some sort of coherence amid the cigarette ends and human spit. But nothing connected. It was all chaos.

We passed a collie and her owner.

'Have you just been to the park?' I asked her, pulling back on my lead.

'Yes, yes. I have, yes. Yes.' I detected from her enthusiasm that she had only just turned full size.

'Was there anybody there?'

'No, no. Nobody. No.'

We were dragged our separate ways but I had got the information I wanted. And when we got to the park I realised she was right.

Nobody.

My plan was simple. Piss, shit and get Charlotte safely home. But then, as I watched her go over to the park wall, I thought: it wouldn't take me long. Just one quick look. Just to check.

So I headed over, past the flowerbeds, the big trees, the bushes which had hidden Joyce's body, the smell-heap and the tangle of twigs, towards the darkest corner of the park.

I turned back and saw Charlotte. Still there. Sitting on the wall. Still safe.

Then I looked down at the drag-trail curving in front of me, the taste of her jacket coming back. And then, nothing. A shallow outline.

No body.

I looked around but there was no sign. Someone had taken her. The killer was close by. But then I noticed something else. There was another drag-trail, a more recent one, leading towards the smaller trees on the other side, beyond the densest area of vegetation.

I followed the flattened plants and long grass until I reached the dark clearing with the smaller trees. I had never been to this part of the park before and felt strangely vulnerable, almost as though I had stepped into a new world.

I saw the muddy corpse of the woman on the ground, twisted to the side, as if in the middle of an uncomfortable night's sleep. She was lying next to a shopping trolley. My nose twitched. There was another scent. Another *human* scent. I sniffed the ground, but realised the scent smelt further away. And so, instinctively, I looked up.

The sight I was faced with was too bizarre to absorb all at once. A man, floating in mid-air, his feet twisting in slow circular movements above my head. Only, when I stepped backward and looked again, I realised the man wasn't floating. He was *hanging*.

I jumped up to get a closer sniff but couldn't believe what I was smelling.

It was Mick, Henry's master.

As I landed back on my feet I lost my grip and slid further back. From this new vantage point, I could now see how it had happened. He had tied Henry's dog lead around the branch of the tree and used the shopping trolley to help him climb up. Once he had managed to tie the lead around his neck he must have kicked the shopping trolley away.

But while I could understand how, I still couldn't comprehend *why*. Was Mick in some way connected to the dead woman on the ground? Was he responsible? Could a man go bad so quickly after his Labrador had left him?

These were questions I did not want to contemplate for long, so I turned around and headed back to Charlotte.

But then as I passed one of the bushes I heard a voice. I looked at the bush but couldn't see or smell anything.

'Prince, wait.'

I recognised the voice, but at the same time knew

my mind must be playing tricks. The bush shook, and struggled. Twigs snapped as a creature emerged. My mind was definitely playing tricks.

For there in front of me, in altered form, was my mentor. My guiding light.

It was Henry.

henry

Henry looked, and smelt, terrible. He'd lost weight, either through death or malnutrition, and his golden coat was barely visible, cloaked as it was in earth and leaves. But it was his eyes that had changed the most. Beneath their milky surface something had been lost. Or taken away.

He could smell my disbelief. 'Yes, Prince, it's me. I'm alive.'

'But I heard you were dead. Your master said you were dead.'

Henry pondered this for a moment. 'Yes,' he said, his voice eerily calm. 'Of course he did.'

'I don't understand.'

Henry looked up at his master, hanging by his lead. 'Some things are beyond understanding, Prince. That is one lesson I failed to teach you.'

'Henry, please. Tell me what's going on. What's happened to you? Where have you been?'

'There are things you never knew about my situation,' said Henry, stepping forward.

'Things? Things? What things? You told me all I needed to know. You always did.'

'No,' he said, kicking soil behind him. 'No. I told you nothing. You see, Prince, there's been a big mess and I've tried to hide it from you. After all, that's what we do,

327

isn't it? We make a mess, we cover it up. But some messes are just too big, aren't they? They can't go unnoticed.'

I was listening to a complete stranger. 'Henry, what are you saying?'

'I'm saying I am not who you thought I was. When Mick left the police force, things started to go wrong with my Family. Things . . . fell apart.' Henry swallowed, then took a deep breath. 'Mick would argue with his wife about anything and tried to stop Sophie, his daughter, from ever going out. He was angry with her. Always angry, although I never knew what she had done wrong. At the same time I went back over the Pact and tried to find a solution. I tried to think how Guru Oscar would have acted, but nothing seemed to work.'

I hesitated. 'So what happened?'

Henry again turned his head up towards his dead master. 'When Sophie was sixteen she left and didn't come home or speak to her parents again. She went to the coast, to be by the sea. And that is when I first met you.'

'But –'

'Yes. I know, it's a strange irony, isn't it?' he said, turning back to face me. 'I was teaching you how to look after the Family and mine had fallen apart. But you must understand, Prince, I couldn't let go. Through you I still felt like I could continue my duty.'

I was devastated. The ground beneath my paws seemed to be crumbling away, but I sensed he had more to tell me.

'So what happened?'

'Mick wanted to pretend everything was normal so he

carried on taking me to the park every morning like he always had. But as soon as he had done that, he would drink. All day he would sit there with the television on and a bottle on his lap. There was nothing I could do. He would sit there, talking to me, thinking I couldn't understand, blaming it all on Sophie and arguing with Claire, his wife, when all the time I knew it was my fault. If I had just tried harder –'

'Henry, you mustn't blame yourself.'

'I just sat there and let it happen. I was a disgrace to my breed.'

'Henry –'

'But things got worse.'

'Worse?'

'When he was drunk he used to get these weird thoughts.'

'What kind of weird thoughts?'

Henry swallowed. 'You know the house I lived in with Mick?'

'Yes. It's over there.' I angled my nose towards the row of houses across the street from the park.

'Well, you can see the park from the upstairs window. You can see everything.'

'I don't –'

'He used to stand there, on a Saturday night, watching the girls and boys. He said they took drugs and had sex with each other. He said they were destroying their Families.'

'Destroying their Families? How?'

'The way he thought Sophie had destroyed his Family. By disobeying their parents, by breaking the human laws

329

and by having sex. He said England was going to the dogs and the teenagers were to blame. I never really knew what he meant when he said that, *going to the dogs*, but I knew he blamed everything on the young people. And the more he drank the more he would accuse them. He told me that England used to be a great country and that it used to rule the world but that the young people made him ashamed to be English. He said that they had gone against Christian values. He said that old people were scared to go out of their own homes. He said that soon there would be no proper Families left and that something should be done. But soon Claire had had enough. She said that Sophie had the right idea, and told Mick that he had driven her away, by not giving her any freedom. Just as Claire had been deprived of the things she wanted. So one day, when Mick was out, she picked up the telephone and asked for a man to come round. The man was young, not much older than Sophie. When he arrived Claire paid him some money and they took off their clothes. Before I knew what was happening they were having sex and there was little I could do.'

I looked at the body of the woman on the ground. 'So what happened?'

Henry remained calm, as he told me what I had already anticipated. 'Mick discovered them. He told the man that he had better leave and then, when the man had gone, he said it was OK and that they knew they were having problems and that they should go to the park.'

'Mick and his wife?'

Henry sighed. 'Yes. And, of course, when he got here, he killed her. It was dark and nobody was around so he strangled her and buried her in the ground. Although I was with him, there was nothing I could do, as I was tied to a tree. I don't know how to slip my lead. I'm a Labrador. After it happened, he carried on as normal as possible, and kept walking me to the park, but soon he realised it was too risky and decided to stay indoors and kept me with him. Although they had no real friends, he knew someone would soon discover what happened. The only time he went out was to get more drink.'

I remembered the plastic carrier bag Mick was holding on the evening he told us Henry had died. I remembered something else. Something more distant. The woman I had once seen, leaving Henry's house. The woman who smelt of sadness. It must have been her, the body on the ground, although the sadness smells were now masked by death. Henry looked at me, a sudden sternness shaping his features. 'He saw you, last night. He saw you and that other dog find the body. He was watching and he knew it was all over. So he took me out again, and dragged Claire's body here, before killing himself. And I have been here ever since.'

'Henry.' I didn't know what else to say. The shock was too much. 'Henry.' His name was the only thing left to cling on to. The only truth I could comprehend.

An aeroplane soared overhead. I lifted my head up and watched its vapour trail fade in the sky. This was all wrong. This was Henry. *Henry*. My mentor. The dog who had shown me the way. Who knew everything.

'I didn't know what to do,' he continued. 'I had to be loyal to my master, the Pact had taught me that.'

As I stared at the two dead bodies, I made another

connection. 'Why did you do it?' I asked him. 'Why did you kill Joyce?'

Henry scratched his ear, and seemed unperturbed by my question. 'She saw everything. She was going to tell you what happened, and then it would have been over. The Labrador Pact would have been a joke in this town if word had got about.'

'So you broke the Pact to preserve it?'

'You could see it like that.'

'And then framed Lear for her murder, pretending to find the body by accident. So I didn't get suspicious?'

'I had no choice. The Pact has to come first. I had let my Family down, but there were still other Families in need of protection. If all this had come out, it would have weakened the entire Labrador cause.'

'But this *will* come out. These bodies will be found and it will be on the news.'

'No one will know they had a Labrador. No humans will be interested.'

'But, Henry, *I* know. You cannot expect me to keep this quiet. We must use this experience, and learn from it. The Labrador Pact isn't enough, we both know that. This does not have to be the end, it can be a beginning. You could come back with me, we could protect the Family together. Everything could work out.'

Henry didn't appear to be listening. 'The Pact must be preserved.'

'But, Henry, it has failed us all.'

He stood up and continued to speak, his voice completely devoid of emotion. 'We must never forget our duty.'

332

'But, Henry, it is right to believe in duty over all, the way dogs always used to – but all the other stuff, it's meaningless. It doesn't work.'

'Labradors must stay strong. If we lose our belief, we lose everything,' he sniffed me, as if he was meeting me for the first time. 'And you have already done enough damage.'

'I'm sorry? I don't understand.'

'Word has started to get round that you killed that man. Your friend, the Springer, he has told everybody.'

Suddenly, I was afraid. 'Henry, come on. You've been through a lot, we'll talk about this some other time.' It was only then that I realised it had been true all along, Henry really *was* gone. The old Henry, anyway. The one who could show compassion, who had a sense of perspective.

'The Pact,' his voice was the voice of the grave. 'Never betray the Pact.'

'Henry –' Before I knew it, he had me by the neck.

'You must die, Prince,' he growled. 'The Pact must be saved.'

'Please, Henry,' I choked. 'Please. I won't say anything.'

'Duty over all,' snarled the monster who now possessed the body of my former friend and mentor.

The pain was unbearable, and I was struggling for breath. 'Please –'

But then I realised what I had to do. I had to fight back. I thought of Joyce, and pictured her lying dead in the bushes, then felt an irrepressible force rise up within me.

I twisted away from Henry's grip as my jaws fixed on

his throat. My teeth embedded deep into his flesh, blood coming fast.

Everything became unreal.

I was watching the scene from somewhere else, from above. It was another park, another Labrador.

Henry rolled over and we fell out of the clearing. We were now in full view of Charlotte.

But we couldn't stop. *I* couldn't stop.

'Help!' Charlotte was running over, I could sense her getting closer.

'No, Prince! No!' she wailed, distressed.

I hesitated, just for a moment. Henry fought back, lifting up, levering my head against my neck. Towards the sun.

My eyes closed and everything was red. Sounds flooded. Henry's relentless, deep-bellied growl. Charlotte running, breathing fast. I resisted, broke free. My jaws firmly clamped back around his neck, shaking away the life. I choked. There was something else in my mouth now. Something soft, hairless. It was a hand.

'Aagh,' she wailed. I had cut her. I had hurt Charlotte. As she bled she dragged me back, away from Henry.

'Help! Please! Help!' Charlotte called to a woman walking past the park wall.

But it was too late. Henry was dead.

The Labrador Pact:
Have faith in the Eternal Reward

If we protect human Families on earth, we will be united with our own in the afterlife.

This is our Eternal Reward.

Provided every member of a Labrador Family tries their hardest to complete their mission according to the rules of the Pact, paradise will be granted. If we stray, or become side-tracked by earthly pleasures, we concede our right to see our parents, brothers and sisters ever again.

Labradors, you must stay strong, and always keep the faith.

muzzle

The muzzle is hurting now, digging hard into the side of my jaw. Adam is no longer shielding my ears, because there is no need – the waiting room is almost empty and all the barking has stopped. Only the young Labrador and myself remain to be seen.

'So you see, there wasn't any other way.'

'What about the man, hanging in the park, and his wife?'

'The humans discovered them, after I was gone. But they made no connection with what had happened, with me and Henry.'

She licks my ear, tenderly. 'But you are leaving your masters early, before your mission is complete.'

'No. The main threats have disappeared. The Family will be safe.'

Before the young Labrador has time to dispute my claim, Nice Mister Vet beckons her master into the surgery.

'Thank you,' she says, standing up.

'What for?'

'For making me understand why you did what you did.'

'I did it to protect the Family.'

'Yes, I can see that now.'

336

'Duty over all.'

'Yes,' she says, as if she has understood for the first time the significance of these words. 'Duty over all.'

And with that she disappears behind Nice Mister Vet, into the room where I will soon enter and never come out again.

I rest my head against Adam's legs while he strokes me. He does not blame me, I know that, as I do not blame him.

He is only here, doing this, to follow his duty. To protect the Family from the violence I have proved able to inflict against humans as well as against my own species. It's easy for me to say he shouldn't have told Nice Mister Vet about Henry or Charlotte's hand or the boy with the damaged skin. But he did. He saw the violence, not the reason. He didn't mention Simon because he hadn't made the connection, but that didn't stop Nice Mister Vet from delivering his fatal opinion.

Charlotte is OK, but it was a terrible mistake. I retch, thinking again of her blood in my mouth.

Beyond the window, on the other side of the street, is a cat. I imagine, for a moment, that it is Lapsang, enjoying the freedom she always used to talk about. It could well be, but it is difficult to tell. The cat turns towards the window, but is blocked from view by a car, parking right outside.

The car door opens and a woman steps out. Deprived of smell, it takes a while for me to recognise her, but once I have my legs feel weak.

She heads towards the window and raps a bent finger on the glass near Adam's head.

He jolts, turns. 'Emily!'

She beckons him outside. Adam gestures towards me and taps his watch, but still she beckons. Adam stands up and pulls on my collar.

'I'll just be a minute,' he says to the woman behind the desk, who is in the process of reapplying her make-up.

Once outside, Emily squats down and strokes my head.

'I thought you were moving,' says Adam.

'No,' says Emily, looking up towards him. 'The energy is too strong here. It won't let me leave.'

'The *energy*?' Adam is unable to hide the despair in his voice.

'I need to tell you something.'

Adam makes a faint whimpering sound, then says: 'How did you know I was here?'

'I went round to your house. Kate told me.' She stroked her golden hair back behind her ears.

'Kate? What? Why?'

Emily stands back up, smiling broadly. 'It's a miracle!'

'Miracle? Emily, look, I'm sorry. I really don't understand.'

'I'm pregnant.'

Adam smells confused. 'Pregnant? But I thought you couldn't –'

'With Simon, no. But with you, apparently, it is possible. I told you – about that night, there were lots of cosmic forces.' She is still smiling a full smile as she places her hand on her stomach.

'With. Me.' Adam looks around anxiously, like a frightened poodle. 'No. Listen, Emily. Have more tests, check everything out. I'm sure you've got it wrong.'

'I have had all the tests. I am pregnant with your baby . . . our own family.'

'Emily, listen. I *have* my own family. I can't do this, I can't even talk to you. You are in a state of shock. You're grieving the loss of Simon. You are still traumatised. You understand my situation, you always have.'

Emily's smile is undented, and happiness molecules still swirl around her. 'Oh dear,' she laughs. 'I can see we are going to have a few problems.'

'Problems? Emily, you can't go through with this.'

This time, Emily's expression changes and the happiness molecules start to evaporate. 'An abortion? You want me to murder our child? This isn't a dog we are talking about. This is a living, breathing human being.'

Adam lets out a low groan. Next, there is the sound of a bell. We turn to see the woman behind the desk who is now standing in the open doorway.

'Would you like to come through?' the woman asks curtly.

'Yes. I'm coming,' says Adam. And then, to Emily: 'I can't talk about this now.'

Emily is already climbing into her car. 'I know, I thought I would come round tonight. Get everything out in the open. Get rid of all the secrets, all the negative energy.'

'No. *No*. You can't! I'll come round and see you.' But Emily shows no indication that she has heard as she slams the car door shut.

I notice something on her back seat. Falstaff, fast asleep. The anger this sight causes is beyond my control.

'This is your fault!' I bark, through my muzzle. 'This is where the Springer philosophy leads to!'

He is awake now, and barking back as the car pulls away.

'And where does protecting the Family get you?' he yells. 'It kills you, madwag, you flaming fool!'

'We can't do nothing!' I respond. 'We can't just sit back!'

Again, he barks, but the car is now too far away for him to be heard clearly. 'It's too late.' Is that what he is saying?

Adam stands still for a while, watching Emily's car disappear into the distance. I wonder what he is thinking. I wonder if he realises the future of the Family now rests on the conscience of the dog on the back seat.

The bell goes again, and Adam slips out of his trance. The young Labrador is leading her master through the door.

'Duty over all,' she says, sniffing me one final time.

'Duty over –' I stop, realising there is something I must say. 'Everything I did, you know, when I broke the Pact. It was wrong. It was all a mistake. Tell every Labrador you see that my example should not be followed.'

'But you said –'

'I know. I'm sorry, I was wrong. The danger never goes away.'

'But –' Her master pulls her from me and holds the door open for Adam.

We head back inside, where Nice Mister Vet is waiting for us.

'Do you want to stay with him, for the injection?'

'Yes, if that's OK.' Adam's voice no longer sounds his own. It is empty, detached, as if his real self is somewhere else entirely. Somewhere words can't reach.

'OK, I'll need your help in getting him up on this table. Yes, that's it. One, two, three . . .'

I am hauled onto a high metal surface, and my paws slide in every direction.

'OK, keep him steady.'

Adam holds my collar and kisses my forehead above the muzzle while Nice Mister Vet opens a cupboard behind him and takes out a capsule of fluid.

'It is always horrible doing this. You never get used to it, especially when the dog is so healthy.'

'Yes,' says the detached voice. 'I bet.'

Adam is now staring into my eyes. We are both trying to connect, to communicate messages we realise won't be understood.

'Right,' says Nice Mister Vet, emptying the fluid into another container. 'There we go.'

Adam's face has changed. Although he is still staring into my eyes, he is now looking at his own reflection. As if he is facing himself on this operating table.

'OK, we'll need to keep him still.' Nice Mister Vet holds up a needle and squirts fluid into the air. 'While I try and find the vein.'

My master closes his eyes and presses his head against my muzzle. We both realise it is time to put me down. 'It's all right, boy,' he whispers, his voice no longer detached. 'It's all right, it's all right, it's all right . . .'